TWISTED

TWISTED

Andrew E. Kaufman

THOMAS & MERCER

Published by Thomas & Mercer, Seattle

www.apub.com

Amazon, the Amazon logo, and Thomas & Mercer are trademarks of Amazon.com, Inc., or its affiliates.

ISBN-13: 9781477829486
ISBN-10: 1477829482

Cover design by Scott Barrie / Cyanotype Book Architects

Library of Congress Control Number: 2014957287

Printed in the United States of America

To Jessica,
for listening to Andrew

Much Madness is divinest sense

—EMILY DICKINSON

1

Dead bolts.

Steel bars.

Metal slamming against metal.

This is my unyielding world, where I mend ruptured minds and fuse cognitive wires. A world that—if emotions were physical— would be a tangled mess of hooks and thorns.

But it's not just the sights and sounds: it's the smell, a musty hybrid of human waste and perspiration. Even the steel has a fug all its own, a mineral tang seasoned by rust and time.

The stench of insanity.

How long have I been here? Six years? Eight?

Sometimes it's hard to remember, and sometimes I forget who's serving time.

"Welcome to the jungle, gentlemen," my boss says, brittle shades of cynicism coloring his words. Jeremy Firestone's sentiment is not unwarranted, but it's hardly necessary. Calling Loveland Psychiatric Hospital a jungle is at best an optimist's euphemism, much like calling hell a tropical destination. And right now we are moving deeper into its cavernous underbelly, a subsurface passageway that dead-ends at a high-security plaster box called Alpha Twelve. Home to the worst of the worst.

The killers.

The rapists.

The dark souls with an incurable addiction to evil.

Dr. Adam Wiley and I exchange vigilant glances. Neither of us knows the purpose of this trip. I steal a glimpse at Jeremy, his steps determined, his gaze aimed ahead, his expression set. On a normal day, our boss is the consummate image of emotional economy, but on this day, reading his face is like studying the side of a concrete slab.

We hit Security Checkpoint One, a gateway that leads to the long corridor, which will take us into Alpha Twelve. The guard spares us a prudent nod, punches a button, and the buzzer goes off. A yellow light flashes once, flashes twice, then turns to green. The gate slides open, and we enter; its bars slam behind us, letting out a thunderous *crack* that cuts the air and ping-pongs ahead through formless shadows.

Something hard and icy pushes through me.

This place is so cold.

But I wonder if my perception is driven more by emotion than climate, whether this hole in the ground is cheating my senses and blowing a chill through my mind.

I try to chase the thought away with a deep breath, but my only payoff is a double shot of noxious-nasty that fills my lungs. I force the air out and with my gaze set ahead, keep walking.

It would be fair to say that Loveland is by no means a modern or up-to-date facility. Calling our setup archaic would be a compliment. Three years ago, Arizona officials agreed. They stepped in and slapped us with numerous building code citations. Once we were on their radar, allegations of human rights violations went flying. Feeling the heat, our board acted quickly, and plans were

soon under way for a new building and a complete program over-
haul. But it will be years before everything is up and running. In
the meantime, we make do with what we've got, watch our Ps and
Qs, and keep guardedly mindful that we're under a microscope.

"So, Chris, how's that beautiful boy of yours doing?" Adam
asks. An obvious attempt to cut through the tension, but I appreciate it.

"Growing too damned fast," I say.

"And the more-than-beautiful wife?"

"More beautiful than ev—"

"Gentlemen." Jeremy interrupts our small talk, his voice boom-
ing louder as we round the next corner. "There's a new patient at
Loveland."

Neither Adam nor I respond. Our boss didn't bring us all this
way just for that.

"And I can't stress enough how important this case is," he continues. "It's one of the biggest we've ever had. Needless to say, we
have to get this right."

Adam raises a brow. "And the mystery patient would be . . ."

Jeremy's gaze drops to the floor, and for the first time, I see
worry break through his stoic demeanor—worry that pulls us
closer toward Alpha Twelve.

"Donny Ray Smith. He's been transferred from the Miller
Institute in Northern Arizona."

"The reason?"

"A court-ordered eval. His lawyers are going for the insanity
defense."

"How come Miller sent him to us?"

"*Miller* didn't—the judge did. The institute had an internal
shake-up just as their review of Smith was near completion. A neuropsychologist working the case is about to get her license yanked.
When the DA found out, he put in a request for reevaluation."

"He got nervous," I say.

"Very nervous. This story's been all over the news up there. Another reason why we must proceed flawlessly. With everything that's been happening around here—"

"We don't need more negative publicity."

"Exactly," Jeremy agrees. "Incidentally, because of all the delays, the judge has us on a tight turnaround."

"How tight?" I ask.

"Your evaluations are due in a week. Until then, I'll be clearing your caseloads."

"Did the folks at Miller reach any decisions before trouble broke out?" Adam asks.

"The psychologist's findings were inconclusive, but the neurologist begged to differ. He concluded that Smith is memory malingering."

My gaze sharpens on the doors leading into Alpha Twelve. "What's his crime?"

"How many would you like?"

"I'd like as many as you've got."

"Murder." Jeremy nods once. "So many young girls, you can count them on two hands. Unfortunately, so far they've only been able to nail him on the last, a six-year-old."

The same age as Devon.

Jeremy eighty-sixes my thought. "That crime will be your primary focus. As the case widens, more charges will likely come down the pike. For now, since Smith's involvement in them is as yet unproven, the information on those cases is for background purposes only. The judge wanted to make this very clear. That said, because the last victim was under the age of fifteen—and multiple murder charges may eventually come into play—this could end up being a death penalty case. So it would be wise to keep in mind the impact of your diagnoses."

"Ten kids? And they couldn't get him until now? How does that even happen?"

He stops to look at me. "It happens when you can't find the bodies."

"Including the last."

"Including the last, yes."

Adam shoves his hands in his pockets and observes Jeremy. "So how come he's being held down in Alpha?"

"It's taken three years to get him into custody, and the DA's not about to take any chances. He requested that Smith be placed within a maximum-security setup. Naturally, we agreed to accommodate."

"Suicide watch?"

"You bet."

We reach Alpha Twelve. Jeremy swipes his card through a scanner slot. The door responds with a sharp, motorized *click;* when it opens, sounds roar out. The kind that can penetrate marrow, the kind that few people—if they're lucky—ever have to hear. Ululating, wordless lamentations. Shrill cries of base terror. Cackling, eerie laughter from men who would not only rather murder you than look at you but also do it in the most heinous and barbaric ways their depraved minds can imagine.

We step out onto the floor. A row of doors faces us on both sides, each punctuated by a steel-gridded window. I see fingers and faces, all eyes aimed directly at us. I see expressions that run the gamut from glazed to goofy, maniacal to menacing, and the rest Just Plain Mad.

"Hurry up!" An urgent whisper sounds from behind me. I turn my head and find Stanley Winters staring at me with pleading distress.

"What the hell are you waiting for?" he asks. "Time is running out!"

I look at him calmly.

"This place is broken!" His voice ramps with frenetic urgency, his body jouncing up and down. "We have to get out of here!"

Stanley tied his wife and three kids to their beds, then set them on fire and watched while they burned to death. He isn't going anywhere. Ever.

"Hey, pretty, pretty . . ."

I swing the other way and lock onto a pair of hungry eyes, a predatory smile dangling just beneath them. On closer examination, I realize the eyes are growing wide as saucers and keenly focused on my forearm, the predatory smile evolving into a shit-eating grin.

"Gorgeous and lovely," the mouth says, nearly salivating. "Gorgeous and lovely."

Adam is now watching, too.

"Gerald Markman," I inform him under my breath.

Adam, a neurologist, works on the medical side of things. He studies imaging tests, lab work, and other diagnostic data, so most of his encounters occur in examining rooms. He rarely makes it down here, but as a psychologist, I often visit Alpha Twelve to observe my patients in their surroundings.

"You know about Gerald, no doubt," Jeremy jumps in, apparently overhearing us.

Adam nods. "Just never had the pleasure of meeting him face-to-face."

"The *pleasure* would be his."

No lie. I've treated Gerald, and he's arguably the most dangerous patient to ever set foot inside Loveland. One of only three serial killers in history to have successfully used the insanity plea, he murdered seventeen people that authorities know of. The news media nicknamed him The Husker—a moniker he earned because killing his victims wasn't enough. Gerald also degloved them, separating their skin from flesh with near-surgical precision. According to detectives, walking into his house was like pulling back the curtain on a grisly horror show. The place was chock-full of biological mementos that included a "mammary vest" fashioned from a woman's torso, a belt adorned with nipples, and Mason jars with preserved human vulvas. When they asked what he'd done with the remains of one particular victim, Gerald Markman smiled broadly and pointed to his shoes.

Everyone at Loveland knows that if you catch Gerald staring, it can mean only one thing: he wants to skin you and wear you.

He's still looking at my arm.

"Back it up, Gerald," Jeremy warns.

Gerald returns a lazy, apathetic I-just-wanted-to-play shrug.

I bet he did.

I shift my attention away, but where it lands offers no deliverance. There's a guy standing toward the back of his room. I know this because, through the window, I can see his head. Not the one on his shoulders—the other one.

"Put it away. Right now," Jeremy scolds.

The patient walks to his window, and I realize it's Nicholas Hartley, revealing his rawboned face and a trembling mouth not indicative of fear.

All up and down the hall, more screams, more laughter, more indeterminate noise.

"An interesting group of patients here," Jeremy comments with a single, downward nod.

"I'm mostly concerned about the one at the end of this trip," I say.

Jeremy holds silent.

"Come on," Adam says, "help us out here. What exactly are we walking into?"

"I'd prefer to let you decide."

A response equivalent to nothing.

We proceed to the end of Alpha Twelve's barrel-vaulted hallway, where an antiquated fixture hangs by a dusty chain, throwing dingy light against the last door on the left. Evan McKinley, one of Loveland's uniformed police officers, stands guard out front. Members of the security staff are normally charged with keeping watch over our more challenging patients, but seeing Evan here underscores the importance of this case: the hospital isn't leaving anything to risk.

A nerve-shattering scream goes off inside the room.

McKinley and I lock gazes, and from his, I get the message: *You've got a live one in there.*

Adam looks at the door. "But we haven't even had a chance to see the patient's files yet."

"You'll get full access to them," Jeremy says. "For now, I've provided most of what you'll need."

"And the rest?"

A guttural yowl, then the sound of rapid-fire chain rattling. Then a bed skidding and squealing along the floor, followed by more screams.

"It's all waiting for you in there," Jeremy says.

He turns and walks away.

2

Evan McKinley peers through the window and into the room, then flashes what might be a mild smirk . . . or maybe I'm just imagining it. He takes a key ring from his uniform belt, unlocks the door, and motions for us to enter.

The moment we step inside, my focus locks onto Donny Ray Smith, but I'm still not quite sure what I'm seeing. I was expecting a monster; instead, this guy looks like he was sent here by Central Casting rather than by another psychiatric hospital. It would appear he wandered onto the wrong set, though, because our new patient in no way fits the role of a serial killer. Striking is the word of the day, and he owns it. With his well-defined physique, jet-black hair, and sculpted jawline, Donny Ray Smith could have leaped from the page of an Abercrombie ad.

A child killer? He's nothing more than a kid himself.

Barely into his twenties, is my guess.

Lying in bed, Donny Ray blinks a few times, then looks down at himself to examine the Posey Net that covers his entire body. Arms, neck, and legs pulled through the openings. Ankles and wrists secured with loop straps. He's sweating, trembling with fear.

Refusing to look at us.

Adam says nothing, but I instantly sense he isn't buying into Donny Ray's fright—not that I am, either. Experience has taught me that psychopaths are quick-change artists who can conform to any shape imaginable. I don't yet know if that's what we're dealing with here, but I'm mindful of the possibility.

Adam and I step forward, and Donny Ray lurches back against the bed, hands clenching the guardrails, biceps flexing, breaths speeding. His restraints clatter; perspiration slides from sodden bangs down the bridge of his nose.

"Why am I being restrained?" he shouts through pallid lips, and I hear his thick southern drawl.

"You've been deemed a danger to yourself and others," I explain.

Donny Ray releases an angry howl and tries to jerk himself free; the bed rattles, squeaks, and shimmies. Recognizing his efforts as futile, he lets out a tiny, helpless moan.

"You're the behavioral guy," Adam mutters to me. "Have at it."

"It's okay," I tell Donny Ray Smith, keeping my body still and my voice level. "Nobody's here to cause you any harm."

A low and inarticulate plea escapes through chattering teeth.

I wait in silence and watch him, my passivity allowing an opportunity for trust. A few moments later, his breath slows and his jaw relaxes, but he still refuses to look at us.

I study him for a few seconds longer, then move closer. Donny Ray reacts instantly, shooting his terrified gaze directly at me, and now I'm the one who's startled. But not by his reaction—it's his eyes, blue, bright, but nearly colorless, perhaps the palest I've ever seen.

Wait a minute.

Because . . .

I know those eyes.

Or do I? I'm not sure. For the life of me, I can't place them. I examine his other features, but . . . I've got nothing, and now I'm more unsettled because this isn't a face I'd soon forget.

And right now, that's not important.

So I try to banish my speculations; but my suspicions may not be unfounded because now Donny Ray Smith is also searching my eyes in a manner that suggests recognition mixed with curious confusion. I study his other features.

A former patient, maybe?

"I'm Dr. Kellan," I move on, still scrutinizing his face as I motion Adam forward, "and this is Dr. Wiley. We'll be working together. I'm a psychologist and he's a neurol—"

"You have to take me out of here!" Donny Ray blurts, those eyes now ablaze and begging.

"I need you to try and calm down," I say. "Do you think you can do that for me?"

A slow nod. A vulnerable expression.

Adam's phone rings, and Donny Ray immediately jerks back. I raise a hand of assurance.

He settles.

"Sorry," Adam says. He checks the screen, silences his phone, then with a nod, encourages me to continue.

Still mindful of my new patient's overall appearance, I say, "I need to ask you a few questions."

Donny Ray is compliant but fearful.

"Do you know where we are?"

"We're at Loveland."

"Do you understand why you're here?"

"Please!" he shouts. "Help me!"

"We're going to find the truth. Whether that helps you or not remains to be seen. Are you able to tell me your name?"

"But you already know all this! What does it have to do with—?"

"I need your name," I say, this time as a firm mandate.

"Yeah . . ." he surrenders. "Okay. It's Donny Ray Smith."

"What's your date of birth?"

"December fourteenth, nineteen ninety-two."

"Can you tell me where you were born?"

"Real, Texas. Why are you doing this to me?"

I circle back to the question he failed to answer. "Do you understand why you're here?"

Donny Ray looks down at his bound hands, looks up, and his expression is markedly changed—something like nervous confusion diluted by distress. "I think . . . I mean . . . I just don't know anymore. They said . . ." His voice falters. "They say I killed that little girl."

Careful to keep my manner nonreactive, I ask, "And did you?"

"They told me they found evidence, you know? Things you can't fake. Like DNA and all that stuff, but as many times as I've turned things around in my head, I can't make sense of them. And then I keep forgetting things, and everything around me doesn't fit, and that just makes it worse . . ."

"Forgetting things," I repeat, because what he describes could hint at some kind of dissociative disorder.

Donny Ray closes his eyes for a moment, opens them. "Like I don't know where I've been for a while."

Tears start as he shakes his head. "Sir, I swear to you—on the Holy Bible—on my own life, even—I never saw that girl before. I mean . . . how do you kill someone you've never met? How can that happen?"

I offer no answer, because I've got none, and because I'm intrigued. Everything I've seen and heard so far rings genuine: his facial expressions, his response times, his vocal intonations and speech pattern. No cues of duplicity. Even his pupils, a clear and clinically proven indicator of tension and concentration, remain dilated.

But a psychopath can achieve all of this, so as a rechecking strategy, I relax my stance, then wait to see whether his presentation changes.

It does not. No loosening of muscles to indicate relief, no altered breathing pattern, no verifiable sign whatsoever of malingering.

There's only about a fifty percent accuracy rate in the study of micro-expressions and body language as indicators of deception, and if I'm indeed dealing with a pathological liar, that would reduce the reliability quotient to zero. It appears as though authorities have compelling enough evidence to prove that Donny Ray killed the girl. If they are right, the only question remaining is whether he remembers doing it. At least one person from Miller seems to think he does. As for me, I'm not yet sure. I can usually reach some level of intuitive deduction after meeting a patient for the first time, but this one has my needle stuck at the midway point. I'm not necessarily convinced he's being truthful—I'm not able to say he isn't, either.

But I don't need definitive answers right now. This is only a preliminary data mining effort, and there will be more opportunities to dig deeper.

Adam's cell vibrates in his pocket. He pulls it out, checks the screen again, then says to me, "I'm really sorry, but I've got to take this one. Go ahead and finish here. We'll catch up later?"

I nod, and he exits the room.

I turn back to Donny Ray. He looks at me with a begging expression, and I still can't shake the feeling we've met somewhere.

But for now, my work here is done, so I tell him, "I'll be back to see you tomorrow."

He's still staring at me. It feels awkward and strange.

Halfway to the door, I hear, "Christopher?"

I reel around, lock onto those eyes.

Where the hell have I seen those eyes?

"Do you think you can help me?" he asks.

"We're going to find the truth," I remind him.

"Maybe we can both find it."

I linger, appraising him from head to toe, and then, "I'm just curious. When I introduced myself earlier, I only gave my last name. How do you know my first?"

"I heard Dr. Wiley call you that."

I nod, then leave.

But as I move down the corridor, a sudden and jarring realization pulls me to a halt, a chill spiking up my spine.

I can't recall Adam saying my first name. We're best friends and colleagues, but he would never address me that way in front of a patient.

And he never calls me Christopher.

This patient knows me.

3

Something definitely isn't right.

While Donny Ray seemed to recognize me, it appeared as though his confusion matched mine; however, since he claims to have memory issues, I wonder if that could be the reason for his uncertainty.

But he said my first name.

And I still can't remember Adam addressing me that way.

I step outside the hospital's heavy entrance doors, and a warm gale of arid air hits my face—another disparity because the weatherman has called for a storm tonight. God knows we could use it after months of drought, but for now it appears any relief has been put on hold. High above the chain-link and spiraling razor wire, I find more confirmation that this evening will be another dry one: stars sparkle like tiny diamonds against a dark and velvety backdrop, not a cloud to be found.

After gaining some distance from Loveland, my mind chatter finally dies down, the day's tension dissipating, thoughts of home easing me down the road. The trip away from work always seems so much longer than the one coming in, almost as if the directional pull can slow time or speed it up. I know it's only my mind bending minutes as I drive, that in reality, the discrepancy is more about what lies at the end of two opposite poles. Going to Loveland is like being snatched up by a rogue wave and tossed into angry waters; coming home is like struggling to escape the current's powerful draw. Each day I move between two different worlds, one occupied by sanity and order, the other completely devoid of either. I do my best to keep them from overlapping, but it never becomes any easier.

Don't get me wrong. I love my work. Except for the parts I definitely don't. I've always been a strong advocate of helping the mentally ill rather than simply warehousing them, and it bothers me that psychiatric hospitals have become a dumping ground for polluted minds. Stowing them away like rat poison for the safety of the community isn't the answer. Furthering their psychological torment isn't the answer, either. Some of my patients have committed unconscionable crimes and destroyed lives in the most aberrant ways imaginable. But spend a few minutes with any of them, and you'll realize their actions were driven by circumstances far beyond their control, that they're already being held prisoners by their own minds. That's not just a professional observation—it's a personal one. Spend another few minutes enduring the hell that I went through as a kid with my father, and you'll understand my reasoning.

Yes, I do want to change the world.

I always have, and I'm driven by a gut-level need to understand the pathology of psychiatric disorders. I know, go ahead and say it: Doctor, heal thyself. To which I respond that altruism by any other name is still altruism, fueled by many different motivations.

As a general rule, it takes me a good ten minutes to recalibrate while swimming toward the distant shore I call home, even longer to once again feel comfortable in my own skin. It's not that I have difficulty working in a violent and pathological environment. Rather, it's the challenge of having to put on and take off the armor.

In order to survive within Loveland's walls, I must remain on high alert at all times. Not keeping sharp-minded can be dangerous, at times even deadly.

And sometimes, that threat can travel beyond the hospital. A few years back, one of my most violent patients managed to escape from the facility—a patient who didn't much like me at all. He made it all the way to the sidewalk in front of my house. Fortunately, the police did, too, and they apprehended him before any harm was done. On his person, they found a butcher's knife, which he'd apparently stolen on his way toward my home. That night was a wake-up call. Soon after, I bought a gun. Neither Jenna nor I particularly love the idea of having a weapon in the house, especially with Devon around, but when it comes to my family's safety, there is no room left for discussion.

So, you can see why once I physically get out of Loveland, I have to mentally get out. Therein lies the struggle, because often there are thoughts that refuse to leave me. Right now, Donny Ray is still doing one hell of a job at spinning my cognitive gears.

Ten kids.

I hadn't allowed my mind to absorb that while meeting with him, purely for the sake of professional detachment, but as I gain physical and emotional distance from Loveland, man, are the feelings coming on strong. I witness so many horrible things at work, but there will always be one that I can never get past and never will: how anyone could intentionally harm a child. I've worked with a mother who drowned her two-month-old twins in a bathtub full of bleach, a father who threw his six-year-old son to his death from atop an amusement park Ferris wheel. In each of those situations, I managed to stay clinical, be objective, even though a part of me wanted to rip out their lungs.

That's not the psychologist in me speaking—it's the father.

Hearing that Donny Ray's last victim was Devon's age is something I can't get out of my head. Reading his case files is going to be a challenge.

Your ten minutes are up, Chris. Home approaching, six miles ahead. Release pressure, prepare for a soft landing.

I take my inner voice's advice and force my mind into some semblance of calm, thankful that the drive affords me this opportunity.

Even more thankful that there's a place of refuge waiting at the end of this road.

4

I arrive back to my settled little home world.

Well, sort of settled.

Somewhere upstairs, it sounds like Devon is running in fast circles, or doing a rain dance, or God only knows what. The ceiling is thumping. Dishes rattle inside the cabinets. And my wife is clearly forcing tolerance, intent on not allowing the commotion to interrupt her phone conversation.

The banging stops—for about five seconds—then resumes.

I grin and take Jenna in, relishing the normalcy, the seemingly mundane, because it's so much more than that. Because beneath the layers, life is all about contrasts and perspectives. After spending time in one of the darkest corners this world has to offer, a walk through our door never fails to restore the balance and order I so desperately need. I credit my wife for drawing those distinctive lines. She knows where I come from, what I lived through as a child. She knows all my demons and offers the security I need to beat them down.

"Yes, I understand," she says, splitting her attention between the caller, Devon's antics, and dinner preparations. Amidst all that, she still manages to brighten at the sight of me.

"Why don't we wait on that one until I look it over tonight?" A few moments later, Jenna finishes the conversation and hangs up the phone.

I walk toward her, kiss the back of her neck. She turns to me, flashing that adorable smile, and it happens once more. I'm overwhelmed. I fall madly and hopelessly in love with my wife all over again. Pulling Jenna toward me, I breathe her in, but even skin to skin doesn't seem close enough. Nothing seems close enough.

We stay this way for several seconds, and I can feel her draw the tension out of me, my muscles loosening, my mind finding its center. She moves back a few inches, doesn't say anything, but I can tell this has been a challenging day for us both.

"Business stuff?" I offer, allowing my hand to slide down toward her waist.

"Business stuff, plus a few hundred other things." She squeezes my hand and tries to smile, then walks toward the stove. Pulling open the oven door, she checks on dinner. "But yes, business at this particular moment."

"The phone call," I confirm.

She nods. "One of the administrators over at Eisenhower. This consulting business is turning out to be so much more work than even I'd expected." She closes the door, lets out a weary sigh. "It's times like this that make me wish I could just go back to being a principal again."

"You're not regretting the decision, are you?"

"Not always. Just sometimes." Jenna pauses for a moment, as if giving the question further consideration. "Then I think about the reason I got out in the first place, how much being here for Devon means to us both, and everything seems okay again. The problem is . . ."

"Starting a business isn't easy," I say.

"Not at all."

"Sweetheart, you're the strongest person I've ever known. You can handle this."

Before the discussion can continue, Devon's pounding intensifies.

I glance toward the ceiling. "What on earth is he doing up there?"

"Being a six-year-old?"

"Dumb question." I laugh. "But he does seem a bit more active than usual."

She frowns.

I answer back with our unspoken language: *Uh-oh. What now?*

Jenna mouths—but doesn't say—*trouble at school.*

And I feel my eyes start to roll.

"We'll just table that one for later," she says. "Okay?"

"Agreed. Indigestion before dinner—bad idea."

Just then, our little devil comes racing into the room with his best buddy Jake, The Lovable Chocolate Lab, trailing closely behind.

"Daddy! Daddy! Daddy!" Devon cries out as he barrels toward me, face lit up like a thousand Christmas trees. He bestows me with an arms-around-the-legs greeting, and despite what my wife has just told me, I can't fight my grin. The pure joy on his face at the sight of me handily trumps all. Because of that, and because of thousands of other reasons, I love the hell out of my son to lengths I often feel are humanly unfathomable. The moment I leave this house each morning is the exact moment I begin missing him, and as the day wears on, I just miss him more. After encountering Donny Ray today, that sentiment is magnified times ten, so I drop to my knees and go in for the hug. He starts to take off, but I tug my son back and give him another, this time clinging to his little body longer. As soon as I release him, he speeds into the dining room, yelling, "Mommy let me set the table! Wanna see?"

I look at my wife and realize she's been watching me.

"What was that all about?" she asks, head tilting, smile half curious, half concerned.

I try shrugging it off. "Just a rough day."

"What happened?"

"Trust me, you really don't want to know."

After so many years together, Jenna is well aware of what that means, knows there are some things better left at the office. She squeezes her mouth to one side in a way that doesn't push the issue but lets me know the door is open for discussion.

I struggle for a moment, trying to temper my statement before it comes out. "I guess I just realized how precious he is."

Jenna's expression softens. Her nod reflects intimate understanding.

"And I don't know what I'd do, if anything . . ."

"Ever happened to him," she says, finishing the sentence that I can't bring myself to complete.

"Daddy! Come on!" Devon yells from the dining room before Jenna can respond. Jake chimes in, barking anticipatory excitement.

I wink at my wife: *I'll be right back.*

She nods and grins: *Your boy needs you.*

I enter and immediately spot the table.

"Um . . . kiddo?"

Devon looks at me with a brightening expression.

"Who's coming to dinner?" My question is actually a rhetorical one.

Swinging his arms back and forth, he considers the table for a moment, then with a shrug, says, "Just us."

"So . . . it looks like you may have a few too many place settings. There are five here."

He proudly appraises his work again. "It was just in case."

"Just in case, what?"

"In case anyone else wants to come."

Kid logic. Gotta love it.

"Okay . . ." I give him an exaggerated, affirming nod. "Fair enough."

Jenna walks in, takes one look at the table, and her expression falls into something like exasperation mixed with learned helplessness.

"We've got this, Mom," I say, offering her a playful grin. "You never know when we might have uninvited company."

Devon giggles.

My wife shakes her head, then goes back into the kitchen.

"Come on, kiddo," I say, "let's show Mom how quickly we can make the table less crowded. First guy to grab two settings wins."

Devon is the victor of our race, and the seating plan is amended and reduced.

"So how was school today, buddy?" I ask, probing to see if he'll volunteer what my wife didn't.

Devon doesn't answer, likely as a survival strategy, likely also because he's too busy rearranging the spinach on his plate.

My son is a fussy eater.

Probably one of the worst I've ever seen. I was, too, as a kid, but compared to him, I was gluttonous. Hard as Jenna tries to spur his appetite, there isn't much he likes or will eat.

"Devon," she says, trying to strike a delicate balance between patience and assertiveness, "moving your food around won't make it go away. Can you at least give it the old college try?"

"I *am* trying," he protests, then continues spreading the vegetable around on his plate. He takes a stab at—but does not put into his mouth—the spinach, then moves his effort to the penne pasta, mashing it with his fork and separating the mess into two nearly symmetrical mounds.

"What's wrong with the pasta?" Jenna says. "I thought you loved it."

"Not this." A nose crinkle. "It's got white stuff."

"That's cream sauce, and it's good."

Devon gives the pasta a disapproving flick with his fork.

"You know," I say, "if you don't finish dinner, we couldn't possibly allow the chocolate cake your mother baked to be your only source of nutrition for the night."

Devon's decision is laser-quick. He digs into the demolished pasta.

Jenna grins. And I'm pretty sure I've won some major points by restoring peace and order to our little world.

Before sleep, I stop by my son's room to say good night and find him waiting in bed, Jake close at his side.

"Great job setting the table tonight, kiddo," I say, taking a seat beside him.

"It was fun. Mom says I can do it again tomorrow." He scrunches his nose. "But she told me not to set the table for company."

"Probably a good idea, unless we're expecting some."

He shrugs. "But you never know."

"True, you never do. Always good to be optimistic."

"I love you, Dad."

His spontaneous and heartfelt sentiment catches me off guard. It fills a void left open from long ago—so many happy endings that never had the chance to happen, so many things left unsaid.

All of it cut too short, and far too soon.

I want to give Devon those things I missed, but even more, I don't want my pain to become his legacy. I know, perhaps better than most, the need to make every second of every day count.

I kiss his forehead, shut off the light, then leave his room.

But opening one door feels like stepping suddenly through another, memories of my own father waiting just on the other side. Memories that are good in so many ways.

But in others, so terribly tragic.

5

A LIE CALLED FOREVER

Summer evenings with Dad were my favorites.

I'd lean back in bed, immersed in the smell of jasmine as it drifted through my window. Distant crickets chirped as cars rolled by, creating music that moved seamlessly to the beat of a soft, settling night.

And I remember the comfort and security of my father's smile.

"Daddy," I said, settling beneath the cool sheets, gazing out at the starry night. "What comes after the sky?"

He looked there, too, and considered my question. "After the sky comes outer space."

"What's after that?"

"Then it's the universe."

"And after that?"

He paused for moment, his expression thoughtful. "Well . . . we don't really know what comes after. Nobody's ever gone that far."

"How come?"

"Because it just goes on and on. And it's a long way back."

"You mean like, forever?"

"That's what some people think, yes."

I fell silent and considered the darkened skies, my young mind trying to process the massive complexity of eternity. Turning back to my father, I said, "But nothing lasts forever."

"Some things do."

"Like what?"

His warm smile. "Like my love for you. That will never end." Then he looked more serious. "My love will always be with you, Christopher, and you'll always know where to find it."

"Where will it be?"

"Deep inside your heart."

I had no way of knowing that disaster lurked silently in wait, ready to take a chunk of my heart and eclipse that love. Each day, I struggle to find balance between the before and after, clinging to the good. But while these fond memories of my father are so very precious, they are also far too few.

The bad ones, painful and far too many.

6

As I enter our bedroom, Jenna looks up from her laptop. With a soft, welcoming smile, she pats the spot beside her on the bed and says, "Come here."

I gladly accept the invitation.

She rests her head on my shoulder, and we indulge in the moment. No words necessary, just silent commingling that feels profoundly exhilarating.

A few minutes later, she exhales softly, and waves of unrest roll across her face.

"Talk to me," I say.

"It's about your son."

"I sort of gathered . . . Wait. *My* son?"

"Yes. He's always yours when he misbehaves. We've discussed this."

"Got it. So, what has Devon the Mischievous done now?"

"It would appear that he hasn't been eating the lunches I've been making."

"But I thought he liked your lunches. Isn't that the whole reason you started packing them? Because he hates the cafeteria food?"

She serves me a deadpan stare.

"Point taken," I say. "He's a fussy eater."

"But now with a disturbing new twist. Not only hasn't he been eating his meals"—she pauses—"he's been selling them. It seems our young entrepreneur has been holding auctions at the lunch table."

"Auctions," I repeat, trying to get a visual on this.

"And my lunches have been quite the hit. For everyone except Devon, of course."

"How long has this been going on? The lunchtime profiteering?"

"There's no telling."

I fall back onto the pillow, shake my head. "This food thing . . . It's like—"

"Totally out of hand."

"I mean, I was bad, but this kid?"

"He's got you beat by a country mile, sweetie."

"So how do we handle this?"

She flops back next to me. "*We* already have. Or I did. There was a discussion. Also a lot of defensive posturing and a lot of yelling. Perhaps a protestation or two of basic human rights violations."

"Which, judging by his behavior at dinner, didn't appear to sink in."

"Setting the table was actually part of the punishment. Of course, as only our son can do, he turned it into a carnival."

I pull Jenna against me, run a hand up and down her back. "I'm afraid punishment doesn't work so well for him."

"Ahh . . . the psychologist speaks," she says, walking her fingers along my arm. "But unfortunately, there's more to this sad little tale."

I don't answer. I'm afraid to.

"According to Dr. Fratiani," she continues, "the situation went to hell in a hurry today."

"Oh, jeez . . ." Fratiani is Devon's principal. Adding to the problem, this is the woman who replaced Jenna after she resigned, so there's always been an underlying note of territorial friction on Fratiani's part.

My wife goes on. "Apparently, one of the kids got a little too excited over my apple cobbler. He tried to outbid a boy who'd offered up his Xbox."

I cover my face with one hand, motion with the other for her to continue.

"Kid Number Two volunteered his mother's Maserati, which our son graciously accepted, then demanded payment. That's when the fight broke out."

"Oh, God. There was a fight . . ."

"There was, indeed."

"Anybody get hurt?"

She shakes her head, expression grateful, bemused even, but nevertheless distraught. "Luckily. But Devon got very upset. He left school and walked home."

Tension pinches the back of my neck, and from Jenna's slightly narrowed eyes, I can tell she knows where this one is going. Where my worries always do.

"It's okay," she rushes to reassure me.

"It's really not." And as my words come out, the Donny Ray case—the children he abducted and murdered—again puts a stranglehold on my mind.

"Chris, he was fine . . . Everything is okay."

"But it might not have been. He left school, and nobody knew where he was. Kids can't just walk the streets alone in the middle of the afternoon these days."

"Sweetie, I know what you're saying, but the media exaggerates those risks. The chances that anything could have happened are so slim. You're forgetting that I've worked in the school system for years. I know a lot about the dangers kids face."

"But I work in a psychiatric hospital. I see the other side. Hell, I work with it every day. I know what kind of evil is out there. The predators and killers."

"I get that—I really do—but look, school is just a few minutes away, and the important thing is that he made it home safe."

"And the other thing? The part where he might not have?"

"I had a talk with him about that and explained the importance of safety. He's promised to never leave school without permission again."

I shift my weight, cross my arms.

"Chris, please stop worrying about him so much," she says. "Overreacting causes more harm than any potential danger he might face."

"I got a new patient today," I say, trying to explain my reaction.

"And?"

"Ten kids are missing. They think this guy killed them. The last one was Devon's age."

Jenna's lips part with unsettled understanding, and all at once I know she gets the full context of my edginess from earlier this evening. Admittedly, I do worry too much about Devon's safety but now perhaps reasonably so.

This conversation has become way too dark, even for me. *Leave work at work*, I think. Pulling Jenna close, I place an arm around her, and she again rests her head on my shoulder.

"Well, there is one good thing," she offers brightly.

"What's that?"

"Kid's got a good business sense. Could really pay off for us someday."

I shift my shoulder, raise Jenna's head so we're face-to-face, and inspect her for evidence of sarcasm.

She manages to hold an impressively solemn expression in place. For a few seconds.

Then she cracks.

Now we're both laughing, and I'm reminded again that life is indeed all about the contrasts and perspectives.

7

IT'S JUST A SHADOW, DARLING

My mother was the classic example of magical thinking in motion. A woman who believed she could manipulate reality simply by ignoring it. A woman who preferred to avoid the complexities of life rather than live in the messy parts.

Southern raised, born and bred beautiful, Virginia Lucille Chambers was a stunning redhead, the kind most men could only dream of. And while she was indeed a sight to behold, everything on the inside seemed to contradict what the outside was doing. There was something so broken about her, so incomplete. The short version: my mother was like window dressing draped over a cracked cinder block wall.

From the start—and at their best—my parents never had the high-functioning or strong-loving marriage that I think was my father's dream. Mom was skilled at projecting a facade of buoyant optimism, which along with her beauty made her an easy sell to men. But beneath the surface, she was a jumble of complexity. Unfortunately, by the time my father figured that out, it was too late.

Whenever anything went wrong—she forgot to pay the gas bill three months running; she gave away my father's heirloom casserole dish as a gift for a neighbor—Mom flashed a little charm, poured a nice glass of sweet tea, and pretended whatever it was had never happened. That would be my father's cue to come swooping in and turn her fantasy into reality. He'd clean up the mess, make it go away, and then, *presto change-o*, that was that. This crazy, backward dance became our family blueprint, our baseline for normalcy, while our foundation progressively crumbled.

The evidence of my mother's pathology was both illustrative and endless. One day, while driving me home from school, she decided that applying lipstick was more important than watching the road. Seconds later, we hopped a curb and hit a trash can, which flew into a speedy roll, dead-ending in a neighbor's cellar window.

And she kept driving.

"Mom! What are you doing?" I said, watching as she made her mistake disappear in our tracks.

"It was only a trash can, dear," she replied, then stepped on the gas. "It's nothing."

"But that *trash can* just broke a window!"

A mild shrug, an oblivious smile. "I didn't see that happen."

"But I did!"

"And you didn't, either."

"How can you just—"

"I said, *you didn't, either.*"

Whether we saw it was academic, because the homeowner most certainly had, and about ten minutes later, he came stomping up our front walkway. When he banged on the door, my mother ignored it, continuing to unload groceries. Dad, by now an expert at sensing this kind of trouble, immediately headed for the front door while keeping a wary eye on my mother.

Several minutes later, it was all taken care of, my dad apologizing profusely for his wife's derelict behavior and writing a check to cover the damages, his wife acting as if none of it had happened.

Problem solved.

Business as usual.

But living with such lunacy eventually took its toll, and my father wasn't the only victim. Struggling to survive inside this thickly encapsulated, reality-skewed world was no way for a kid to grow up. It was shaky footing indeed, one that continued to chip away at my ability to trust the tangible.

Me at age ten. "Mom! There's a giant spider on the ceiling!"

Painting her toenails, refusing to take her eyes off them, "Nonsense. There are no spiders in this house."

"But you're not even looking at it!"

Finishing one foot, moving onto the next, "It's just a shadow, darling."

"It's not a shadow. It's got legs!"

"Such a willful mind you have," she replied through a dismissive laugh, wiggling her toes and admiring them. "I swear I don't know where that comes from."

The irony.

The following afternoon, still bothered by the incident, I asked my dad, "How come Mom pretends?"

His smile was tolerant and knowing. "Your mother's a bit, well . . . she's different."

"Different."

Sensing my confusion and taking the cue, he said, "Or maybe a better way to say it would be *fragile*."

I still didn't get it.

"Think of it this way," he went on. "What happens when you drop a tomato onto the ground?"

I shrugged. "It smashes?"

"And how about an orange?"

"It's okay."

"Do you know why?"

"Because of the outside?"

"Exactly. Some are tougher than others."

"Which one is Mom?"

He laughed. "Probably somewhere between the two. But that's just how she is, and we love her anyway because of what's on the inside."

Well-meaning but completely flawed logic that, as the years wore on, would continue to fail the test of time.

Logic that would eventually backfire in the worst possible way, leaving my dad to pay the biggest price.

8

The hospital seems busier than usual—more people, more noise, more chaos. I've worked here long enough to gauge the activity without actually seeing it. Built in the 1930s, this building is so frail and rundown that sound travels easily through walls. Besides the structural shortcomings, poor planning has placed my office beneath Acute Care, a sort of psychiatric emergency room. There's a lot of foot-pounding, cart rolling, and screaming, all of which at times make concentration difficult. Above that are six stories filled with treatment facilities and rooms for our patients, making Loveland often feel like a loose house of cards just waiting to buckle and collapse at any minute.

On this day, I'm also aware that my perceptions are more heightened than usual. I've been worn out from working too many long hours lately, and the pressure of Donny Ray's arrival to Loveland only adds to my distraction.

Not a single body found.

I'm still stuck on that one. How do you strip ten people from the world without leaving any trace of them? In the pursuit of supporting logic, I start digging through Donny Ray Smith's case files—at the same time, I hope to perhaps jog my memory and figure out how we might know each other.

Six-year-old Jamey Winslow vanished one morning while walking to school.

I stop right there.

Jenna said I shouldn't worry so much about Devon, but this new information only confirms my fears. I may be overprotective of my son but only because of a deeper understanding about how truly vulnerable children are these days.

Now another concern pokes at me, this one just as relatable.

A child walks out the door one morning, and, by evening, her short life is a tragic memory.

Ten kids means at least ten parents trapped in a cycle of relentless agony. Ten parents who have not only lost their most precious young ones but also their ability to begin the healing process. No bodies to bury. Nothing tangible to prove their children are actually dead. To walk into a tiny bedroom and feel a void so powerful and deep, so excruciatingly endless. To realize you've lost something that can never be replaced. I try to imagine what that must feel like, whether I could accept or even believe my son was really gone.

I take a sustaining breath and move on through the file.

The detectives got a break in the case. Not far from where Jamey disappeared, they discovered small sneaker prints in the mud leading down toward a ravine. After combing the area, crews unearthed a clump of hair partially hidden beneath a small boulder. Hair that not only matched Donny Ray's color and texture, but also his DNA.

It appeared the girl had fought to her death.

I swallow hard, feel the skin on the back of my neck turn cold. Picturing these details brings on an intense moment of conflict, squaring my personal and professional objectives directly at odds with one another. The commitment I made a long time ago to defend the rights of the mentally ill, now pitted against love for my child.

I remind myself to remain impartial, to keep things clinical, to compartmentalize and gather facts, even though the emotional toll is steep. As a regrouping effort, I return to the task at hand, or more specifically, to the question: Does Donny Ray Smith remember murdering Jamey?

I begin sorting through the nearly fifty pretrial motions, most of them from Smith's lawyer, a guy by the name of Terry Campbell. He claims that, evidence or not, his client isn't guilty by reason of insanity because of a closed head trauma he suffered at the age of eleven. The theory, according to Campbell, is that Donny Ray went into a dissociative state—induced by the injury—before murdering Jamey and is unable to recall the event. Therefore, he can't be held responsible.

And then I keep forgetting things, and everything around me doesn't fit, and that just makes it worse . . .

Donny Ray's comment boomerangs back, along with my previous thoughts about a potential dissociative disorder. Of course, until I dig deeper and examine that possibility, there's nothing on which to base a concrete diagnosis. Since my patient is suspected of malingering, he could have thrown out the comment as a means to plant doubt. But his panic and confusion yesterday seemed so real. Is he sophisticated enough to lie that convincingly?

I keep reading.

As for his alleged intent to cover up the girl's death by disposing of her body (an insanity plea no-no, which often indicates knowledge of wrongdoing), that's explained away as also occurring during his temporary amnesia.

I consider the likelihood, and something else flags my interest. Hiding a victim after murdering her can be an act of remorse. But people who dissociate aren't able to feel much of anything, which is why they check out in the first place. If Donny Ray went into an altered state during the murders, his hiding behavior could have been part of an unconscious pathology. Since he allegedly racked up ten victims, I'm even more curious. But what would be the trauma trigger?

While consistently concealing bodies is indeed an interesting and definitive pattern of behavior, it's not yet at direct issue here. Until evidence is found linking him to the other disappearances, my patient only has to account for Jamey's.

Reading on, I find more to pique my interest. Donny Ray Smith is no stranger to disappearing bodies. The first person in his life to vanish was his sister, Miranda, when they were children. At that time, detectives zeroed in on the father as their prime suspect, but they were never able to bring charges because the evidence wasn't strong enough.

Miranda was never found.

Just a coincidence?

I scroll forward to the information about Donny Ray's head injury. According to the medical reports, he claimed to have fallen onto the family tractor's front bucket loader but couldn't recall the exact date. Only that it happened the summer his sister disappeared. Nothing from detectives on whether they contacted the originating hospital to zero in on when the incident occurred. Nothing mentioned about it in the attorney's notes, either.

Interesting.

About six months prior to Miranda's disappearance, their mother passed away. Nothing suspicious about it: she had cancer of the pancreas. The father died about a year later of a massive heart attack, and Donny Ray spent the remainder of his childhood bouncing between foster homes.

I'm about to open a file containing photos of the ten victims, plus Miranda Smith, but that last bit of info about his lack of a stable home life tugs me in another direction—or rather, the potential for answers does. An increasing pattern of antisocial behavior can often be a precursor to psychopathy, so I investigate whether Donny Ray Smith has a juvenile record. After scrolling through more pages, I find a section titled "Criminal History," but just beneath it is a rather rough-looking blank space.

That's not right.

A juvenile's criminal records are expunged when he reaches eighteen, but the defense team usually makes them available to experts. If Donny Ray has no history of illegal activity as a minor, this document would state so, as would be the case if his records remain closed. But seeing the header with only a gap beneath it raises my suspicions.

I dial Donny Ray's attorney.

"Terry Campbell, please," I tell the receptionist when she answers.

"I'm sorry. Mr. Campbell is no longer here."

I check the screen to make sure I didn't miss something. "This is Dr. Kellan at Loveland Hospital. My records indicate he's representing one of my patients."

She hesitates. "Unfortunately, not anymore. Mr. Campbell passed away."

"Oh . . . I'm so sorry. When?"

"Last week. It was an accident off the coast of San Diego. They found his boat but no sign of him."

"Dear Lord. How awful."

"It is."

"Well, I was just calling to get some clarification on my patient's criminal records. Donny Ray Smith?"

Silence.

"Are you still there?"

"Yes . . . sorry. I'm here."

"Is there something wrong?"

"No." But she answers a bit briskly, nearly gulping down the word. "That case is in the process of being reassigned, but there have been a few unexpected delays."

"What kind?"

"I really don't have that information."

"Do you know when the new attorney will take over?"

"I'm sorry, I actually don't. But I can call you when we have more information."

I give her my number, then hang up.

The receptionist was a bit closed-mouthed, but given how high profile this case is—plus having an employee tragically die—I suppose it's not a complete surprise.

Hoping to find concrete instead of sand, I turn to the reports from Miller Institute, but that only lands me in another quagmire of ambiguity. Donny Ray's imaging tests show none of the physical evidence typically seen with a moderate head injury that could cause lapses of memory. The EEGs, however, potentially suggest otherwise—they show slight abnormalities in some cognitive functions.

I flip to comments from the attending neurologist at Miller, Dr. Stephen Ammon, who says that despite the conflicting test results, he's confident Donny Ray's head injury has no bearing on this case. His reasoning is based on a review of the patient's educational history following the accident: Donny Ray was never placed in any special ed classes, and, in fact, his grades were just fine. With that as a baseline, Ammon concludes that enough time has since passed for the brain to heal. In plainer language, Donny Ray's defense is trying to parlay an insignificant head injury, which happened eleven years ago, into a Get Out of Jail Free card.

Diagnosis: malingering.

The psychologist, Dr. Sherri Philips, ran a different course with her opinion. Donny Ray's assessment tests split right down the middle. His MMPI-2 validity index suggests he wasn't being forthcoming about his stated psychiatric illness, but the PAI validity scales were within normal range. Because of that disparity—and because some of the PAI scales typically associated with trauma were slightly elevated—Philips felt there might be some other psychological disorder at play that she could not yet identify. According to her notes, she was working on a provisional diagnosis but needed more time to evaluate Donny Ray's childhood history and get him to open up about it. Apparently, that was when she got pulled off the case, because her notes end there.

Diagnosis: incomplete.

I search the Internet for details about the scandal that broke out at Miller. As the two doctors were wrapping up their reports, accusations started flying that Philips was having inappropriate sexual relations with a patient. The judge, anticipating the potential fallout and a media firestorm, got Smith the hell out of Dodge, parked him on us, and requested a new evaluation.

My mind is flip-flopping like a skillet pancake in a greasy-spoon diner. The reports from Miller have potential to go in either direction: nothing to indicate Donny Ray's crimes are psychopathic, nothing to indicate disassociation as the culprit, either.

I'm scoring goose eggs.

Then I get another knock to the chops. Under the "Additional Comments" section is a notation from Ammon, the neurologist, which sends my heart into palpitations.

Three words.

Be very careful.

9

The temperature in my office feels as though it's dropped about ten degrees. Outside the window, dark clouds tumble by, casting murky shadows across my desk.

The storm is finally coming.

I read Ammon's comment again, this time not so much because of what it says, but rather what it does not. In our profession, we deal with a different kind of patient. Warnings like this are not uncommon, but it is very unusual to find no explanation.

I need answers, so I reach for the phone and dial Ammon's number.

"Miller Institute," a detached, almost mechanical female voice recites, "how may I direct your call?"

Okay. Apparently it's not Ammon's number. It's the main switchboard.

"Can I help you?" she says, more as a prompt than a question.

I clear my throat. "Yes. Sorry. Dr. Christopher Kellan at Loveland. I was trying to reach Dr. Ammon."

She doesn't respond.

"Ammon," I repeat.

"One moment, please."

Click.

It seems customer service is sadly lacking at Miller Institute—either that or Robo-Receptionist is due for a tune-up.

About twenty seconds later, I hear someone on the line. "Hello?" The voice is male, older, but definitely human.

"Dr. Ammon, it's Christopher Kellan over at Loveland. I was hoping to ask about your—"

"I'm sorry," he interrupts, "this isn't Dr. Ammon. I'm Dr. Pritchard."

"My apologies, Doctor. The receptionist must have made a mis—"

"No . . . It wasn't a mistake," he says, voice taking a noticeably deeper tone. "His calls are being forwarded through the switchboard for now. I'm the hospital administrator. Is there something I can help you with?"

"Well . . . you could start by telling me how I can reach Dr. Ammon."

"That is a good question."

I tell him I'm confused, and he responds, "You're not alone. He failed to show up for work about five days ago and hasn't been seen since."

I skim Ammon's report. His disappearance happened a few days before Donny Ray was transferred to Loveland.

The hairs on my arms flick up.

"Are the circumstances suspicious?"

"No . . . no . . . ," he says through a drawn-out sigh. "Nothing like that. At least, the authorities don't seem to think so. No evidence of foul play."

"Do you have any idea why the doctor would just take off?"

"Unfortunately, I might. A few weeks ago, Dr. Ammon became extremely depressed, and it kept getting worse."

"Do you know why?"

"We have a pretty good idea, yes," Pritchard says. "We'd just lost another doctor. A suicide. They found her at home."

"I'm very sorry to hear that."

"It's been a rough few weeks around here. Dr. Ammon took it especially hard. He and Dr. Philips were very close friends."

"Wait a minute." Heat flushes my forehead as I check the report. "Doctor, I'm calling in reference to Donny Ray Smith. Philips was the attending psychologist on that case."

"Correct. I'm sure you're aware that she was under review."

"She killed herself over it?"

"That seems to be the consensus, yes."

I look at my screen and wonder why Jeremy never mentioned this, then dismiss the thought, deciding he probably felt it was irrelevant to Donny Ray's case.

"And still no clue where Dr. Ammon might be?"

"Not a one. It's like the man disappeared off the face of this earth."

A man who stood in the way of Donny Ray's insanity plea.

I try to connect dots I can't yet see. "Dr. Pritchard, did Donny Ray Smith leave the hospital at any point during that period? Perhaps he was transported for ancillary medical care? A court hearing, even?"

"No, and he remained under high-level security the entire time he was here. Why do you ask?"

I hang on to my suspicions because I've got nothing to support them. Ammon and Philips are adults, not young girls. And the cryptic warning—plus a lack of explanation—could have easily been a product of Ammon's depression.

"Just covering all bases," I say. "One last thing, Doctor. I'd really like to get more information about Donny Ray. Is there a chance you could provide some?"

"I'm afraid I wouldn't be much help in that respect, other than reciting what's already on Ammon's evaluation. I had minimal contact with Smith. Practically none at all, actually."

I thank him for his time, hang up the phone.

What exactly do I have here?

Bodies falling away all around this guy.

And those hauntingly familiar eyes.

My persistent and unsettled feeling creeps back. I need to get to the bottom of it, prove or disprove whether Donny Ray and I have met once and for all.

I begin with our patient database, narrowing down my search to male patients only, then narrowing further by age group. A more manageable number of files come up, but they reveal zilch. Nothing to indicate that Donny Ray Smith has ever set foot inside Loveland before now.

I go back to the Internet. Donny Ray has been making headlines for months. With headlines come in-depth background pieces and, occasionally, older photos. I search through all the links for anything that might indicate we've previously crossed paths.

Nothing.

I continue skimming through headlines, then land on video coverage from one of the TV stations. About a minute in, it seems there's nothing new here, a repeat of information I already know. Just as I'm about to move on, I zero in on footage of Donny Ray Smith as he's being moved from a transport van to the court building for one of his hearings. Cuffed, shackled, and wearing a jail-issued, orange jumpsuit, he shuffles forward, then looks directly into the camera lens.

My skin flashes hot and cold.

Because I just saw something pass through those eyes, which, during my meeting with him, never once did I witness. An unforgiving cloud of darkness, devoid of anything that resembles even a modicum of human emotion.

Now a biting chill arcs through my entire body.

Which throws me back into a sea of swirling uncertainty. I still don't know what to think. Everything associated with Donny Ray Smith seems laden with equivocality and unanswered questions: his appearance so innocent, the accusations so drastically opposite. Then there's the odd string of disappearances all around him.

And that look I just saw.

Maybe we can both find it.

If it's the truth my patient is after, he's sure taking a circuitous route in getting to it, and so far, pulling me right along with him.

I need to talk this through with Adam.

10

"People do seem to vanish all around him." Adam leans back in his chair and looks like he's thinking. "But only one of the doctors is actually missing, and as for his attorney, he was all the way clear over in San Diego. I can't imagine how Donny Ray could have anything to do with that. He's been locked up. Besides, adults don't seem to be his forte."

"I know, but it does seem awfully coincidental."

Adam shrugs. "I'd leave it at that."

"But what if it's not a coincidence? What if Ammon knew something? Or maybe Philips didn't actually kill herself."

He grins, and I catch that twinkle in his eyes I know so well.

"What?" I ask.

"We're docs, remember?"

"I know what we are," I say a little too defensively.

"We're not detectives."

I nod at his tie.

He looks down at it, then back at me.

"You're wearing Scooby-Doo on your chest," I say. "Doc."

"Hey." Adam straightens his tie. "Don't go hating on Scooby, okay?"

"Yesterday it was George Jetson."

"Don't mess with my man George, either. Guy's an American icon. His feet never touched earth. Like to see you do that." He protectively rearranges the rubberized Gumby, Pokey, and Prickle figurines on his desk.

I'm positive there's some sort of neurosis at play.

Adam takes a sharp poke at the air. "And don't go analyzing me, either."

"Doctor *and* mind reader, no less." I grin. "Impressive."

"Can we get back to Donny Ray?"

"Okay . . . Okay. Back to Donny Ray. So what do you think?"

"Well . . ." He runs a finger across his chin a few times. "The note from Ammon does seem to indicate a concern of some kind."

"The question is, what?"

"Could be something less sinister than what you have in mind. He thought the patient was malingering, right? Maybe it was just a warning to be on the lookout for that."

"Or maybe it was something more."

"Well, I don't know what he meant, but from one neurologist to another? I'm with Ammon. I think Donny Ray Smith is trying to sell us a bill of goods."

"Your reasoning?"

He shrugs. "Tests don't lie, and I've seen this scenario play out more times than I can count. From a purely medical standpoint, I can't believe the defense is trying to use a minor head injury from childhood to explain ten dissociative episodes."

"Just the last one," I remind him.

"Right now, but trust me, that will become the precedent once those other charges start rolling in."

I nod. He's right.

"From where I stand, his legal team is just blowing smoke up everyone's ass. What we have here are lots of moving parts and plenty of missing pieces. It's quack science. Nothing adds up. I just can't see this any other way."

I don't respond.

"Your turn now," Adam says, not affording me the luxury of silence.

"I'm thinking."

He motions with a hand. "Care to externalize?"

"I'm not saying I think he's innocent."

"But?"

"But my mind keeps seesawing."

"Between what and what?"

"Stages of indecision? I'm just not sure what we have here."

"You think he might be telling the truth."

I shake my head. "I'm not willing to take that leap yet. But something's missing here." I tell him about Dr. Philips' mention of an unidentified psychological issue and the conflicting test results.

"Well?" he says. "Do you think she was on to something?"

"Not sure. I mean on one hand, having her license suspended, and then committing suicide, definitely compromises her credibility."

"But on the other?"

"It doesn't mean she didn't have the skill to see things as they were."

"So, what's your plan?"

"I need to finish what Philips couldn't. Dig into Donny Ray's childhood and confirm whether this psychological issue she mentioned actually exists."

"Fair enough. I'll do my medical thing, and you do your clinical stuff. We're good at that. But we don't have much time, so you'd better get busy fast."

I glance at my watch. "How's five minutes from now sound? That's when our first session starts."

11

I reach the consulting room in a wing that connects to Alpha Twelve. Evan McKinley stands at the door. He greets me, and I peer inside. Donny Ray is seated and waiting at the table, wrists and ankles under restraint, body slumped forward, elbows jammed into his sides.

Holding the floor firm under his gaze.

I enter, then keep silent and still, not only to prevent my presence from feeding his apparent distress, but also as an opportunity to more closely scrutinize and process his overall presentation. The perspiration that soaks his collar. The disheveled hair. It's safe to surmise that Donny Ray had a rough night. I can also deduce through these physical cues that he's trying to make his body appear as small as possible, which would seem to indicate fear. But not just any fear—it's powerful. So close to his skin I can almost smell it hanging on the air.

I take a few steps forward, and Donny Ray shoots his head up to look at me, then just as fast, he lowers it.

Whether those actions were reflexive or for my benefit, I don't yet know. With a patient suspected of killing ten kids, anything can be possible. I move closer toward him, and he again acknowledges my presence—albeit only by pulling his feet in beneath the chair and latching them around the legs. Not exactly what I'd been hoping for, but from what I've seen so far, I'm already aware that getting him to warm up could take some time.

"It's okay, Donny Ray," I say, voice quiet yet assertive.

The corded tendons in his neck loosen and smooth. By no means is the response anything earth-shattering—however, if genuine, it's perhaps a small opening. A start to the process of gaining trust.

"But I can't help you," I continue, "unless you give me your attention."

Donny Ray slowly lifts his head again, vision still aimed at the floor.

"We're just going to talk today," I say, taking my seat across from him. "I'll ask some questions, and you can answer them to the best of your ability. Do you understand what I'm telling you?"

He nods but still won't look at me.

"Donny Ray." I raise my voice. "Your attention, please?"

He at last shows me his face. Despite all attempts to keep my emotions steady, his blue gaze rattles me.

This is driving me crazy. Where have I seen those eyes?

"Before we start, I was just wondering. Have you heard anything from your attorney lately?"

He lifts one shoulder, shakes his head.

I pause to deliberate on Donny Ray's indifference. His attorney disappeared a week ago. Has nobody told him, or is he just stonewalling me?

"Let's start off by backtracking a bit. Are you able to recall memories from your past at this time?"

Donny Ray offers no answer.

I allow the silence to linger.

"Backtracking . . . ," he finally says. His thick southern drawl carries a new rasp that sounds like tension or exhaustion or maybe both.

"Yeah," I say. "Like for instance, when you were younger. How did things go in school?"

A listless shrug. "Okay, I guess."

"Okay, as in . . ."

"Nothing great."

"Did you get along all right with other kids?"

"Yeah."

"So then what did you mean by *nothing great*?"

"Just that I never fit in real good."

"How about your friendships during that period? What were those like?"

His expression appears a little vacant, but I'm not sure why, so I press. "Did you have friends?"

"No, sir, not really," he replies.

"*Not really*, meaning, not many or not any?"

He pulls his knees together, shifts his attention off to one side.

"Donny Ray?" I probe.

Then, through a weak sigh of surrender, "No, sir. I didn't have any friends."

The only expression he'll find on my face is empathy. I want to avoid any physical cues that could indicate I'm passing judgment.

"You know, as a kid I didn't have a lot of friends myself," I say, "because my dad was sick, and I spent most of the time taking care of him. It was awful. Lonely. I can't imagine how you must have felt not having any friends at all."

Donny Ray levels his gaze on me as if trying to verify the authenticity of my story. Then, for the first time since we've met, his legs move out from under the chair. His shoulders fall ever so slightly. Like he's releasing some of the tension—perhaps fear even—that he's been clinging to for days.

An inlet. A start.

"What about pets? They can be a lot better company than most people." I smile at him.

He fights back a smile of his own.

"Did you have any?"

He shakes his head rather adamantly. "No, sir. We didn't."

"How come?"

"Because of my dad." Donny Ray lifts his hands a few inches from his lap, almost as if unsure where they should go. Discomfort, and I'm curious what's causing it. "My dad always said that animals weren't worth anything unless they were used for work."

"And did you feel the same way?"

Donny Ray nods.

I ask if he can explain.

"Guess I never really thought about it. Maybe since we didn't have any animals, it was hard to know what I was missing?"

I find his response curious. He refrains from saying *pets*, instead referring to them as *animals*. This, of course, could merely be a product of his rural upbringing. But what has my interest more is not just his answer, but rather what rode just beneath it. A note of detachment that, along with his social history, may give my previous questions about him new context: no friends, no affection for animals. No relationships, period. This is a common building block for a lack of compassion and love, a tenet in the development of a psychopathic mind. Am I sitting across from a man who grew up isolated and lonely, or is he simply modeling the effects of what those circumstances should look and sound like?

Hoping to at least find the start of an answer, I go a little deeper. "It sounds like you didn't have a lot of allies in this world as a kid, Donny Ray."

He looks down again, says nothing.

"How did that make you feel? Having nobody you could turn to."

"Alone." His voice cracks on the last syllable. "Really alone. You know?"

And I do know, more than he realizes.

I push the feeling aside, smile sadly, and nod. But I'm also watching him carefully. Checking his demeanor. Trying to see through his outer layer. Yet, hard as I attempt to find even a shred of disingenuousness, I cannot. Donny Ray radiates vulnerable innocence. Then I think about all the people in his life—past and present—who seem to have mysteriously disappeared. My wrinkles of doubt. Adam's comments about Donny Ray's immaterial head injury. All of these troubling undertones run counterintuitive to the candor I've just witnessed here.

I'm stuck.

I look at my watch and realize that our session is drawing to a close. Evan waits at the door, ready to escort Donny Ray out.

"We have to stop for now," I say, giving Evan a nod. "We'll continue this in a—"

"Okay," Donny Ray interrupts softly, then with a polite smile says, "Have a safe night, Christopher."

An eerie sensation wriggles down my back.

12

I head toward the hospital parking lot and realize the weather fore-caster wasn't exactly wrong—just a day late. Those swirling clouds outside my window were indeed the first clue of an approaching storm, and now the moist air and hint of drizzle offer more tangible evidence.

Five miles up the road, the proof manifests in a thick curtain of downpour that drops on me suddenly, boosted by a powerful, ramping wind that kicks up loose gravel into my windshield. The horizon is dense and inky, trees bending to the threat of a vengeful gale. As I drive on, the storm gathers intensity, making my tires wayward and slippery.

Have a safe night, Christopher.

I can't seem to let Donny Ray's parting comment go. On its face, the statement would seem innocuous, and his manner appeared innocent enough. But there was something else enmeshed within his words. A tone that seemed to resonate with both insight and ambiguity. Almost like a warning.

Or was it?

I scrutinize my reaction. Am I exaggerating? Would I be so unsettled if another patient had made the same comment?

Do I really think he was threatening me?

Another strong wind forces the car into a shake, jangling my nerves and blowing the thought away. I fight for control of the wheel, but it does more harm than good. My tires hydroplane along flooded pavement with building velocity. Water blankets the windshield, creating instant road blindness that makes it nearly impossible to steer forward safely.

Out of instinct, I slam the brake pedal, but the engine grinds out an angry complaint, and my car jerks sharply to the right. My head rams into the side window, and for a few seconds I see stars. When they fade, I find myself midway into a dangerous skid.

Again, I struggle for control. About fifteen heart-stopping feet later, I manage to gain an upper hand as the wheels find traction, at last allowing me to slow. Just as my respiration starts to even out, reality settles, telling me I've just escaped what could have been a nasty smack-up.

My relief is short-lived. Several feet ahead, a rubber kickball rolls directly into my path, a teenaged boy in a red hoodie chasing after it.

Oh shit, oh shit . . . OH SHIT!

I yank the wheel to the left, trying to avoid the kid, but the wheel seems to have other ideas—it resists the effort and jerks out of my hands.

The boy freezes in my headlights, body rigid, eyes rounded by terror. My stomach roils, my pulse pounds, and I slam my foot against the brake pedal, but wet asphalt instantly counters the action, forcing the car into a screeching skid, propelling me even faster toward him. As a last-ditch effort, I wrench the wheel into a half turn that sends my car charging off the road. But now I'm hurtling toward a giant and unforgiving oak tree. I missed the kid but may end up paying for it with my own life.

I try to veer toward safety, but wet, slippery ground greases the wheels, fast-pitching my car right at the tree. I can't get my breath. A speeding pulse hammers through my ears.

It's over. Done.

A flash of light explodes with blinding fury, and the last thing I hear is glass shattering.

The last thing I see, a pair of eyes staring directly into mine.

Eyes so sharp, so evil, they could have claws and teeth. Eyes burning like the blaze of a hundred suns, waves of heat shooting out of them. Just below the eyes hangs a poisonous smile—I can't see it, but I don't have to. I can feel it.

Christopher, wake up. Can you wake up?

I have to wake up . . . Something's telling me I have to wake up.

My body jolts.

I'm gulping air down a throat that feels thick as rope and coated with wax. My vision is soupy, my eyelids heavy. Everything is tilted, and I don't know where I am. I'm not even sure whether I'm actually alive.

I see light.

My filmy haze clears enough to reveal the dashboard in front of me.

I'm in my car.

Then my mind kicks into gear.

The tree. I hit the tree.

I raise my head and peer out through the unbroken windshield.

No . . . no . . . that can't be.

My mind fumbles for purchase as my gaze travels to the tree, then reality pitches me a wicked curveball, revealing exactly how close I came to losing my life—about seven feet, to be exact, the distance from where my car has stopped before a steep bank that drops into one of the deepest parts of Anderson Lake. The fear of God sweeps through me, because if this tree hadn't done me in, the lake surely would have.

So, to what do I owe this miracle?

I open the door, stick my head out, and find the miracle itself staring up at me.

Saved by the ditch.

A look at the dashboard clock tells me I only lost consciousness for less than a minute. Then my memory comes out of hiding, and panic steams through me.

The boy.

I strong-arm the door open and leap from my car. Running alongside the road's shoulder, I search for him, but the terrain beneath my feet betrays me, becoming unbalanced and thick. My effort proves futile anyway because the boy is nowhere in sight.

What the . . . ?

Confusion sends me racing across the road and looking for the rubber ball, but it's not there, either.

I'm positive I saw both.

There's a park about a hundred feet off to my right. Maybe the kid came from there? Then common sense throws me a dummy-slap.

A boy. Playing with a ball. In the middle of a storm?

Wait, what storm?

I look up. The sky couldn't be clearer, covered only with a blanket of stars. My gaze drops to the asphalt, and I'm even more bewildered: dry as sandpaper.

How does that happen? Rapid evaporation?

Before I can ponder the laws of physics, pain knifes at my skull, followed by a dull throbbing ache behind my ears. I touch my forehead, inspect my fingers: blood.

Injured.

That's not good.

I stagger back toward the car, but about halfway there, it's clear the rest of my body isn't catching up with the plan. My equilibrium falters, and the earth turns to rubber. I stumble, then lean forward, and with hands rested on knees, try to find my balance.

Inside my car, the rearview mirror reveals the damage: a nasty gash just above my left brow, complemented by an unforgiving lump near the right temple. I remember smacking into the side window. I must have hit the steering wheel after my impromptu landing in the ditch.

Now I'm starting to worry just how serious my injury might be. I reach for a penlight, shine it into my eyes, but the pupils don't appear dilated. I find some relief in that, because it indicates that even if I've suffered a concussion, it's more than likely minor. After locating a box of tissues in my glove compartment, I apply gentle pressure to the wound and dab away the blood.

Back to the tree again. I take a closer look and see its trunk is split wide open, the base littered with pieces of jagged, rusted metal and broken plastic.

That could have been me. I could be dead right now.

I remind myself how notoriously dangerous this road is, how I'm constantly hearing about accidents on the news involving horrific injuries or even fatalities. It would appear I'm among the luckier ranks.

So what should I do now?

Call for help, idiot.

Help . . . yeah . . . Get help, that's it. I find my phone on the floorboard, but there's no signal. A quick glance around reminds me why. The road is situated in a low point with foothills all around. I can't count the number of times my phone has dropped calls while passing through here. I set my gaze uphill, knowing I'll be able to get reception there.

After turning the ignition key, I'm thankful to hear the engine start. I straighten my wheels, put the car into reverse, and rock my way out of the ditch. Seconds later, I'm racing up the hill.

13

Or maybe I was wrong.

I'm at the summit's peak, but my phone still isn't showing me the love. No bars.

To my right, I spot a potential explanation, another taller foothill that's likely blocking the cell signal. But I also see a clearing about a hundred feet away, so I get out of the car and trot toward it.

When I arrive, the bars at last make an appearance, only three, but I'll take them. I dial my wife and wait for her to pick up.

She does.

"Hi, honey . . . ," I say, for the first time realizing how thick my tongue feels as it wades through the sentence. "I'm okay, but I . . . but I've accident."

"What?"

"I mean . . . I . . . I've had an accident."

"How bad? Are you okay?" Jenna's voice grows more distraught with each syllable. "Where are you?"

"Yeah . . . my think my am . . ." I try to assure her, but my hoarse voice and jumbled words strain credibility beyond reasonable limits.

"Where are you?" she again asks.

"I was on Saxony . . . I lost control in the rain, swerved to miss a tree but . . . but ended up running . . . off the . . . I ran off the road."

"Chris, I don't like the way you sound at all."

"I hit my head on the steering wheel."

"*What?* Have you called an ambulance?"

"It's not that bad."

"Baby, you can barely even speak."

"I checked my pupils. They're fine. I can handle this."

"You can't, and I'm not about to let you try. I'll be there in—"

"*No!*" I cut her off. "Don't!"

About five seconds of quiet.

"It's just . . . ," I say, hearing desperate urgency in my voice that I'm unable to conceal. "I don't want you driving so late with Devon. This road is dangerous enough."

"Chris, this is not a good time for your persistent worries about Devon. You've been hurt. I can handle the road, and I'll call for the sitter."

"No. Absolutely not."

"But you can't possibly think you're getting behind the wheel like this."

"Honey, I'm more . . . I'm qualified to say I can drive or not."

You can barely put two words together, Dr. Moronic.

Shut up!

"I'm sorry," Jenna says, "but not on my watch. Either call Adam, or I'm on my way."

"I can't just leave my car here," I say, at last finding a foothold on clarity.

"That's not important now! We can get it in the morning."

I let out a long sigh. My wife's got me beat in the persistence department. Has the stubborn down pretty well, too. After a few seconds, I relent and say, "Okay, I'll get a hold of Adam."

"Call me when he's there," Jenna adds, then without allowing me a response, hangs up.

I scowl at the phone, but in all honesty, she's right. I probably shouldn't be driving—it's just that suddenly, and for reasons I can't explain, bad vibes are rocking through me. I don't like this place. I need to get out of here.

In my car, the throbbing resumes behind my ears with ferocious intensity, followed by skull-crushing tension. I lean back against the headrest and pray for deliverance from this pain.

My phone rings.

"Is Adam there?" Jenna asks.

"Well, no . . . not yet."

"What? Why?"

"Honey, please. We just got off the pho—" But as the dashboard clock comes into focus, my reprimand grinds to a scrambling halt. Forty-five minutes have passed.

"Chris?"

"Yeah," I answer, a little too rushed, a little too distracted, and then, "He'll be here soon."

"But he should already be there by now. What's taking him so long?"

What's taking him so long is that you never called, because you took a nap instead.

"He'll be here soon," I say again for lack of a more reasonable response. "I'll see you in a bit."

To avoid further explanation, I hang up, then take one last look at the tree resting downhill and obscured beneath shadows. The wind takes a sudden shift through the branches, opening them up like wide, outstretched arms. But this is no welcome—this is a warning.

A swath of red moves out from behind the tree. I get a fix on it but can't believe what I see. The teenager I nearly hit earlier is running away, and the farther he goes, the more his image becomes lost in the cover of night.

A vile sensation claws its way through my stomach and up into the back of my throat. And I know—without a second of doubt or a moment of hesitation—that there is indeed something terribly wrong with this place.

You've got to get the hell out of here.

I have to get out of here.

I turn the ignition key, slam the gas pedal, and before I know it, I'm flying up the road.

14

I make it home in one piece.

My body does, anyway. As for my mind, that's becoming more questionable by the minute. I'm not a medical doctor. I'm a damned psychologist, and that doesn't make me anywhere near qualified to determine whether I should drive with a head injury—it only makes me impulsive and thoughtless.

When I walk into the kitchen, Jake is lying on the floor asleep. He stirs, flicks his attention at me, then withdraws, appearing lethargic and detached.

"You okay, boy?"

The dog lifts his head, gives my leg a gentle nudge with his nose, then with chin resting on paws, stares absently ahead. Troubled, I watch him for a moment, but something dark on my pant leg distracts me. I inspect closer and find a muddy splotch.

I look back at Jake. His nose is covered in mud.

There are two problems here. First, I know his nose was clean just a moment ago. Second, I've got no idea where the muck could have possibly come from. Arizona is in a drought, and while I may or may not have seen rain before my accident, everything I've witnessed since has been bone dry.

I return to Jake and flinch. His nose is clean.

Before I can reason my way through this unsettling mud quandary, Devon darts into the room. He throws his arms around my legs, forcing my weight to shift abruptly, which sends an instantaneous stab of pain through my side. Now I've got bruised ribs to contend with, and as the initial shock wears off, I'm aware that more troubling injuries from the accident could soon surface. But for my son's sake, I try to conceal both the pain and worry.

"Daddy got a bad cut!" Devon proclaims, pointing to my forehead.

Jenna rushes in. As soon as she sees me, her expression bounces from relief to serious worry.

"Chris, sit down right now," she says. "You're bleeding."

I gingerly touch my head and feel dampness, now with added heat and a marked increase in swelling.

Jenna sits me in a chair, then heads for the sink. She runs a towel under the faucet, brings it back, and begins applying first aid.

"You look awful," she says, blotting the blood off my forehead.

"Just a small cut. It actually looks worse than it feels."

She pulls back to frown at me. She's not buying it.

Devon now sits across from me at the table, leaning forward and watching. "Does it hurt, Daddy?"

"Not too bad," I say, then throw in a wink to go with my little white lie.

"I don't like the way this looks at all," Jenna says. "I think we should take you to the emergency room."

"It's not necessary. I'll be fine."

"What if it's something serious?"

"Sweetie, believe me, I'd know if it was. I'll have Adam check me over tomorrow."

She gives me another look, then goes back to work and shakes her head. "I think you need some treatment."

I'm with the wife on that one. Seeing and hearing things that don't exist isn't exactly small potatoes.

"Stuff it!"

Jenna pulls back to look at me again, only this time it's not worry I see but, rather, injured surprise. Add me to the startled list because I've got no idea how my thought transformed into spoken words. It's like my brain sprouted speakers.

I go for the save. "I said *I'll tough it.*"

Jenna watches me, but I'm not sure whether she's measuring the veracity of my statement or still assessing my condition.

"Please don't worry, sweetheart," I say.

But it seems my assurance is only worth a frustrated sigh, followed by, "Your head is so damned hard that I'm actually surprised the crash managed to break skin."

For the first time in the last hour, I grin.

Jenna bustles for an ice pack, and I retreat to the couch, thoughts funneling past my headache like cloudy dishwater. Devon perches in the easy chair across from me, and his company is a welcome distraction.

Jenna enters the room. She doesn't look concerned about my injury right now. She looks . . .

"What's the matter?" I ask.

"Your car is in the garage."

Oh. Shit.

I meant to explain that earlier, come clean right away, but it's too late. I'm in trouble.

"Yeah," I say. "About that . . ."

"Please tell me you did not drive home."

"I sort of did."

Jenna points to the staircase but keeps her eyes nailed to me as she says, "Devon, please go to your room."

Devon looks at his mom, looks at me, and gets the picture. He's out of here.

"You drove yourself."

"Honey, I just wanted to get home."

"After I told you not to."

"Basically, yes," I say, then quickly add, "But I swear, I wasn't trying to make you mad." I inhale sharply. "It was something else . . ."

Jenna must sense my distress because her expression softens. Her tone, too. "Chris, what are you saying?"

I draw some more air, let it out slowly. "Something happened. I got scared."

She takes a seat at my side, studying me with guarded concern.

"I told you I lost control, but what I didn't tell you . . ." I steeple my hands, keep my eyes aimed on them. " . . . is that I saw things."

Jenna's body relaxes, but the action doesn't signal relief—it's recognition—and without speaking, she says: *I get it.*

A few seconds of quiet stretch between us, and I need them, because I'm not sure what to say, and because the fear I was speaking of earlier now seems that much more real.

"Baby," Jenna whispers, "you are not your father."

All I can do is shake my head.

"This isn't the same thing." She reaches for my hand, gives it a squeeze. "It's not him."

"It *is* him. It's always him."

"You're upset. That's making everything seem worse."

"I know . . ."

And I do know. I know that my exhaustion from work could have played a part in what I saw before the accident, then my head injury further precipitated the visual distortions after. But that doesn't make this any easier. Jenna is well aware of my fear, knows that I battle it every day. Fear that any misperception, anything strange, could be a whisper from the past, coming to pay a most unwelcome visit. That what happened to my father will happen to me.

"Just a few moments," I say, "that's all it takes. Just a few moments of uncertainty, and I'm there again."

"The accident played with your mind."

I nod.

"Please promise me you'll have this looked at tomorrow."

"I'll have it looked at."

"You still should have told me."

"I know."

"But I also understand how you can get."

"I shut down. I close up."

She smiles a little. "Let's keep working on that, okay?"

I try to smile back.

"And do me one more favor? No more driving with a dented head again. Ever. Got it?"

"I promise."

"And if you get scared like that, you tell me." Jenna leans over, gives me a kiss, and I feel a little better.

That is, until I catch sight of Jake over her shoulder, body inert, expression stoic and fixed on the front door. Like he's waiting for someone.

Or something.

15

THE MAN IN THE DRAIN

Trouble was on the slow burn and moving through our home, through our lives.

My father began acting just a little odd. At first it didn't feel like much cause for alarm. I'd occasionally overhear him mumble quietly while doing things around the house, but it seemed more like thinking out loud than anything else. So I brushed it off.

Until the mumbling turned into what sounded like an exchange with a voice only he could hear. Then, little by little, his comments took a disturbing turn, straying far outside the lines of normalcy, his shades of gray falling deeper into darkness.

My mother, just like always, pretended nothing was wrong. She wrote off the statements as his offbeat humor. Then in a fleeting moment during dinner one evening, the earth shifted beneath our feet, and just like that, we found ourselves on a whole other planet.

"There's someone inside the drain," my father proclaimed matter-of-factly, speaking around a mouthful of potatoes.

"What's that, darling?" My mother regarded him briefly, her smile revealing negligible interest as she placed a bowl on the table.

After swallowing his food, he said, "In the drain."

"There's something in the drain?"

"Some*one*."

"James, take some collard greens. You love those." That was her response.

My father shrugged, then scooped greens onto his plate. "He's in the bathroom. In the tub. A man—or I'm pretty sure he is, anyway. It's hard to tell sometimes."

"Stop being silly," my mother said with a dismissive giggle, then with a grin of encouragement, motioned enthusiastically toward his plate, "Try those greens! Tell me what you think!"

"I've seen him there twice," he said, throwing me a confidential wink and smile, as if revealing some secret we'd been sharing.

I wasn't smiling. I was unnerved. Not only because of his nonsensical observation but also because there was something in his demeanor I didn't recognize—as though a stranger was posing as my dad.

"Honestly, James," my mother remarked, "the things you say sometimes."

Dad reached for a slice of bread and shrugged again. "He's there. You'll see."

"I forgot the dumplings!" And with that, she was gone from the room.

After she returned, dinner went on for several minutes in tight silence, until my father shook it loose.

He pushed his plate away, leaned back. "He says he's going to kill us all."

It was as if every bulb in the room had blown because all I saw was utter darkness. My father's mind had turned inside out and landed smack dab on the dining room table. Even Mom couldn't ignore that one, and her face—blank and nearly bloodless—showed it.

But the dinner horror show paled in comparison to what I saw a few hours later.

I walked into the bathroom, and my legs went flimsy.

There was my father, inside the tub and hunched over the drain.

Talking to it.

Pleading.

16

My headache refuses to let up.

The ribs aren't cooperating much either, shifting from sore and tender to stabbing and stinging. Despite how lousy I feel, I stop by Devon's room to tuck him in.

Entering through the doorway, I find him belly to floor and searching beneath his bed.

"What are you looking for there, kiddo?"

He draws his head up to look at me. "My pajamas."

"Unless I've missed something, Mom doesn't keep them there."

"But they were just on the bed a little bit ago."

"Then they have to be somewhere." I give the room a cursory inspection.

Devon stands up and frowns.

"No worries, buddy." I pull open his dresser drawer, grab another set of pajamas, and hand it to him. "I'm sure there's a logical explanation."

As he begins changing into his PJs, I take a seat on the bed and notice Jake several feet away, chin resting on paws, foreboding eyes aimed at me. Again, I'm baffled. Long before my son's body can hit the sheets, without fail, Jake is already there and waiting. This is a constant, one I've been witness to for years. It's their pattern.

But not tonight.

Devon crawls into bed, and I nod toward the dog. "Is he doing okay?"

Without so much as sparing Jake a glance, he says, "Uh-huh."

"Are you sure?"

"Uh-huh," he says again.

"Because he seems a little down."

"He's okay." Devon pulls the blanket up and over his chest.

"And he's usually in bed with you by now."

My son shrugs and reaches across the bed for Jake's favorite toy, the rubber bone, then tosses it onto the floor. The bone drops beside Jake's head. Jake doesn't seem remotely interested. I puzzle over the strange dynamic playing out between boy and dog, wondering if there's more to this than Devon is telling me.

"Daddy?"

I look quickly back at my son.

"The accident hurt you bad."

"Not so bad," I say and notice that Jake is now sitting across from Devon's door and gaping at it. Just like earlier. As if he's waiting for something.

"Daddy?" Devon says again, and I look back at him.

"We forgot liftoff last night," he informs me.

"You're right." I consider Jake again, still troubled by his behavior.

Liftoff is our secret evening ritual. Actually, it was how I used to get Devon into bed when he was younger. We never said *bedtime* or *sleep*, because for most kids, those are dirty words. Instead it was a *time travel mission*, and he wasn't sleeping, he was transforming into a special crime fighter to rid the world of evil. It worked like a charm, and even though he eventually wised up to my game, our little routine has endured. I'm not really up for this, considering how I feel, but his eager expression makes it hard to say no.

"Ready?" I say.

"Ready," he replies through a big, gap-toothed smile.

I pull the covers up snugly around him, then intone, "This is Ground Control to Spartan Newberg." He still loves when I use his covert crime fighter code name. "Do you copy?"

"Copy!" He squirms, then settles.

"You are clear for liftoff."

Devon makes rumbling rocket sounds with his mouth.

And I begin the countdown. "Five . . . Four . . . Three . . . Two . . ."

"One!" he shouts with glee, then does the liftoff noise.

"Go get those bad guys, kiddo. The clock is ticking, Spartan, and only you can restore order to the world."

I straighten the covers, kiss his forehead, then step softly toward the door.

Before leaving, I steal one last look at Jake, still parked there, still with that desolate, edgy, ominous expression.

17

I spend most of my night riding the Insomniac Express, bouncing between brief periods of turbulent sleep and wakeful, agitated tossing and turning. My head and ribs take their shots at keeping the action going.

With a new sun now on the rise, I look at Jenna beside me in restful slumber, kiss her cheek, and she blearily opens her eyes.

"Come closer," she says with her sleepy little smile, softly brushing a hand across my cheek.

I do, and she returns a sleepy little kiss.

"Feeling any better?" she asks.

"Some." I force a comforting grin.

She doesn't say anything, but I know the look. My wife is worried. For reassurance, I kiss her again, then drag my aching body from bed to shower, hoping the warm water will deliver some relief.

Unfortunately, the payoff is marginal at best. I'm a bit more awake, but that just makes everything hurt harder.

I dry off, then check my injury in the mirror. The forehead swelling has gone down, but . . .

Something doesn't look right.

I move in closer, study myself, then discover the problem. My hair looks odd and unfamiliar. Different, but I have no idea how. Still, looking into the mirror is making me terribly uncomfortable.

I try to concentrate on brushing my teeth but can't let the uneasiness go. I keep glancing up, and the more I see myself, the more on edge I feel. Finally, I can't stand it anymore. I turn on the faucet, throw my hands under the water, then run my fingers across my scalp. I grab a comb and restyle, but the result ends up exactly the same.

My hair is still wrong.

"Honey, you'll be late," Jenna calls from the bedroom.

I look at the clock and realize she's right.

Another glance in the mirror only fuels more frustration, so I reach for the comb, move my part to the other side, and find a small measure of respite from my bad hair day.

Strange things are happening.

And they're scaring the hell out of me.

18

There's something so very peculiar about revisiting the scene of an accident, especially your own. It's knowing that, in a heartbeat, you've had a glimpse at just how precious and fragile life can be, how quickly it can be taken away. Those lingering emotional remnants often speak louder than any skid marks or jagged, twisted metal ever could. The physical traces can be washed away, but a cerebral imprint never leaves, time only making it that much more powerful.

I feel all of this, and maybe more things I can't even begin to describe, as I approach the tree on my drive toward work. Though daybreak has come, it feels like darkness still surrounds the tree, just a few bright slivers of sunlight shafting through a bruised and battered sky, striking the branches like fiery daggers.

As my car reaches a point where the trunk sits closest to the road, I feel more agitated. Now the tree has taken on a more threatening aura, standing tall and firm as if making a bold statement of power. I study its immense branches, like giant, mythical arms that want to reach out and pull me into a swirling vortex of pernicious evil.

Just as we cross paths, I see it flaunting its bare wound like some sinful badge of honor. I push hard on the gas pedal, and my car surges forward, picking up speed.

Not fast enough.

Because I don't like that tree. Don't like it one goddamned bit.

19

I reach for the door handle at Loveland, and my ribs deliver a ferocious objection. Then my head joins in with ruthless and grinding pain. I grimace, assuring myself that this is to be expected, that neither are signs of anything serious. So far, everything around me looks normal, but I remain watchful for any weird sights or sounds.

When I step into the building, it's like I've flipped a switch in my mind, and thoughts of Donny Ray shift to the forefront.

Have a safe night, Christopher.

Not so much.

In retrospect, and for obvious reasons, his comment needles under my skin. But there's something else about it that's niggling at me—something less obvious, something I can't even quantify.

I try to chase the thought away, tell myself I'm being ridiculous, and continue through the hallway toward my office. But much like the aches and pains waging war on my body, Donny Ray's message is doing the same to my mind. So I unload my belongings, deciding it's at last time to prove he's not the villain I've made him out to be. I head for Alpha Twelve to check on my enigmatic patient.

But after stepping onto the floor, I stand amid punctuated silence, and it's not the soothing kind—it's the weird one.

Alpha Twelve is rarely quiet this time of day, and even when things are relatively calm, it only takes one visitor to stir things up—then before you know it, faces thrust against windows, voices shout, and the momentum of chaos continues to build. But that's not happening today. No mattress springs bouncing or creaking, no feet shuffling across the tiles. Not a single voice to be heard. Even as I step down the hall, every window remains vacant, every patient beyond it lost in some sort of commanding, dead hush.

I look ahead through the Plexiglas window at the nurses' station. No sign of anyone around, and my concern ramps up. There's another problem I can't describe but can definitely feel: the air surrounding me is not just silent—it's still. Unreasonably still, as if someone or something has turned it dormant. Alpha Twelve is never predictable, but it does tend to have established patterns of nuttiness, and what I've just witnessed strays wildly from any of them. If I've learned anything around here, it's that more than disorder, quiet can often be a precursor to trouble. At least with the latter, you can see it coming.

I move forward on edge. The flooring beneath my feet feels atypically uneven, the walls around me atypically narrow. Peering into the first room, I find that my ardent admirer, Gerald Markman, doesn't seem so keen about anything right now. He stands in a shadowy corner and faces the wall, his body rigid, his feet firm to the floor like bolted fixtures.

"Gerald," I say.

He gives no response.

Another disturbing abnormality. Like the ward itself, most of our patients have established baselines, which the medical staff document and rely on as predictors, both in giving care and to detect potential danger. Gerald has taken a distinct and oppositional shift.

An indiscernible whisper pulls me away from Gerald. I wheel around for a better listen and realize it's coming from Nicholas Hartley's room.

I pad that way, and the tone becomes clearer, but the words do not. He's rambling and delirious with a scrape in his voice you'd hear after someone's been screaming too loudly and for too long.

I find Nicholas in bed, hands no longer working the pleasure zone; in fact, his appearance is downright distraught: head to chest, arms wrapped around knees. Steadily and rhythmically rocking himself. Still whispering, but faster now, as if my presence demands it. I try to make out what he's saying, and one sentence emerges from the chatter.

"That sleep of death, Christopher."

Ice water spills down my spine.

I check the remaining rooms, but all I find is more of the same: patients oddly subdued and detached, none of them wanting to so much as look at me.

Except, that is, for one.

20

Donny Ray Smith peers out at me through his window.

I walk toward him, and those cold blue eyes beam into mine like beacons. Then in an instant, they change, and something flashes through them—a fleeting moment of stark transparency, a portal into some dark place where I don't want to go.

Much like what I saw in that video clip.

Uneasiness shakes me, but at this point, I don't know whether to trust my perceptions, and really, I shouldn't. I'm rattled, well aware that in this state, distortions can abound.

And whatever I did or didn't see in Donny Ray's eyes is now gone. His face is calm and blank as he walks away from the window.

I reach for the door handle, but it offers no resistance, spinning freely within its tumbler. I jump back. Now I'm more than uneasy—I'm actually very nervous. Jeremy made it abundantly clear that Donny Ray is being held under the strictest of protective measures. An unlocked door definitely falls below that standard.

And where's Evan?

I grab my phone and call security to request assistance.

A few minutes later, Evan arrives.

"Where have you been?" I ask.

"What?"

"Why is nobody standing guard outside Donny Ray's room?"

"Shift change."

"You guys don't cover the gap between them?"

"Normally, but we're short one person. I got called in early, because Peters hasn't shown up for work in two days."

"What do you mean? Is he sick?"

Evan shakes his head. "Nobody knows. He didn't answer his phone, and when we sent somebody by his house, the place was empty."

"Empty, as in . . ."

"Everything. No furniture, no car . . . no Peters."

I look at Evan for a good five seconds, then nod toward Donny Ray's door. "It's unlocked. This could have been a serious problem."

Evan immediately inspects the door, but when he attempts to turn the knob, it won't budge. He looks up at me.

I step forward and try it myself.

Locked.

"I swear the thing was unsecured just a few minutes ago."

Evan scratches his head. "Could be something with the mechanism?"

I'm still staring at the door.

"I'll radio for backup," he says, "and try to figure out what happened with the lock."

I explain the other patients' strange behavior to Evan, then he enters Donny Ray's room to check on him.

"Nothing suspicious with the patient that I can see," he tells me after returning outside, then with cautious steps, proceeds up the hallway, looking carefully into the other rooms.

Evan comes back and says, "They all seem fine to me."

I'm stunned and speechless.

"You're clear to go inside if you want," he says, reaching for his key ring.

Wary and watchful, I enter Donny Ray's room.

Inside, I find him sitting up in bed. A pair of fluorescent tubes hovers overhead, bathing his face in blue, sulfurous light. I move toward him, observing that his restraints are now gone. In and of itself, that's not unusual. We don't keep patients bound unless they pose a threat to themselves or others. Apparently, he's calmed down enough to warrant this, but with the lock to his door acting wonky, I'm not quite loving it.

I step closer and find more to bristle my nerves, because Donny Ray is clearly in a different state than yesterday. A far better one. His posture is firm, his hair combed neatly in place. Face fresh, skin more evenly toned. Judging by his much improved appearance and manner, it would also seem that whatever moved through Alpha Twelve missed this room—either that or it was no match for Donny Ray Smith.

Is he in some way connected to all this?

The thought is fleeting, but I consider him more closely.

"Is something wrong?" he asks in his southern twang.

"I feel like I should be asking you that question," I say, still observing him, still trying to sort through my mixed-up impressions.

He shakes his head, appears confused.

"Donny Ray," I say, standing just a few feet away from him now, "what's going on with your door?"

"My what?"

"It was unlocked when I arrived."

He gives the door a baffled glance. "I can't tell you."

"What's that supposed to mean?"

"I didn't know it was unlocked," he says.

I study his affect, trying to discern whether he's telling the truth. "What about before I arrived?"

"I'm not sure what you mean."

"Outside. On the floor. Did anything happen? A disturbance of some kind? Maybe something to upset the other patients?"

"I don't think so."

"You don't sound very sure about it."

Donny Ray looks past me, face blank, eyes shooting back and forth like dancing blue flames. "I'm really *not* sure. I was dead asleep, Christopher."

That sleep of death, Christopher.

A sharp and fiery sensation twists through me.

"But Nicholas was having bad dreams all night," he offers rather quickly.

"Donny Ray, I never mentioned Nicholas. What made you think I was talking about him, specifically?"

"I heard him." He shrugs. "Anyone could."

Nicholas' room is a good fifty feet from here. Would his mumbling whispers actually penetrate these thick concrete walls? My nod feels hesitant. Since I wasn't here earlier, there's no way to verify whether what he's telling me is true.

Before I can press further, there is noise and motion through the window in Donny Ray's door. Evan and some other members of our security staff are talking, and one of them is turning the knob to inspect it.

I get a little lost inside my head.

"Christopher?"

My attention jerks back to Donny Ray, but when I look at the bed, it's empty. I blink a few times, then swing my gaze to the left. He's now standing on the opposite side of this room. I didn't see him get up, didn't even hear or sense it.

His face reads like an empty page.

"You've lost something." He holds up my pen.

I pat my shirt. The pocket is empty. I feel unhinged, unsure what's going on.

"We're not supposed to have these," he tells me, as if I don't already know that patients are forbidden from having sharp objects.

My fingers feel a little numb, a little cold, as I take the pen from him. Then I glance back at the window. Evan and the security officers are gone. I never saw or heard them leave.

"Thanks for clearing things up," he says appreciatively. "It was very helpful."

What is he talking about?

"Sure . . . ," I say, angst juddering my response. I've got no idea what I'm agreeing to, but at this point, making him aware of my confusion doesn't feel professional. "I'll be seeing you soon."

"Okay." He smiles politely. "Careful on that road from now on. It sounds like a nasty one."

Razor-edged fright torpedoes through me. "What are you talking about?"

He points at my forehead. "The car wreck."

"How did you know about that?"

"You just told me."

"No, I didn't."

"Yes, sir, you did." He's nodding, but not in a manner that challenges. More like a kindly reminder. "You said you lost control and had a horrible accident."

I most certainly did not tell him that. Maybe he's just taking a stab after noticing my bruise?

Or is it my bruised mind? Is it possible that I actually *did* tell him?

And in that moment, looking into those infernos of blue, I can no longer contain my curiosity.

"Donny Ray," I say, "have we met somewhere before?"

He offers no answer, but his blank expression snares my nerves, subtle shades of doubt telling me what I already know.

I shouldn't have asked.

I feel pressure near the right side of my head. I reach up and find something tucked behind my ear. I pull the object out and look at it.

My pen.

But I was just holding it in my hand.

I turn quickly and head out the door, but about five feet down the hallway, I get hold of myself. Too much weirdness going on, and I can't leave here without figuring out the cause.

After returning to Donny Ray's room, I look through the door and find him standing before the rear wall window, back facing me, arms hanging loosely at his sides, body motionless. I take a shaky step closer.

Donny Ray steps toward his window.

The hairs on the back of my neck start to rise—I run a hand over them.

Donny Ray does the same.

Am I imagining this?

I shake my head in bafflement.

He shakes his head.

There has to be a simple explanation. He can see my reflection in the glass.

No, that's not possible.

It's broad daylight outside—there *is* no reflection. Besides, Donny Ray's window is positioned off to the left, placing me out of the glass' line of sight.

A quiver rips up my spine. I need to get the hell out of here, and my feet can't carry me fast enough.

21

Something very peculiar is happening, but I haven't a clue what.

I do, however, know one thing. I've got a bad case of the creeps, and it's drilling deeper under my skin.

What was Donny Ray doing by that window?

Then there was my pen.

Which seemed to move from one place to the next completely independent of my will or awareness. I have no memory of removing the thing from my pocket or even dropping it. Much more unsettling is that it ended up in a violent patient's hands and could have been used as a shank—an error with repercussions I don't even want to consider. His reminding me of it only added to all the strangeness.

I reach my floor and see Adam stepping out of his office. He takes one look at my dazed expression and says, "Whoa. What happened to you?"

"There's a problem in Alpha Twelve," I say, winded and trying to slow my spinning thoughts.

Adam throws me a look of confusion.

I give him one back.

He says, "I was actually asking about your forehead."

"Oh, that." I glance up and down the hallway. "I kind of had a car accident last night."

"*Kind of?* Looks like you did one hell of a job at it. Why don't you come in and let me have a look?"

I'm in no condition for this right now, but he isn't leaving me much choice, so I follow him inside his office. He points me to the visitor's chair.

I lower myself to sit, then explain about the accident. But not about the vanishing rain, and definitely not about the boy and his ball. I trust Adam but don't want to alarm him, let alone create awkwardness by making him doubt my mental stability. I'm still convinced my audiovisual distortions were brought on by stress, then exacerbated by the two knocks to my head.

He narrows in on the cut above my brow. "You worried about it?"

"A little. I can't seem to shake this headache."

"You could have a concussion." He reaches into a pocket for his penlight, clicks it on, and says, "Look straight ahead."

He checks my pupils, then administers a few coordination and balance tests.

"You seem okay," he says after finishing. "If there's a concussion, it's probably minor and should resolve itself. I don't see any cause for concern."

"Great, and thanks." I gently run a finger over the wound. "Jenna's been worried."

Adam is staring at me again. He nods toward the top of my head. "Trying something new there, sport?"

"Huh?"

"The 'do."

I look away from him, scrub a hand through my hair. "It's no big deal. I just moved the part."

When I turn back, Adam is now giving me another look—it involves one cocked brow and one emerging smirk. I give him a look back, but mine's not so jovial.

He takes the hint, raises his hands in surrender, and makes a negligible attempt at taming his smirk. "So what's this about Alpha Twelve?"

"Something very strange was going on."

"Strange is kind of how they roll down there, right?"

"But it was uncharacteristically so. I walked onto the floor and everything was eerily quiet. Not a peep from any of the patients—they were all so subdued, then Nicholas Hartley whispered to me."

"Nicholas who?"

"The guy we saw that first day. You remember."

"I was too busy watching Jeremy for signs of life. Anyway, what did he say?"

"Something about 'that sleep of death'?"

Adam shakes his head, confused.

"Strange, don't you think?"

"If you ask me, it sounds like just another day at Loveland."

"But he also said my first name."

Adam shrugs. "He could have heard Jeremy say it, right?"

"And none of the patients would so much as look at me. They were in some sort of weird and altered state. I've been on that floor more times than I can count, and I've never seen them so subdued."

"But you're not there all the time, right?"

"Well, no . . ."

"Besides, since when is it a problem if the patients are quiet instead of unruly?" Adam's smile is amused, and now I feel silly for even bringing it up.

The conversation stalls. Then he says, "Did you see Donny Ray while you were down there?"

"I did," is all I offer.

"And? Anything new with him?"

"Just his entire attitude."

"Really . . ." He straightens his posture. "Like, how?"

"Like he seemed a lot more comfortable than the first time we saw him."

Adam crosses his arms over his chest, leans back in his chair. "Couldn't keep the scared puppy routine going for very long?"

"Maybe."

"Can't say it completely surprises me."

"I'd imagine not. It sounds like you're pretty close to a decision about him, anyway."

"Actually, I've already reached one. I'm just finishing up my eval."

"Already?"

"Well, yeah. It's kind of a no-brainer from my end. I've gone through all the tests and Ammon's notes, and I've concluded my physical exam of Donny Ray, which answered any remaining questions."

I look at his computer screen, then back at him. "So, you're going to say he's malingering."

Adam laughs. "You look more surprised than you should there, buddy. What's up?"

"No . . . nothing, really. Just seems like you turned it around pretty fast."

"With only five days left 'til deadline, time is a luxury, partner." He taps his watch. "You saw Jeremy cracking the whip."

"I figured maybe you would have consulted with me, first."

Adam gapes at me.

"Sorry . . ." I try waving off my concern. "Guess I'm just feeling pressured because you got done so fast."

But to be honest, because of all the mixed messages Donny Ray has been sending, I feel even further away from the truth than before.

And I'm still slightly irritated by how Adam just minimized what I saw in Alpha Twelve.

He squares his focus on me. He knows me all too well, can easily detect when something is bubbling inside.

"Chris," he says with a sidelong look. "Is there anything else going on that you're not telling me?"

"No, why?"

"You seem—I don't know—a bit high-strung?"

"I had a car accident last night," I remind him.

"Right . . . right. Of course," he says with a smile, but the slightest trace of hesitancy strains it.

He knows.

Knows what?

"Oh, jeez." I check my watch, but the action feels a little too abrupt and perfunctory. "Didn't realize how long I've been here. Better get busy on that evaluation."

I don't wait for Adam's reaction as I head for the door. But after turning back to smile my good-bye, I catch the fretful look on his face.

22

I was wrong.

The tree looks worse at night, and drawing closer, I could swear the big ugly thing is staring at me, its gnarled roots bulging from the ground like giant arteries full of poison, waiting to wrap themselves around me.

Devour me.

As my car's headlights hit the trunk and our shadows cross, a brittle sensation claws through my intestines. At first, I'm unable to name it, but as the road curves away, and the unsavory and magnetic draw diminishes, my emotions take shape.

I feel anger.

Anger so gritty, so carnal, that I can taste the rancidness on my tongue. Anger that grabs hold and shakes me, anger that refuses to let go; and in that instant, I come to an agreement with myself.

I hate that Evil Tree.

Hate it more than I've ever hated anything before. A new brand of hate, caustic, corrosive as battery acid. Hate running deeper than those roots could ever reach, farther than those branches could ever stretch.

I know the feeling is mutual, that we share an understanding, this tree and I.

We are mordant and dangerous enemies.

And that once this battle is through, only one of us will be left standing.

23

Before entering the house, I strike a deal with myself to leave today's stress at the door. Home is my safe harbor, my distant shore, and I won't let what happened at Loveland rob me of that. I've worked too hard at drawing the line. I'm not going to stop now.

Jenna catches sight of me, and her expression falls. I get a little wobbly and wonder whether my attempt to appear calm is perhaps too transparent. Then I'm relieved to see she's actually looking at my forehead.

I tell myself to settle, that everything's fine, that allowing her to see me flustered will only bring on more worry about the accident.

I kiss her on the cheek. "Looks better, right?"

She pulls back to inspect the wound. "Still not great, but yeah, better. A little time is what it needs."

"Not sure the guy playing bongos on my head got the memo."

"Oh, dear. Did you have Adam take a look?"

I open the fridge, reach for a soda. "He said everything's fine."

When I turn back, Jenna's expression softens with observable relief. She smiles, but then the corners of her mouth sink appreciably.

"Something wrong?" I ask, unsteadiness making an unwelcome return visit.

"What did you do with your hair?"

Oh, God. Not this again.

I break from her gaze, move to the counter, then mindlessly thumb through a stack of mail. "I just changed the part."

"How come?"

"I don't know. Trying something different, I guess?" I glance back at her. "Why? Don't you like it?"

Her shrug is tentative.

This morning, my style adjustment seemed reasonable, but now, in retrospect, it feels sort of silly.

"No Corvette next," I say, trying to create diversion through humor, "I promise."

My joke falls flat. Jenna's smile seems obligatory.

"Gosh," I say, then head quickly into the dining room, "I'm really hungry."

I make it to the dinner table without further conflict, helped in part by my son, who's stirring up trouble of his own.

The food skirmish continues.

At the moment, he's practicing his spatial reasoning skills, carefully manipulating the items on his plate to create an illusion of emptiness. His least favorite, the peas—but typically any vegetable—are exiled to the outer rim of his plate, circling it like a pretty wreath. His second least favorite, the rice—but as a rule, any starch, except for spaghetti or macaroni and cheese—has been expertly spread out and distributed with near-perfect symmetrical balance.

"I can still see the peas, sweetheart," Jenna says with a patient smile.

"Peas suck!" my son shouts.

Jenna frowns, and I've got to cut off any argument at the pass. With a stern look as my warning, I say, "Devon, there are better and nicer ways to state your likes and dislikes. Mom works hard to prepare dinner for us each day, and it hurts her feelings when you say things like that."

"Sorry," he mutters. Not the most earnest apology but hopefully enough to facilitate peace.

Jenna still looks mildly irritated. I offer her a warm smile of diplomacy: *He's just a kid.*

She rolls her eyes: *Boy, do I know.*

Our smiles broaden. Mission accomplished.

Until less than four minutes later when, with his plate still full of food, Devon gleefully announces, "Okay. I'm done now."

"No," Jenna says, "you are not."

"But Moooom!"

I'm about to step in again when a wave of pain chisels through my head, so severe that it makes my teeth chatter. I close my lids and try with everything I've got to endure the agony.

Jenna and Devon are still debating, but I can't hear any of it. I'm too busy trying to ride out this bone-crushing agony. A few deep breaths later it eases, allowing me back into the moment. Devon offers Jenna his signature scowl, then gives the plate his signature grimace. He goes back to rearranging—but not eating—the food. Jenna scolds. He whines. The collective tone grows more heated by the second. With evident frustration, my son finally makes a token attempt, forcing himself to eat a single pea, while holding his nose and squinting at the offending vegetable.

"I ate it," he says.

"Not one pea. All of them."

"Mom!"

"SHUT THE FUCK UP!"

My wildly inappropriate profanity leaves me thunderstruck. I heard it but have no idea where it came from. I look at Devon, his eyes wide and brimming with tears.

"Chris!"

I swing my head toward Jenna. Before I can respond, a blinding flash of white light goes off, followed by the sound of shattering glass, which scares the bejesus out of me. As the light fades, my wife reappears, but her expression has changed. Though she apparently didn't see the light, she clearly observed my reaction to it, and her face now mirrors my confusion.

"I'm so sorry," I offer, voice sheepish, mind reeling further into disorder and uncertainty.

The lines on Jenna's face deepen. Devon is stunned into silence, staring at me with unfamiliar—and heartbreaking—fear.

I'm just as appalled by my behavior. No, I'm horrified, because the words shot out so fast that my conscious mind never had a chance to see them coming. It felt like somebody else was talking. Now, in addition to the shock, I'm frightened.

I look at Jenna.

I'm also in deep trouble.

"Wow," she calmly says to Devon but keeps her eyes pinned onto mine. "Daddy's very upset right now. Everything's going to be okay. Why don't we set you up with a movie so that he and I can talk about it?"

My son makes tracks toward the staircase, but, to my surprise, Jake stays behind. Much like last night, he's lying on the floor, head resting on paws, same desolate look painted across his face.

Staring at me.

And I'm even more confused, but lately that seems to be the flavor of the day. Jake follows Devon everywhere but now seems to be detaching from him, and I don't understand why.

"What the hell was that all about?"

Jenna's voice jars me from bafflement, and all I can manage is, "I don't know."

"What do you mean, you *don't know*?"

"It means what I said."

"That's not acceptable," she replies, the heat of her glare nearly scorching the hairs on my arms. "We had an agreement, Chris."

"I know."

"That we would never speak that way in front of our son, especially directly *to* him, and especially not *that* word."

My own anger unexpectedly flashes red. "You don't have to recite the rules to me! I'm not a child. I didn't forget!"

"Well, apparently, you—"

"I slipped, okay?" I slam my fist on the table with such force that silverware rattles and dishes clank. Jenna falls silent, and I know in an instant, without a shade of doubt, that I've managed to turn this mess into a disaster. And the worst part is that, with all the rapid-fire distractions going through my mind, I can't remember how it all began. I start to apologize again, but before I can finish, Jenna gets up and leaves the room.

And here I sit, off-balance, bewildered, but most of all, deeply troubled.

Seconds later, I'm climbing the stairs. Though I don't understand what just happened, I can't leave my son feeling lost in it.

When I reach Devon's room, he's in bed and watching his movie. He looks up at me, but before I can speak, my face goes bloodless and my stomach shrinks into a rock-hard knot.

Sloppily scrawled across my son's blanket is one word.

MUD.

Written in mud.

24

WITH A WAVE OF HER WAND

My mother and I watched a stranger emerge. An intruder. A thief who, little by little, was stealing my father away. It was frightening and infuriating, but most of all, it was so utterly brutal.

The day after I found Dad talking to the drain, we received a new and unsettling surprise.

My mother stepped inside the bathroom and turned on the shower, then went to the bedroom so she could change into her robe. When she returned, the floor was flooded.

"What happened?" I asked, watching her sop up the spill.

She squeezed out a waterfall into the bucket, thrust her mop at the floor as if it had caused the mess, then with a fixed smile replied, "It's just a little water."

I edged past her to peer inside the tub. A towel was stuffed down the drain, so far that we had to call a plumber to get it out. Apparently, my father had had a disagreement with the man taking up residency there.

After the plumber left, I showed the towel to my mother.

"I wonder how that happened," was her reply, with a forced expression of vacant surprise.

Business as usual.

Deny, deny, deny.

It was more of the same when we started finding our family photos turned facedown in the living room. In robotic fashion, my mother would set them back up. After finding the pictures flipped over again, she'd simply start the process all over. But while she did her level best not to show it, I could see the cracks beginning to form, her facade of normalcy breaking down.

One evening while setting the dinner table, I looked inside the silverware drawer, then at my mother. "Where are the knives?"

"In the dishwasher, dear," she replied, not bothering to spare me a glance. "Where they always are when they're dirty and someone forgets to run the machine."

I opened the door, looked inside, looked back at her. "Not there, either."

She walked over and checked the washer herself. "Then they must all be upstairs where you left them. Even though I've asked you not to bring food to your bedroom."

"But I don't—"

"Because everything always piles up there." She flashed the smile of a cynic. "Honestly, Christopher, did you actually believe they'd just get up and walk their way back here?"

Not once had I ever brought food to my room. Not that it mattered. Reality wasn't up for discussion in our home.

Case in point: for dinner the next evening, she simply ordered out for pizza.

Problem solved.

At least in her mind.

The next day, my mother went for a different strategy, sending me into the basement to retrieve the fancy wedding silverware stored there. I flicked on the switch, looked at my father's workshop corner, and stopped in my tracks.

Intricately woven into a mangled tower of metal were all the missing kitchen knives, points protruding in every direction and at every angle, a series of colored wires looping in and out between them. And at the very top, a large serving knife aimed directly at me.

It was the strangest thing I'd ever seen.

I edged closer and found pages and pages of notes, drawings, and diagrams—all in my father's haphazard handwriting. Blueprints for his metal monstrosity. Barely legible maps of our house with arrows pointing to every door and window. Some kind of bizarre and frightening electrical device he'd apparently designed with steel clamps and sharp teeth.

"Take it down."

I wheeled around and found my mother standing at the bottom of the staircase, her expression so sober that I barely recognized it.

"I *said,* take it down." She pointed to a pail in the corner. "And when you're done, bring the silverware upstairs to the dishwasher."

Then she marched up the steps, hard and fast footfalls speaking what she would never dare say.

A day later, when I tried to bring up my concerns, she said, "It didn't happen."

"But you saw it."

"I didn't, and neither did you. End of story."

And just like that, with a wave of her wand, she made reality vanish.

But this was one rabbit that wasn't going to stay put. Mom had at last met her match. My father's insanity was gaining frightening momentum, and it was about to blow down the walls.

Both hers and the ones around us.

25

I wake up in a chair.

Wait. What chair?

I look around.

The family room?

I rub my bleary eyes, try to find a sense of balance—or something like it.

An infomercial plays on the TV, hawking a contraption that promises to shed ten pounds in ten days. Looks more like a medieval torture device.

My sleepy fog lifts, but beneath it I find only another layer of wavering disarray. Moments ago, I was walking into my son's room, but I've got no memory of what occurred after, no idea how I ended up here. Or is it actually a memory? Did the trip to my son's room even happen?

I don't know . . . I just don't know . . .

My headache is raging.

I check the clock.

Wait. Moments ago?

It's after midnight. Not only don't I know how I got here, I also have no idea where the last several hours have gone.

Losing track of time is a problem. Drastic mood shifts are a problem. Violent and uncharacteristic outbursts . . . those aren't so great, either. Any one of these symptoms on its own would be cause for worry, but combined—

That sleep of death, Christopher.

I startle, spin, and look around. Then I realize I'm now standing in the center of the room. I don't remember getting here. Another problem, but right now I'm more concerned about the voice I just heard inside my head. While it seemed so real, I know it wasn't.

My mind is getting worse.

I lean forward, bury my face in my hands, and search for clarity in a place where there seems to be none. Adam said I was fine, but what if I've suffered a potentially serious brain injury? If that's the case, I'm now at a significantly higher risk for secondary trauma, the effects of which could be even more serious. I can't afford that. Ultimately, these symptoms could affect my ability to work, and then I'll really be in trouble.

Now, there's this voice I keep hearing, which could point to another possibility—one far worse.

It can't be that. It will not be.

I refuse to surrender to my past. To my father's past. I've made it this far, fought for years to recover from the damage his mental illness caused me. I'll be damned if I'm going to let him win now.

Mud.

The memory resurfaces, and all I can think about now is Devon. I'm unsure if what I saw on his blanket was actually there, but I do know one thing: I can't afford to take chances where my son's safety is concerned. Someone could still be in the house and trying to harm him.

I rush toward the stairs.

On the way up, my mind shoots into rewind, still trying to track the evening's events. Then I wonder why Jenna didn't come down to wake me.

Because you scared her, you idiot, this new voice tells me, *and put the fear of God in your son.*

I try with all my might to ignore the voice and climb the steps faster.

I'm not an idiot, but I *am* an ass, and my behavior at dinner was deplorable. I know this, not only because of the horror I saw emanating from my wife but also because, during all our years of marriage, she's never gone to bed angry at me. I'll make it up to her, but first I need to see my son. Make sure he's safe and take care of what I'd set out to do earlier—or what I think I did, before my mind decided to skip through time.

The instant I enter Devon's room, my vision zooms to his covers. Though it's dark, there's enough moonlight through the window to see there is no mud on his blanket.

Another hallucination. Another sign of trouble.

Jake is lying on the floor.

Of course he is.

I send the thought packing and focus on Devon, lying in peaceful sleep. I lean over and kiss his forehead, still fearful that I may inexplicably find myself back downstairs.

Devon responds with a gentle stir and tries to narrow his focus on me.

"I love you, kiddo," I whisper, "and I'm very sorry for getting upset earlier. It wasn't your fault. It was mine."

He gives me an eyes-half-closed smile that, while shrouded in sleepy fog, tells me he's already moved past it. That all is well. Seeing him this way leaves me tongue-tied. It's as if the earlier incident never happened, as if he's pulled some giant lever, putting our turbulent world into reset. This amazing child finds forgiveness so easily, is so secure in his love.

"It's okay, Daddy," he says, voice weakened by sleep. "It was just an accident, that's all."

I run my hand over his head, watch him surrender to repose.

And I smile—I can't help it—because despite what I've been through tonight, despite everything, I still have him. Right at this moment, that seems like more than enough.

I take an extra few seconds to enjoy the comfort of that feeling, then head for the door.

"Daddy?"

I turn back.

"I want you to be okay now," Devon says.

I'm not sure whether he's talking about the accident or my outburst downstairs, and I'm afraid to ask, so I simply say, "Me too, buddy . . . Me too."

He slips away again, the only sound now, his soft and easy breaths falling into a tranquil, sleepy rhythm.

I move toward our bedroom, the weight of information overload heavy on my mind. So much happening, so much of it I don't understand.

I want you to be okay now.

If only it were that easy.

Just an accident.

There have been a lot of those lately.

Joining Jenna in bed, I wrap myself around her and take in her scent. The warmth of my wife's body feels like a needed layer of comfort. She stirs, and in a whisper I say, "I'm sorry for tonight, sweetheart. I was wrong, and I'm . . . well . . . I'm just so sorry."

Moving into my arms, covering my hand with hers, she looks up at me. Through the dim light, I see forgiveness in her half-awake smile. I bury my head in her shoulder, feel her body flex and relax into the contour of my arm. I become one with her.

And there you have it. Why each day, without fail, and with astounding strength, I find more reasons to love my wife in ways no words could come close to describing.

I kiss her lips, and she reciprocates, and in this moment, we are again good. No, we're better than good.

We are amazing.

26

Just a few feet into the hospital parking lot, something yanks at my nerves. At first, I'm unable to peg it, then I pull into my space and feel a peculiar sense of absence.

I look out my window at more empty parking spots than I've ever seen before.

Odd.

At least for this time of day, it is. Thinking I've perhaps arrived a bit earlier than usual, I check my watch, but I'm actually a few minutes late. I peruse the lot once more, then get out of my car and hurry toward the building.

Inside, I head directly for Adam's office.

"Got a minute?" I say, my steps unsteady as I enter.

He looks up at me from the screen and abruptly closes a red folder on his desk. "Sure, pull up a seat."

Eyeing the folder, I lower myself to the chair and try to think for a moment before speaking.

"I need your help," I say.

"Done. What's up?"

I drop my gaze, fuss with my hands, then look up at him. "I

wasn't going to involve you in this, but you're the only person I can trust."

Adam's lids flutter with one part apprehension, one part concern. He leans forward and gives me his full attention.

"What we talked about yesterday—my edginess over the accident—it's all true, but there's a little more to this. I've got some concerns about my head injury. There have been other symptoms. I didn't mention them yesterday, because they seemed to be going away, then last night . . ."

Adam pulls back a few inches to study me. "What symptoms? And how serious?"

I tell him about my sudden and furious outburst at dinner. I confess the reason for changing my hair, how my perception seems inexplicably distorted. I explain how my thoughts at times are confused. That I'm scared. But I play down the hallucinations, the distracting sounds, and flashes of light. The loss of time and the voice in my head. I don't like hiding the truth from Adam. I trust him like a brother, but this isn't just about protecting myself. While I know he'd keep things in the strictest of confidence, I don't want him to shoulder that kind of pressure. If my condition is indeed serious or permanent, I'll be the one who lets the higher-ups know about it. I don't want to throw him into a situation where he feels conflicted because of our friendship.

Adam holds silent, but concern washes across his features, maybe a few other things I can't quite gauge. Tiny grooves form around his mouth when he says, "We need to get you an MRI."

I nod. "That's what I'm thinking. I was going to ask Steve Miller over in radiology, but I figured it wouldn't be the best idea."

"Steve's not here anymore," Adam says, shaking his head.

"Where'd he go?"

"He quit."

"Just like that? Guy's been here for over twenty years."

"I got the info secondhand, but rumor has it there was some kind of out-of-town family crisis that needed to be taken care of."

"So he left permanently?"

"There's probably more to it. Anyway, I can send you to see Rob Jennings," he says, resolve lending firmness to his voice. "Rob's a good friend, runs an offsite neuro practice. I'll put a call in to him right away."

"That would be great, but if it's okay with you, I'd prefer keeping this . . . you know . . ."

"Only between us," he finishes for me. "Absolutely."

"Just for right now. It may very well be nothing serious, but I'm obligated to make sure."

"Understood." His smile is solid and comforting, as if he knows exactly what I need to hear right now.

"I really appreciate you doing this."

"We're friends, and for what it's worth, I'm still pretty confident this won't be anything significant."

I don't answer because I know his intentions are good and because I still feel horrible about deceiving him.

"I'll let you know the second I hear from Rob," Adam says. "Okay?"

I attempt a smile, then turn to leave.

Be careful. He knows.

Knows what?

You'll see . . .

That voice returns. The one I'm coming to know, the commanding and evil whisper that never has anything good to say.

The one I'm learning to despise and fear.

27

I'm trying not to chew on things where my mental health is concerned, not to let worry escalate, but I know too much about this subject for my own good, with a perspective both professional and personal. My training tells me that there's nothing to indicate the car crash should have caused a traumatic brain injury, especially since I was unconscious for only a brief period, an important guideline in diagnosing neurological damage. But what if it did?

And with that thought, like a villainous blast from hell, my biggest fear since childhood comes back to haunt me with vengeance.

Like a monster.

I tried to deny it last night, but after growing up with my mother, and as a student of the mind myself, I should certainly know better. Denial only fertilizes fear, making it stronger and more virulent. Adam doesn't know about my father—nobody does, except Jenna. Being a psychologist, it serves no benefit to make my family's past known. Plenty of professionals in my field have mental illnesses running through their bloodlines, and some even speak publicly of their triumphs over them. But that's not me. It never has been.

Statistically speaking, I'm almost three times more prone to suffer the same mental illness my father did, and the head injury only raises those odds. Hard as I try, I can't hide from that fact because it's staring me directly in the face.

I thought you weren't going to chew on this.

I ignore the voice.

Focus on the work. I have to focus on the work. I turn my computer monitor toward me and shift my thoughts to Donny Ray Smith. Our session is fast approaching. I need to get things in order, read up further on dissociative amnesia, and organize some thoughts.

My phone goes off.

I look at the screen and see Jenna's number.

"Hi, honey," I say, trying to camouflage the garbage floating rampant through my mind.

"Just checking on you," she says with a drag in her voice that I read as fretfulness, still probably trailing from last night. "You doing okay?"

"Yeah . . . fine."

"You don't sound fine."

"You know me too well."

"It's my job," she says with a smile I can not only hear but see in my mind's eye.

As we talk, I make an internal decision not to mention my conversation with Adam. It will only exacerbate Jenna's concerns, and I don't need to hand her any additional worry. I'll tell her about the MRI when one is scheduled.

Another headache fires off, and it feels as if someone's mercilessly slamming a boot heel into my forehead. With teeth clenched, I try to endure in silence, hoping Jenna won't catch on. As the head trouncing continues, a dizzy spell sends the room swimming around me. I squeeze my eyes shut and search for balance, stability, anything, in my increasingly out-of-balance world.

After what feels like a decade of screaming misery, the pain subsides. I open my eyes. Jenna's been talking, but I haven't heard a thing she's said. I check the phone screen. About four minutes have passed. Four minutes I don't remember at all.

More loss of time. More trouble. It just keeps coming.

"Chris?"

"Huh?" I say, trying to snap to.

"Did you hear what I just said?"

"Yeah . . . Sorry. Just got distracted for a minute."

Times four.

Knock it off! Okay?

"Look, sweetheart," I say, "I've really got to cut this short. I have a lot of work to get done."

"Of course," she says, leaving so much unspoken between us. "We'll see you tonight."

28

I enter the consulting room and immediately observe that Donny Ray continues to show signs of improvement. His cheeks, though still a little pale, have gained significant color. Even more interesting is his shift in demeanor. He's calm, lips leaning toward what could be an expectant smile, like he's been waiting for me. His composure does nothing to abate my lingering discomfort over what happened on Alpha Twelve yesterday, but I have to push those feelings aside. I've got four days to complete my evaluation, and while Donny Ray may be strange, none of his strangeness adds up to a diagnosis—nor does it mean that he deserves a prison sentence or the death penalty.

I settle into the chair, bring up his case files on the consulting room computer, then an odd sound from above distracts me, as does a quick and vague movement off to my side. I glance to the left, then at the ceiling, but see nothing. I swing toward Donny Ray, but he seems more surprised by my jitteriness than anything else.

Was it nothing?

Concentrate, Chris.

I refocus on Donny Ray. Prepared to look at him more objectively, I observe as he now curiously—and rather leisurely—takes in his surroundings.

Today, his striking appearance is even more evident. While this, of course, has no direct bearing on whether he's malingering, it's still worth noting. Physical beauty can have interesting effects on the psyche, not to mention on those who fall—willingly or unwillingly—into its path.

I return to his files. A short while later, I look up and realize that he's been observing me with interest. I stare back, and he quickly, perhaps even bashfully, averts his gaze.

"How are you feeling today?" I ask.

"How are you feeling today?" he replies.

"Fine, thanks," I answer a little hesitantly. It wasn't what he said, but, rather, how he said it. The inflection in his voice sounded like he was repeating my question instead of asking one himself.

I'm reading too much into it, I decide. After taking another look at his files, I roll my chair toward him until we are face-to-face.

"I'd like to continue," I say, "with what we were discussing before."

"Before," he repeats.

"Yes. Going back to when you were a kid."

"Going back."

"Donny Ray," I say, "are you having difficulty understanding me?"

He shakes his head. His expression appears innocuous, and yet . . .

"Can you give me just a minute?" I ask.

He nods.

I return to the computer and skim his case files. The automatic and repetitious vocalization pattern he's exhibiting has overtones of what could be echolalia. Since the action can be the byproduct of a closed head injury, it's worth examining. I didn't pick up on this during our last session, but with the behavior very prominent now, I feel certain in identifying it. Did I miss something in the notes about this?

But after going through Dr. Philips' file again, I find nothing to reference any sort of speech abnormalities. No differential diagnoses of autism, Tourette's syndrome, epilepsy, or any other disorders that might also be culprits.

Strange.

"Is something wrong?" he asks, as if unaware that anything might be.

Not wanting to further influence his behavior until I get a better understanding of it, I smile and say, "No. Just checking on some information about your case."

"Oh." He smiles back.

I roll my chair toward him and continue. "I was thinking about your mention of feeling alone as a kid. I'm just wondering how your sister played into all this. Did you have a relationship with her?"

"I adored her," he answers immediately.

I hear the statement but detect an odd glitch in his tone—not quite the level of detachment I witnessed while he spoke of having pets but something similar. Of course, since Miranda disappeared, and since his father was at one point the key suspect, Donny Ray could be blocking out tragic feelings about his sister.

"How close were the two of you?" I ask. "Can you tell me more about that?"

"More about that . . . ," he repeats.

I elaborate. "You said you adored her. How did she feel about *you*?"

"I guess the same," he says, and I notice his hand closing around the chair's arm.

"You guess?"

"No, she did. We got along great."

"So, did that connection between you help at all? With the loneliness?"

"In some ways, yeah. But she was so much younger than me, you know?"

"How about your father? What was your relationship like with him?"

"Okay . . ."

"Just okay?"

Donny Ray is silent for a moment, then says, "He worked a lot."

"Meaning?"

"Just that he wasn't around much."

"And Miranda? How did she get along with him?"

"She was always his favorite," he says through a laugh that sounds a little tight.

"Do you know why?"

Donny Ray shrugs and shakes his head with an indecipherable expression.

"Were you bothered by that at all? Your sister and father having a relationship that you didn't?"

"I don't know." He rubs the back of his neck. His foot is bouncing. "It was what it was, I guess."

"But you'd said you felt lonely as a kid, so why *wouldn't* that bother you? I mean, it would be natural to feel some jealousy."

He looks down at his feet and shuffles them back and forth along the tile. "Maybe it did, sometimes."

"Can you tell me about specific times when it felt harder than others?"

"I'm not really sure if I can remember anything."

With a raised brow, I wait him out.

"Well . . . there was this one thing," he says a moment or two later. "They used to go off together a lot and leave me behind."

"Where would they go?"

"I didn't know."

"You never asked?"

"No."

"How come?"

"Because it was their thing. I wasn't a part of it."

"Okay. How did you feel when they'd go off without you?"

"Kind of lonely."

"Anything else?"

"Angry, maybe?"

"Anger's a pretty strong emotion." My smile challenges him. "There aren't many *maybes* about it."

"I guess you're right. It did make me kind of mad."

"What made you mad about it?"

A dimpled grin appears, and he shakes his head as if admonishing himself for the next thought.

"What is it?" I ask.

"It's really kind of dumb."

I motion for him to continue anyway.

"It's just that . . . like . . . when they'd come back, she always had an ice cream cone. I was just a kid and all, but I'd get jealous. She really pissed me off that way, know what I mean?"

"So your *sister* pissed you off. Did your sister do anything in particular to make you feel that way? Did she . . . I don't know . . . Did she brag about getting something that you didn't?"

"No. Not at all."

"Then why were you angry at her instead of your father? After all, wasn't it his decision to give her the ice cream cone? To spend time with her and not you?"

"Yeah . . . but it wasn't really his fault," Donny Ray says, and now he's not just gripping the arm of his chair—he's white-knuckling it.

"Why not? He was the adult, and it was his choice."

"Because that's how little six-year-old girls are. They know how to get what they want."

Cold goose bumps scale up my arms. The hair on my scalp tingles.

Donny Ray squirms in his chair.

"I'm not sure I understand," I say. "What do little six-year-old girls want?"

"Everything." He spits out the word, then instantly sees my uneasy reaction and schools his expression into one of remorse. His lips start to part, but nothing comes out.

Tension twists through the air.

He breaks it. "Or at least that's what I thought."

I let my silence indicate he should continue.

"Because I realized I had it all wrong . . . So very wrong . . ."

"Had what wrong?"

"Everything," he says again, but this time in a manner so feeble and fragile, it seems as though he could crumble and fall within seconds. A manner that surprises me, because in a flash, Donny Ray has flown from one end of the emotional spectrum to another, first disconnected, and now, quite the opposite. The only problem is, both seem so convincing that I can't determine the validity of either.

"I'm a little confused here," I say.

"Imagine how I felt."

I wait for him to explain.

"One day," he goes on, "I was sitting on a swing in the front yard. My dad and Miranda were taking off again." Donny Ray looks off to one side as if watching the scene play out. "The second her feet hit the driveway, a hard rain started to fall, and she immediately turned back my way. So slow . . ."

"What was?"

"The way she waved at me . . . and so sad."

"Did you know why?"

"No . . ." He looks past me and into some distant place, seemingly lost in the retelling. "She'd never waved good-bye to me before going off with him. It was so strange. Then they were gone."

"What happened next?"

"The rain fell harder, but I just sat on the swing. I must have been there for two hours. I'd never felt so lost before in my life. When they finally came back, Miranda got out of the car. This time"—a sad smile crosses his face—"she had two ice cream cones in her hand. She walked up to me and gave me one. Then without so much as a word, she just walked away."

"Did she seem upset?"

"No . . . She seemed empty."

He falls into a hush, as if thinking about that.

"I sat and watched her disappear into the house. Water was pouring down my face, and the cone was melting in the rain. I had ice cream dripping down my wrists, into my lap, but I couldn't move a muscle."

"Did you ever find out what was wrong?"

Donny Ray looks at me. A tear rolls down his cheek.

"I never got the chance."

29

The ice cream cone story carried a disturbing—but as of yet unproven—undertone of Miranda's sexual abuse. If true, it could lend reasonable support to the cops' suspicion that the dad was a viable suspect in her murder. And while Donny Ray stopped shy of revealing those dark circumstances, he came close. My goal now will be to glean that information from him, then determine whether it has any bearing on Jamey's murder or my patient's alleged inability to remember it.

Still, Donny Ray's comment about six-year-old girls was chilling, not just because it seemed off-color, but also because Miranda and Jamey Winslow were the same age when they went missing. Then before I had a chance to form an opinion, he threw me for a loop with his heartbreaking story about sitting alone in the rain that day.

But is the story true?

I just don't know. Once again, his emotional response seemed right on cue—and once again I find myself lost and searching for truth between layers of doubt.

After leaving the consulting room, I pass through Alpha Twelve, and a pocket of brightness off to the right flags my attention.

I don't like what I see.

Nicholas' door hangs wide open, fluorescent light spilling out onto the floor like something toxic. I look inside: empty, not only of him but also all his belongings.

What the hell?

I quicken my pace toward the nurses' station. Melinda Jeffries, the head nurse, is working at her computer, and while I know my footsteps are loud enough to hear, she doesn't look up.

"Hello?" I say upon reaching the counter, urgency and impatience ramping up my voice.

Melinda raises her head, but when our eyes meet, something in hers strikes me as peculiar—cold and detached. I nod toward the room and say, "What happened to Nicholas?"

"He's no longer here," is all she offers and goes back to typing.

I look at Nicholas' room, then at Melinda, then back at the room. "But I just saw him yesterday."

"And now you don't."

"Yes, I realize that. I was hoping you could tell me why."

Typing faster now. "He's been transferred out."

"*Where* was he transferred? And why?"

"Smithwell Institute."

I shake my head. "I've never heard of it."

"In Billings, Montana."

"Why would he be transferred to a facility in Montana?"

"I don't know."

"And why wasn't I informed of this?"

"You're not his doctor."

"I realize that, but I'm just wondering if—"

"You'll need to take that up with the actual doctor."

Getting information from this woman is like trying to swim

through a sea of cable-knit sweaters. She's being disrespectful—I'm not sure why, but I've had enough.

"Let me ask you another question, Nurse Jeffries," I say. "Were you trained to treat *actual doctors* with contempt, or was that a self-taught skill?"

I have Melinda's full attention, but her once-apathetic eyes now look as though they're about to spin out of their sockets.

"Don't you have somewhere else you need to be right now?" she barks.

I give no response—I'm about to blow a gasket.

She's already returned to her typing. My choice is to either make a scene or report her, but all Jeremy's likely to do is raise a brow and say, "You'd go crazy, too, if you had to sit down there all day." Instead, I zoom from the nurses' station and burn off my frustration with a fast walk through Alpha Twelve.

"Pssst! Hey, Christopher!" a whispery voice says.

I turn around. Stanley Winters looks eagerly at me through his window.

"Bitch Face at the counter ain't gonna help you." He throws a surreptitious glance up and down the hallway, then with a voice to match says, "You want answers? I got 'em."

I step toward him.

He flashes a stained-in-yellow, snaggletooth smile. "Cost you a pack of smokes."

"Stanley, you know the rules," I say with a shudder in my voice that I'm unable to curb. "That's not how things work around here."

"Nothing works around here!"

I shake my head.

"We have to get out of this place!" he loudly states. "It's broken!"

I step back from Stanley, and he lets out a sharp yowl, so loud, so menacing, that it carries through the entire floor.

"THAT SLEEP OF DEATH, CHRISTOPHER!" He explodes into maniacal laughter. "IT'S THAT SLEEP OF DEATH!"

The other patients parrot Stanley's message, shrieking, howling, and banging so hard on their doors that the reverberations beat against my chest.

I bolt toward the exit and leave Alpha Twelve, nerves buzzing, Stanley's remark whipsawing through my head.

30

The patients are speaking to me.

That sleep of death, Christopher.

A message now poking at my psyche like a puppy's needle teeth. Once was obscure enough to be the ranting from a mind gone sour, but coming from an entire floor?

And now Nicholas has mysteriously vanished.

What do the patients want me to know? The only way to get some peace of mind is to stay rational and seek information. So in my office, still trying to warm my shivers, I take a wild stab in the dark—or rather, at the Internet—and to my surprise, I score a direct hit.

Shakespeare?

Okay, so we have some lovers of classic literature among the men of Alpha. The phrase is part of the opening soliloquy in Hamlet's nunnery scene.

> *To die, to sleep,*
> *To sleep, perchance to dream; Aye, there's the rub,*
> *For in that sleep of death, what dreams may come,*

When we have shuffled off this mortal coil,
Must give us pause.

A whole lot of talk about death there, but whose? I'm a bit rusty on my Shakespearean studies, so I examine the words individually, hoping they'll reveal some kind of hidden meaning.

Sleep.

Death.

Dreams.

I was dead asleep, Christopher . . . Nicholas has bad dreams all the time.

Now Donny Ray's comment comes back, and although the connection might be somewhat loose and far-reaching, I have difficulty ignoring it.

From the relative safety of my desk, I revisit Alpha Twelve. Lots of disturbing activity happening there, which I've yet to understand, let alone figure out. But one thing seems more than evident. An aggressive and sinister pestilence is snaking its way through Loveland's basement floor.

Something that feels disturbingly prophetic.

"The patients are trying to communicate with me," I tell Adam as we move through the cafeteria line.

He stops sliding his tray. "Come again?"

"They're exhibiting some sort of peculiar mass reaction. It's like they're trying to give me a message."

Adam moves on but doesn't respond. When we get to the cashier, he turns back to me and says, "A message . . ."

"Yeah, 'that sleep of death' thing I mentioned. I've heard two different patients say it, first Nicholas, and just a little while ago, Stanley. Then right after, the others started in."

"The patients are constantly saying crazy things. That's why they're here."

"All of them? Repeating the same phrase?"

"And they're constantly repeating each other."

"Okay, but now Nicholas has disappeared."

I reach for my wallet, but Adam moves faster. After paying the cashier, he says, "*Disappeared*, like, how?"

I tell him on our way to a table.

"I'm not sure I'd exactly call that a disappearance," Adam says as we take our seats. "I mean, patients get transferred out of here all the time."

"To Billings, Montana?"

"Why not? They could have a specialist who's better suited to treat him."

"It's a place I've never heard of. Smithwell Institute. And besides, it seems like they rushed him out of here pretty fast."

"His transfer was probably already in the works. These kinds of things are planned months in advance. You know how that goes."

"I feel like the information was intentionally kept from me."

Adam looks up from his lunch.

"And Nicholas has been a fixture in this place for years. Why now?"

"Could be for any number of reasons. New complications, new treatments."

We continue eating.

A few minutes later, I say, "It's from Shakespeare."

"What is?"

"'That sleep of death.'"

"Okay . . ." He chews but doesn't say anything more.

"*Adam*, everyone on that floor was acting very strange yesterday. I told you about it."

He stops chewing, stares at his food for a few seconds, then looks up at me. "Chris, they're mental patients."

The conversation stalls out, and for the rest of lunch, neither of us speaks.

31

I leave the building to head home when my phone vibrates. After checking the screen, I see two missed calls from Jenna.

Wait a minute.

Why is my ringer turned off?

Wait, again. Jenna's cell?

She usually calls from home at this time of day, because she's usually getting dinner ready. I click the answer button, but before I can speak, she says, "Where are you?"

"I'm just leaving work." I glance at my watch and wonder if I've once again lost time. Nope. I'm good.

"Leaving work," she says.

"Yeah. What's wrong?"

"Why are you just now leaving?"

"Because that's what I do when I'm done?"

"But you're supposed to be here."

"Be where?"

"Chris, we spoke about it this afternoon. On the phone? You couldn't have possibly forgotten. You were supposed to take off early. Adam's already here."

I still don't know where *here* is, so I ask.

"At Adam and Kayla's. For dinner." Her voice trails into apprehensive concern. I feel her on that one. "Chris, what's going on?"

I'm not so sure that I know. I don't recall her telling me about this, don't recall agreeing to leave work early; but I do remember losing a block of time during our conversation.

"Didn't you see Adam this afternoon?" she asks. "He was supposed to remind you."

"I actually did. At lunch. But he didn't mention anything."

It was intentional.

What was?

Adam didn't tell you on purpose. He doesn't want you in his house. That's where he keeps the files.

Which files?

The ones with all the information he's been gathering on you.

"I'm so sorry, honey," I say, trying to block out the voice and get back to my wife. "I got really busy after we spoke. It completely slipped my mind." Not exactly a lie but perhaps my biggest understatement of the year.

Jenna sighs. "It's okay. Just get here as soon as you can, all right?"

"On my way." I hang up and hurry through the parking lot.

32

The lost time during my earlier call with Jenna.

Stanley's frightening and hysterical declarations.

Nicholas' unexplained and secretive disappearance.

The list keeps growing, my stress keeps cannonballing, and any attempt to hold my mind together seems like a job unto itself.

On the road, I make a concentrated effort to gather myself, to block out the crazy taking up residence in my mind. At the same time, I'm well aware this dinner may only throw more hurdles into my path, because there is yet another problem waiting for me there.

When I met Adam, he was single. A few years later, Hurricane Kayla blew in, and before I knew it, she was part of the deal. Not that I have a problem with Adam finding love—it's just that he really didn't. He instead found Kayla, a woman incapable of giving or receiving anything of the sort. It's my professional opinion that Kayla suffers from an acute personality disorder. Diagnosis: Histrionic Hot Mess.

Drama queen on steroids pretty much nails it. Kayla is ridiculously eager for attention, inappropriately demonstrative, and if pretentiousness and superficiality are her goals, she's cornered the market. As much as I love Adam, I could have predicted that Kayla—or someone like her—was a problem waiting to happen. His judgment is fairly sound in most aspects of life, but somewhere deeply embedded within him is a noncognitive wrinkle, a psychic blemish that greatly impacts his relationships with women. Because of that deficit, he drifts into the same hapless pattern, making mistakes that seem to fall far beyond his learning curve. To put it plainly, Adam turns to Silly Putty for any woman with good looks and a rocking body. Kayla has both, and she works them with skill—or as other friends have rather crudely observed, Kayla has Adam's dick in an iron vise. But because I care a great deal for Adam, I force tolerance and try my best to ignore his wife's antics.

However, it's not always easy.

When I walk through the entryway, Jenna and Kayla are sitting and talking. Actually Kayla is talking, and my wife is making a valiant effort to listen. Jenna looks at me in that special and subtle way we have, the one that speaks our universal language: *Get me out of here.*

"Christopher!" Kayla says with a nerve-grinding shriek. She deploys from her wing chair like it's got a built-in ejection handle, the under-seat rocket motor launching her the distance between us. She lands against my chest, throws her arms around me, and kisses the air next to my head on both sides. Over her shoulder, I catch one of those corny leg lifts you see in movies but never in real life.

Jenna looks like she's about to barf.

I work to paint a smile on my face and swallow bile.

I'm also trying to suppress a malicious laugh over Kayla's clothing choice for the evening—or perhaps, more appropriately, her costume. An angora sweater, pink, fuzzy, and barely legal within a public context. Same goes for the skirt—or at least I think that's what it is—with a hemline that would leave nothing to even a sailor's imagination.

A pink beret. Eyeglasses without any lenses.

Adam enters the room and the fray.

"Honey, Chris is here!" Kayla announces, emphasizing the syllables as if her husband were hard of hearing or an idiot.

Adam nods and smiles. This is his standard. Whenever Kayla states the patently obvious, he blows it off while simultaneously excusing her overbearing and vainglorious behavior.

"Hi, Chris," he says. "Get a little mixed up today?"

He has no idea just how mixed up, but I ask what he means anyway.

"About coming here. Jenna said I never mentioned it to you."

"But you didn't."

His head pulls back in surprise. "Yeah, I did. I told you at lunch."

"I don't remember that at all." And I don't, but Subject to Change seems to be the flavor of the day in my world lately, so I add, "Maybe it was just a misunderstanding."

It was no misunderstanding. It was intentional.

Knock it off.

He can't get you out of here fast enough.

Shut up!

Adam starts to say something, then thinks better of it, and I see traces of apprehension drift across his face, possibly left from our discussion at lunch, now made worse by a conversation we either did or didn't have.

"It was probably my fault," I add, trying to ease the unspoken tension between us.

It was his fault.

Kayla flutters over to us and says, "Come on, you guys! Dinner's ready!"

Adam smiles blissfully at her.

Kayla flutters off.

And I wonder if being crazy is a good enough excuse to get me out of here sooner.

33

Dinner is served.

Kayla holds the conversation on her own, Jenna and I try to hold down our food, and as usual, Adam holds firm to oblivion. Also as usual, my nerves are screaming for deliverance. It's not just what Kayla says, or how much—it's her voice, a high-pitched nasal tone with a handful of gravel thrown in for added irritation. The cathedral ceilings only amplify the sound and make her all that more difficult to endure. It's like having dinner with ten Kaylas, when even one is far too many.

The meal drags on, then mercifully comes to a close. Adam takes Jenna outside to see the new roses he planted, which leaves me alone with Kayla. It's awkward and tense, at least for me, because I honestly don't know what to say, although I'm sure she'll have no trouble filling the gaps.

"So, Chris," she starts, "I've always wondered . . . Does it bother you talking to all those crazy people every day?"

"Actually, we don't like to refer to them as—"

"Having to listen to all those horrible, *horrible* stories? From criminals? Killers even?" She shivers, and a tiny moan escapes her thin lips. "I just don't know if I could do it."

"Well, then it's probably good that you don't," I say with diminishing patience. "But what do you think your husband does all day?"

"Oh, that's different. He's a *medical* doctor." She takes a sip of coffee and nods as if agreeing with herself. She looks back at me. "But have you ever considered doing something not so creepy?"

"I don't find it creepy. I'm giving help to people who need it."

With a patronizing simper that one might offer a toddler, Kayla says, "Well, that's nice for you." She grabs a few dishes from the table and heads for the kitchen.

I lean over to spit in her coffee.

A few moments later, Kayla returns. She settles into her seat again, sips her coffee, then delivers a tacked-on smile.

I return one.

Jenna and Adam reappear. Kayla's mouth is once again off and running, and I've got to find an escape hatch before she sucks the last bit of oxygen from this room.

I stand.

Kayla ignores my departure signal, then with a kittenish grin asks, "Has anyone noticed something different about me today?"

Has anyone thought about putting the bitch out of her misery?

"No, but if I had a gun, I'd happily fire the first bullet."

Oh. Shit.

There is charged silence.

Kayla, for once, is speechless. Jenna is clearly shocked. Adam is motionless, but I sense it's not just because of my rudeness toward his wife. Something else is going on, something that feels a lot like creeping suspicion, similar to what I saw during our earlier conversation, only far more pronounced.

Now I've done it.

And I don't know where that awful remark came from, or even more, how to fix this mess I've created. Still, I try.

"Settle down, everyone!" I say, forcing a laugh as an attempt to backpedal. "It was a joke!"

Nobody sees the humor.

I'm mortified, and now I really need to get the hell out of here, so I abruptly leave the table and make a rush for the bathroom.

Inside, I lock the door. I check myself in the mirror. I run the sink water, stick my hands under the faucet. I yank a tissue from the box, throw it into the toilet. I flush.

But really, I'm trying to figure out what's going on with me. It's like some stranger is taking over my actions, my speech, and even worse, my thoughts. A stranger who flies into fits of rage, makes inappropriate and now even frightening comments. Who can't keep track of time.

I fall against the wall and slide to the floor. I hit bottom, drop my face into my hands. I'm so terribly frightened. I feel so humiliated. So goddamned broken.

And here I am, doing the same thing my mother did, the thing I hated most about her. I'm trying to make the pain go away by running, trying to compartmentalize the inevitable when I should be dealing with it. That strategy never worked for her, it certainly didn't help my father, and it's not working for me. I need to go out and apologize. Kayla is many things that I don't like, but my behavior makes me no better, and in some ways, far worse.

As I walk down the hallway and toward the dining room, a glimmer of vibrant light steals my interest. A glass knickknack glistens from high atop a shelf, a globe, no larger than a golf ball. I pull the object down to inspect it, admiring the filamentary spatters of iridescent color in each continent. Beautiful in many ways, this tiny glass world, yet in others, so very fragile and vulnerable.

So completely loaded with aching truth.

I smile with sadness, lift the globe higher, and a ray of light shoots through, igniting it with even more color, more life. It's the most beautiful thing I've ever seen.

So I slip it into my pocket, then head back to join the others.

34

Adam and Kayla make an earnest attempt to accept my offer of reparation, then Kayla launches into her next topic; but I don't hear much of it. I'm too distracted by an expression on Jenna's face that seems to work its way deeper into her as the evening wears on. Uncertainty. Fear. The look of someone pulling away.

Silence widens the fissure between us when we arrive home. Jenna goes upstairs and leaves me standing in a vacuum of uncertainty. I can't endure another minute. It crushes me to see my wife hurt this way.

When I reach our room, she's still fully clothed and sitting up in bed, expression stoic, knees to her chest, arms wrapped around them. I close our door, and the sound brings her attention to me momentarily before she takes it away again.

I walk forward, then lower myself slowly to the edge of the bed, keeping my back to her.

Again, there is silence. And again, it's stifling.

"I don't know what to say." I turn to look at her. "All I know is that I'm so very sorry."

Jenna searches my eyes. "Chris, tell me what's happening. Give me the truth."

I vacillate for a few beats. "I'm not even sure."

"You scared the hell out of Devon last night, and tonight it was as if I didn't even know you."

Like an axe, her comment cleaves a plumb line through the center of me, breaks me in two, because she's the last person in the world I want to hear that from. It reactivates so much old pain that runs so deep. Pain that lies heavy at my core like some rotten and stinking piece of meat. I turn away because seeing my wife like this is excruciating—and I don't know how to fix myself. I feel so powerless.

Jenna must sense my agony because I immediately feel her hand on my shoulder. Still, I can't bring myself to meet her gaze.

"Chris," she says. "Look at me."

I shake my head. My hands are trembling.

"Don't do this," she persists, firming her hold on my shoulder. "Don't shut me out. Not now. Not when you need me the most. I know it's your old pattern, what you had to do in order to survive your father, but . . ." I hear her soft, labored breaths. I hear her pain—no, I feel it—which gives me the courage to finally turn around. She's biting her bottom lip, shaking her head. I look at the tears filling her bottom lids.

Sliding over, I place an arm around her body, pull it against mine, but still I don't know what to say, don't know if there's anything in me that can make this better. Instead, I hold my wife tight. I cling to her, hoping our physical closeness can in some way mend what now seems so terribly torn apart.

"I've been fighting this battle alongside you for years," Jenna says after we've been quiet for a while, "and I understand it . . . and I know your pain as well as any that I could ever feel . . . and I goddamned hate the pain, Chris. I hate it every bit as much as you do, and God knows I'd do anything to take it all away. But what I don't understand—what I can't, hard as I try—is why, after all this time, you still think you've got to go through that misery alone."

"I don't want to," I answer, voice no more than a crippled whisper. "I'm trying not to."

"Baby, I know you are, but you have to try harder."

"I'm not sure how."

"You do it by starting with the truth. Whatever that is."

"Then what?"

"Then you put one foot in front of the other. You walk on faith, and the answers will find you. They always do."

I study Jenna's confident expression, as if it might in some way give me strength to trust her wisdom. I shake my head, feel desperation in my tragic smile when I say, "I think it may be serious. I think I'm losing my mind."

Jenna doesn't appear surprised. It's as if she already knew, like she's been waiting for me to tell her.

"We need to find out why," she says.

"I'm scared." My response comes out fast and instinctual, like it's been fighting for air.

"Then we'll do that together, too."

"Adam is arranging an MRI."

"Good."

"If he's still talking to me."

"Adam will talk to you."

"You don't know that."

"I do. You'll tell him the truth, and he'll understand."

I say nothing.

"He will," she assures me, "and then whatever happens after that, you will not be alone. I won't let you be. Do you understand?"

My nod is barely substantive, not because I don't believe her, not even because I can't trust or feel her commitment. The problem isn't what I know, but rather, it's what she doesn't, what she never could.

That my cracking mind may be the one thing stronger than us both.

35

"I wanna see the ducks when we get there, Daddy! Can we see the ducks like last time?"

"Absolutely." I glance at my son and smile.

It's Sunday. Devon, Jake, and I are on our way to Anderson Lake. After my outburst at Adam and Kayla's, I'm hoping this road trip may restore balance and, if I'm lucky, some calm to my life. But more than that, because I frightened Devon at dinner the other night, I owe him this and want to be sure our relationship is back on solid footing.

"Will the white one still be there?" Devon asks, bouncing up and down with excitement. "Do you think he will?"

"He might be. We'll just have to see."

My son watches the world fly past his window with the steady fascination that only a child can muster. I love watching him in these peaceful moments, and do I ever need one right now.

"Good," he says, turning back to me with an approving nod. He pulls his feet up beneath himself, arms wrapped around legs. "I like the white one, Daddy."

"So do I, kiddo," I reply, then notice his sock choice for the day. Devon looks curious, too, but I can tell our reasons differ.

"Your socks," I inform him. "They don't match."

He studies them and says, "Yeah. I know."

"Is there a particular reason? Maybe some sort of fashion statement?"

He looks out his window again and says, "Uh-uh."

"Okay, then. Care to explain?"

"None of them match anymore."

"*None of them?* You must have over thirty pairs. Where did they all go?"

"Dunno."

"Well, where do you put your socks after taking them off?"

"In the hamper, just like Mom tells me to."

"Hmm, I'd imagine she's not very happy about this."

"Nope. Said she's gonna buy me some more."

We reach the entrance to Anderson Lake. Before slowing, I check the rearview, but it's not the road I see. It's Jake, upright in the backseat. Eyes glued to mine. As if he's been waiting all this time for me to notice him.

A thousand tiny ribbons of amber sunlight dance across the rippling water. I'm relaxed and in the present, simply enjoying time with my son. If it were possible, I would reach out and capture this moment in my hands and hold on to it forever, because the feeling is so authentic, so pure. But I know that's not possible, and with this understanding comes another far more troubling. If my injury is serious, or if history is indeed repeating itself, then I don't know how much more time I've got left before my mind checks out, before I disappear into another place, a much darker one.

Before I lose my son, and he loses me.

I banish the notion, give myself a stern warning not to stray from this moment. To enjoy it, because this moment is the only one that matters.

With that spirit, I settle on a park bench and share in Devon's joy, watching as he runs along the shoreline, splashing water everywhere and having a wonderful time. He kneels to observe the ducks at play, and the excitement in his young eyes captivates me. It's like I'm seeing magic in motion, and I'm compelled to join him.

I kneel alongside my son and place an arm around his shoulder. He looks up at me, squinting in the sunlight, and now we are both smiling, as if we know we're creating this wonderful memory together.

"I love it here, Daddy," he says, mirroring my thought. "Let's stay like this forever, okay? Just like this."

I pull Devon closer and tightly wrap my arms around him.

But the joy dissolves when over his shoulder and across the lake, the Evil Tree towers from a distant hillside. A symbol of impending doom, spreading its bloodred blanket of misery like a giant, toxic cloud. Mocking me, telling me there is no escape from its malignant and calamitous power.

I turn my head but find only a different source of unrest. Jake sits at the shoreline, his body ramrod straight, his gaze nailed to the tree. Then he looks my way, and a bitter chill shimmies through me, and the air in my lungs turns thick and ropy.

The dog is speaking to me.

Not with words. Not even with his stare. This is different and far more powerful. No mental impairment, no distortion. This is genuine. It's primitive, and above all, it's critically urgent. Like some kind of communication custom-made for me, only I still don't understand what he wants me to know.

I glance protectively down at Devon, then amble toward Jake. When I'm about two feet away, he stiffens, lets out a low groan, and I feel another chill, this one absorbing through my bones. I'm still unable to discern what he's telling me, but there's nothing good about it. The message is dark and foreboding and dangerous. It makes my hairs stand on end.

"Daddy! Help me!"

Devon's distressed voice rattles me. I spin around.

"I can't get my sneaker on," he says, looking down at his mismatched and wet socks covered in sand.

I exhale my relief. But then I glance toward Jake and my relief fades because there is an empty spot where he once stood.

I scan my surroundings and find him several feet away, staring at the tree again.

Backing away from it.

Ears lowered and pinned back, tail tucked between his legs.

Like he smells fear.

36

We walk toward a wooded picnic area, carrying the lunches that Jenna packed, but the lingering gloom from my encounter with Jake is a burden I can't seem to lift. The dog trails several feet behind us, and while his mood seems less intense, it's still noticeable. I steal a curious glance at my son, but just as before, he appears oblivious to Jake's peculiar behavior.

"Devon?" I say.

He looks up at me.

"I feel like there's something you might not be telling me about Jake."

His expression falls flat, and he shakes his head. "I wouldn't do that, Daddy."

"Do you know what's happening with him?"

"He's just upset."

"About what?"

"He can't tell me."

"I know, but I was wondering if maybe you had an idea."

With sight aimed forward, he gives a mild shrug. "It's just how things are."

I raise my brows. "What things?"

"Since the accident," he says. "That's when everything changed." Then he bolts toward a picnic table and shouts, "Daddy, can we sit at this one?"

After lunch, I do my best to relax and enjoy the beauty that surrounds us, the sunlight filtering through the trees, the moist tang of soil mingling with a whisper of pine.

A crackling noise interrupts my quietude. I look up and see two birds perched side by side on an overhead branch. Without warning, one of them loses its balance. The bird flaps its wings, flutters, and rights itself back on the branch. The other bird sidles a little closer, and they gaze into each other's eyes. In that brief instance, I sense profound unity between the two creatures that nearly takes my breath away. For them, imbalance and uncertainty have moved quickly into the past. Together, everything is just right in their world, exactly as it should be. I turn to Devon and realize he's been watching, too.

Later, as we sit on a dock by the lake, Devon seems reflective, looking into the water and making circles in it with his feet. I wait, allowing him to find his own time to speak.

Eventually, he turns to me.

"Daddy?" he says, "We're like those two birds, aren't we."

It's not a question but rather a declaration, and the conviction in his voice, the unequivocal confidence, makes my heart swell so full that my chest can barely hold it. He sees us as unshakable, and I couldn't love him any more than I do right now.

"Yes," I say, "we're just like that."

37

You again.

The Evil Tree lies in wait up ahead.

If there were another road, some alternate, high-velocity flight path or time travel spiral, I'd take it. But there is only one way in and out of Loveland, so eluding the monster is unavoidable.

As I approach, I size up my opponent and see things are much the same—still hideous and threatening, intrinsic evil oozing from every branch like poisonous sap.

I hate that thing.

Burn it down.

Are you crazy?

No, but you are, so burn the motherfucker down.

I clench the wheel, angst and sweat holding my palms to it like epoxy. Now the tree is less than ten feet away, challenging me, daring me to cross its path.

Wanting to get past its powerful, toxic draw, I punch the accelerator, and like a gun throwing lead, my car fires forward and away from what I'm now sure is the filthiest patch of hell on earth. Though I maintain a fast and steady pace for the next several miles, I can feel that the Evil Tree has still sent its noxious vibes on the hunt for me.

That's when I realize the beast's control is more powerful than I'd first thought, its reach stretching far beyond the cursed spot where it tore through the ground to wreak havoc on my life.

38

The morning can often bring clarity. It can bring perspective. But on this morning, there is neither. In fact, this morning—as I return to work and know that seeing Adam is inevitable—I'm even more restless as my mind hashes over the embarrassing scene I created in his home. Humiliation has washed into regret, shock into achy disquiet, all of it pumping like dirty blood through my veins and out to every part of me.

This isn't just about my off-color behavior or even about my inability to control it. What wrecks me is that I've hurt my closest friend. As messed up as I know Kayla is, as difficult as she can be, and even though I know she's not right for Adam, I've worked hard to respect their relationship. What I did last night may have destroyed a friendship that means a great deal to me.

I really screwed this one up.

I'm fully aware that my effort may be in vain, but I've got to try and fix this, to reconnect with Adam, to make this right.

At the office, I rise from my chair, draw a breath of courage, then head down the hall. I give Adam's door a faint knock and poke my head inside. He looks up from his work, expression at first attentive, then after seeing me, strained by awkward discomfort.

I'm feeling it myself, probably more than he is.

I clear my throat, then say, "Got a minute?"

"Sure." Adam nods. He motions me inside with a warm gesture that gives me the courage to step forward.

I drop into the visitor's chair. I try to think.

"There is no excuse for my actions the other night, Adam," I say, remorse giving me the proper amount of resolve I need at this moment, "so I'm not even going to try making any. All I can tell you—and all I want you to hear—is that I deeply regret what I did, and I wish there were a way to—"

"Chris," he interrupts in a tone of compassion that I wasn't at all expecting. "It's okay."

"It's not."

"Well, no." He laughs a little. "It's not *okay,* but my concern for you far supersedes that. Look, I know you, Chris. I've known you for years, and that guy the other night? It wasn't you."

He has no idea.

He has every idea. He's yanking your chain.

"That guy was someone else," Adam continues. "Chris, you're one of the kindest, most thoughtful people I know. So . . . I guess what I'm trying to say is that, well . . . I've been worried about you, buddy."

I lower my head, close my eyes. "Me too."

"And even though I can tell you've been trying to act strong, to keep your feelings from showing, I know you well enough to see past all that."

"I feel so goddamned bad about this. How I hurt Kayla."

He levels his eyes with mine. "Kayla will be just fine. Trust me. She's the least of your concerns right now. If you really want to fix this . . ." He hesitates ". . . What matters most now is that we fix *you*, and I want to help."

"You already are. You're arranging the MRI."

"That's not what I'm talking about. I'm talking about the more important stuff. Look, I understand how you are, maybe even better than I understand myself, sometimes. I know what you do when you're scared. The hiding thing, how you shift into that place where you think you've got to fight the toughest battles alone. Don't do that. Not now, not at a time like this."

His sentiment sounds painfully familiar.

"I'll try," I say.

"Look, we'll get the MRI set up for you tomorrow, but listen to me very carefully when I say this. Please don't let that be my last effort in helping you. I want to be here. I want you to lean on me if you need to, okay?"

"Okay."

"That doesn't sound so convincing there, partner," he says, a careful undertone of humor in his voice. "Can I get a side of emotion with that boilerplate?"

I try again. "Okay."

"Better, but still not so great. It'll reflect in your tip."

I laugh a little.

"Adam?"

"Yeah?"

"Thanks."

"Just please take care of yourself, Chris."

I try to smile my compliance. He does know me well enough to recognize my pain, even when I'm trying to hide it, but most of all, enough not to let it come between us.

I'm so lucky to have a friend like Adam.

Adam is trying to destroy you.

39

I enter the cafeteria—or start to—when my legs feel soft, my stomach a little narrow. Checking my watch, I see it's five past noon.

I scan the room.

And now my reasoning feels wooly. On any given day, the traffic at this hour is at its peak, but on this day, that's not the case. While many tables are occupied, an unusually high number are empty.

My feet shuffle forward, but I barely feel the flooring beneath them. I swing my vision to the line of hospital employees and visitors that normally extends out toward the exit doors, but today it's only about half that long.

I try to strike a deal with reason and tell myself that perhaps the nursing staff is rotating through an offsite training program. That there's some kind of flu bug going around, vastly diminishing the hospital's staffing power.

That it's not what I think.

But none of those explanations work for me.

In line, I slide my tray along the track, eyes suspiciously shifting from side to side. Observing.

"Sir?"

I follow the voice and find a worker staring at me expectantly.

I clear my throat. "Just the soup, please."

She dips her ladle into a recessed pot, dumps the brown liquid into a bowl, then slings it onto the raised counter. I reach for the soup, place it on my tray.

Don't eat that.

Huh?

It's laced with poison. What do you think is happening to all the people here?

I lurch back and, in the process, knock my tray off the track. The bowl goes flying. Glass breaks, soup splatters everywhere. Silverware slides across the linoleum.

I take a flustered look around me. Everyone is staring.

"I . . . I'm so sorry. I didn't—"

Don't!

Don't what?

Don't talk to these people.

Why not?

They're in on it. They've been sent here to watch you.

I rocket from the line and dash toward the exit like my ass is on fire.

40

How can I pull my mind together, when all the pieces are not only out of reach but twirling around me like scattered windup tops? With the deadline for my evaluation just two days away, I've got no time for crazy. I have to focus on this moment. I'm so close to breaking through Donny Ray's defenses, to figuring out whether he's malingering.

On my way to the consulting room, I inhale a staggered breath, try to collect myself. Several feet later, I reach a point of clarity, telling myself that I work best under pressure, that I'm competent, that I know how to do my job.

Now I can think.

I have to think . . . In our last session, Donny Ray was teetering closer toward revealing a significant piece of his past—then he pulled back on me. Miranda was his hot button, and I pushed it. Hopefully, with this new day, those emotions won't betray him, and we can try again.

When I walk into the room, Donny Ray is the image of ebullience. His skin isn't just clearer—it glows, the color in full bloom, the light enhancing his squared chin and chiseled cheekbones.

Even his lips, pale during our first meeting, have warmed into a full, rich pink. But it's not just his face: Donny Ray's overall presentation is stronger, chest muscles well-defined through the T-shirt he wears, posture firm, head held high.

And then there are those eyes.

Still penetratingly sharp, still indefinably familiar, and—to be completely truthful—hard to turn away from.

I observe as he takes a seat across from me. Never before has the contrast between body and mind—between the outer beauty and inner darkness—been more striking. With his arresting good looks and athletic physique, he could be anyone's all-American boy. Throw a few textbooks under his arm, and he's rushing off to his next class. Toss on a ball cap and sweats, and he's heading to the gym for his afternoon workout. Then I remind myself that Donny Ray Smith is nobody's all-American boy. Regardless of whether or not he remembers his crimes, Donny Ray Smith is a deeply disturbed young man.

A killer.

I try to keep that in mind, to look past his aura of purity, of innocence. To understand that everything about his physical presentation seems tailored to entice, to charm and seduce.

To manipulate?

I'm still not sure, and watching him now, it almost seems impossible to believe. In fact, Donny Ray appears completely unaware that his good looks even exist, let alone the power they might hold.

An undulating noise from overhead distracts me, then a shadow from above drifts across the table. I follow the tail end onto the floor as it zooms across my shoe before rapidly fading.

I glance up toward the ceiling: nothing there.

"Christopher? You okay?"

Donny Ray is staring at me.

Hold it together.

I can't afford to fall through the cracks of my mind right now. I have to do my job.

"You seem a lot better today," I say.

He looks down at himself, then up at me.

"So . . . when you . . . When we first met you'd mentioned that you were from Texas?"

"Yes, sir. Born and raised."

"The reason I bring it up is that I am, too."

"Yeah?" His expression brightens a few shades. "Whereabouts?"

"Johnson City."

"Hill Country, right?"

"Right," I say, feeling relieved, on solid footing again. "But I'm actually not very familiar with Real, Texas. What was it like there?"

"It was a small town . . . Well, it still is, really." He lets out a small laugh. "My mother used to say it was the kind of place where there's nothing to do every minute, and every minute counts. But that was her."

"What was?"

"I don't know . . . how she always saw things."

"So she had a positive outlook."

"No . . . that wasn't it at all." He looks down, shakes his head, and suppresses a grin as if trying to figure out how to explain something. "It was more like she *pretended* to have a positive outlook. You know the kind, right?"

I hesitate, because I do know all too well, but also because I'm trying not to let my past experiences, my personal bias, eclipse what could be an important communicative moment between us.

"How did that affect you?" I ask. "The way your mom was."

"Sometimes it was okay."

"Can you tell me about the times when it wasn't?"

"Well, I guess it bothered me."

"In what way?"

"How she liked to shove stuff under the carpet. You know, when things went wrong."

"What kinds of things went wrong?"

Donny Ray turns his head toward a cheap painting that hangs on the wall. I look, too. Some generic street scene. A little girl wearing a blue dress stands in an open doorway, her expression pensive yet sad.

I give him time and space to sort through his thoughts, but his eyes seem slightly unfocused. A bit vacant, even. Much like our last session, he seems to be traveling back, revisiting a long-ago place. I observe his hands, opening up and falling gradually to his sides. I study his breathing, slower now, shallower. His face is expressionless. Though I've got no indication of his specific thoughts, my suspicion is they're not particularly happy. I also have a feeling they might center on Miranda.

"Donny Ray?" I say. "Are you okay?"

He doesn't respond.

I lean in closer, speak louder. "Donny Ray."

He looks back at me, and as our eyes connect, I realize that whatever was on his mind is now gone, like he's found his way out of it—or perhaps pushed his way out—and has no intention of going back.

Edging closer to what I suspect is his point of vulnerability, I ask, "What about your dad? How did he deal with difficult things? Did he avoid them, too?"

Donny Ray's movements are slow and cautious. He seems more alert but also significantly more distressed.

"Uh-uh," he finally says. "My dad wasn't like that at all."

"How was he?"

No answer.

I push a little more. "What was it like for you after he died?"

No answer for that one, either.

And now I realize we've uncovered the weak spot in Donny Ray's armor. Not a complete surprise, considering what he spoke about during our last session. My job now is to take him down that rocky path.

"And your home life?" I ask. "How was that?"

"There wasn't much to it." Tension rushes his speech. "We lived in a double-wide. A trailer park. It was on the outskirts of town."

"What was life like *inside* that trailer?"

"Not so great, but I don't think I realized it. Not at first anyway."

"Can you explain?"

"I guess it's just that when you're young, it takes time to figure out there's more to this world than just what you see around you."

"What did you see around you?"

No answer again.

"Donny Ray," I say, knowing it's time to guide him into that dark place. "What was your relationship with your father like?"

In a heartbeat, all the color I saw before in his face evaporates, and I'm again looking at the frightened young man who first presented himself when we met.

"A foreman," he abruptly says. "My dad was a foreman."

"Okay . . ."

"And we didn't have much, but there was always food on the table. We were never hungry. We always had clothes on our backs."

"It sounds like your dad was a very good man."

Donny Ray doesn't respond. He lowers his head, hands repetitively flexing into and out of tight fists.

"*Was* he a good man, your father?"

"I . . . I don't really like talking about that part."

"Can you tell me why?"

"If it's okay, sir, I . . . " Voice getting shakier, words coming out pressured. "I'd really prefer not to right now."

I wait and watch.

With slow hesitation he looks up at me, as if the silence has given him much-needed courage to finally do so. And in his eyes, I no longer see the piercing intensity, the bluer-than-blue disconnect. There is vulnerability. There is deep inner fear.

Fear that I know so very well, have seen reflected back from countless patients. The kind that, from the moment of inception, never leaves, getting tangled and integrated into every thread of their physical being.

The kind of fear that I'm pretty sure still lives within my own eyes.

41

REFLECTIONS OF FEAR

The scales had finally tipped.

I no longer loved the man in our house because the man in our house was becoming a stranger. Now I only feared him.

That man wasn't my father, anyway. Even when I caught familiar and fleeting glimpses of him, they were so fractured and shallow that I felt only a vague tug of recognition. It was like looking at a picture of a picture. A disturbing cardboard cutout. A fraud.

With his outbursts becoming more frequent and unruly—and despite Mom's resolve to deny and detach—there was no other choice but to get him medical attention. Soon after that came the bombshell diagnosis: adult-onset schizophrenia. As for my mother, her early-onset now-you-see-it-now-you-don't was progressing just as steadily, which only made things worse. She added pain on top of more pain, and I was the one feeling all of it.

Dad's speech was frequently disjointed, rambling, and nonsensical. He had also developed a peculiar giggle that began as a barely audible grunt and culminated with a high-pitched titter.

"What's so funny, dear?" my mother asked one day as we all drove from the grocery store.

He gave no answer, but from my place in the backseat, I could see his reflection smiling in the window glass. Then the grunt started, and I knew what would soon follow.

Apparently, so did my mother. "Oh, Christopher!" she said, loud enough to cover my dad's cackling, "look at all the pretty heliotrope on that fence! I do love the heliotrope. They have a glorious aroma, just like cherry vanilla pie. Brings back so many happy memories of my life as a girl. Nature has such a wonderful way of showing us beauty!"

And sometimes irony, too.

My father quietly stared out the window and watched his world go by—whatever that was—smiling and shaking his head.

I couldn't have smiled, even if I'd wanted to. I felt too torn over which was more worrisome, his madness or Mom's continued and unshakable avoidance of it.

Just as I was about to look away, I saw my father's reflection change in the glass. His smile disappeared, and his eyes narrowed as they stared directly at me, mouth moving silently with slow precision, as if he wanted me to read his lips.

Get out, or I'll kill you.

Terror shot up my spine as we turned onto the next road. Outside, the scenery changed, a dark row of trees further clarifying my father's reflection. There was no mistaking his sentiment: angry, hostile, and filled with vitriol.

A few seconds later, his smile returned, but this one raised goose bumps all over me. Never before had I seen him look at me with anything other than kindness and love. Now this impostor, this alien, glared at me with hatred and contempt.

As our car continued down the road, I tore my attention away from his evil gaze and stared instead at my sweaty palms. Tears rolled down my cheeks, prompted by fear and heartbreak.

I looked up and out through the front windshield, but all I could see was the unavoidable truth.

Danger ahead.

42

I try to reject the empathic feelings that Donny Ray is prompting.

I'm not supposed to have those. They compromise objectivity, stand in the way of diagnostic progress, which is crucial if I'm going to do my job effectively. And this particular patient, more than any other, is an extremely important one.

But it's difficult to ignore what I'm positive I saw, and yes, what I felt. Everything I witnessed from Donny Ray—the implicit fear he showed when his father entered the conversation—rang true as a product of deep, intrinsic, and profound mental suffering. Human emotion, pain so commanding, so visceral, and so very powerful. Pain I can relate to on a personal level. While the fear Donny Ray had of his father was likely very different from the fear I had of mine, I can still understand it. I know how it feels.

But maybe I can make our commonality work in my favor and uncover what others might have missed. I just have to climb outside of myself, to separate my own feelings from his. To use my personal experience as a stepping-stone to facilitate a better and more complete understanding of what's happening inside Donny Ray's mind.

I pass through Alpha Twelve, and it's like the mental clarity I worked so hard to regain earlier has tripped a fuse. My steps fall out of synch, then awareness jerks them to an abrupt standstill. At first I wonder if I'm seeing double because, at this point, it would not be the unlikeliest of scenarios, but a quick survey of my surroundings sinks the theory, and I know that I'm staring at not one, but two open doors. Nicholas', and now Stanley's.

Something very bad is definitely going on.

I move toward Stanley's room, look inside, and it feels like an instant replay of the other day. Same scenario, different patient. The place is stripped, not a single sign of human habitation.

Another one, gone.

That sleep of death, Christopher.

I practically fly to the nurses' station. Melinda managed to knock me off guard last time, but this time she'll be no match for my resolve.

She looks up from her computer screen, appearing more startled than compliant, but, once again, oddly detached.

"What happened to Stanley?" It's not really a question—it's a demand.

Melinda gives the hallway a negligible glance, then goes back to her work. "He went to St. Mary's Hospital."

"What for?"

"He had a heart attack."

"Two patients gone from this unit. In just a few days."

She offers nothing.

"And again, I haven't been notified." Obvious, I know, but I'm making a point. "Why is nobody telling me these things?"

Still typing. "It just happened this morning. Maybe the news hasn't reached you yet."

"Like it didn't reach me the other day?"

No answer.

"What time did you say this happened?"

"I didn't," she mutters and punches more keys. "About three a.m."

"I feel like information is being intentionally kept from me." Anger burns through my throat. "This isn't right. I want answers."

"I don't have any."

"Find them," I say, getting louder. "And while you're at it, find out why Nicholas was sent all the way the hell out to Montana."

Melinda reaches for a notepad and scribbles something.

I storm away.

But when I head back through Alpha Twelve, those two open doors stare back at me like menacing signposts. I've got no idea where they're pointing, but I do know one thing.

It's no place good.

43

My cell rings as I head back toward the office,

"It's your lucky day, partner," Adam tells me.

"Man, could I ever use one of those."

"Huh?"

"Nothing. What's up?"

"Dr. Rob found an opening in his schedule. Can you get there by two?"

He doesn't have to ask twice. I click off my phone and head for the exit.

"You're doing the right thing," Jenna says when I call from the car to let her know.

"I hope so."

"You are. Let him do his job, and then we'll take care of the rest, okay?"

"Okay," I reply stiffly, then hang up.

I want to believe her, want to face the truth, then walk on faith. But the rails are shaky when you're hopping from one fast-moving train to another.

I wait in the examining room for Dr. Rob to materialize. About five minutes later, he walks through the door.

"Dr. Kellan," he says, reaching out to shake my hand.

"Thanks so much for fitting me in, Doctor. I really do appreciate it."

He waves it off and smiles. "Not a problem. Adam's a great guy."

Adam is vindictive and evil.

"I'm happy to help a colleague and friend of his." Rob pulls up a chair and sits across from me. "So what can I do for you today?"

"I think Adam might have explained a little about my situation." I shift my weight. "I had a car accident several days ago."

"How many days, exactly?" He moves his gaze to the mending bruise over my eye.

"Five. I hit my head on the side window first, then the steering wheel."

"I assume you're still having symptoms."

I give him the same ones I told Adam about. I have to play this down. If news gets around that I'm losing time and seeing things, it will be a prescription for disaster. I've already created havoc at home; I don't need to add more by losing my job and causing financial problems. My goal today is to get the MRI and see if it reveals brain damage from the accident, then hopefully, through the process of elimination, rule out heredity as a precipitator for all the abnormal things I've been seeing and hearing.

"You waited a while to see me," he says.

"Yes." I nod. "At first the effects seemed mild enough not to worry."

"And now?"

"Now they're persisting, so I just want to be sure there's nothing more serious going on. Not that I suspect there is. It's more of a precautionary measure. You know, peace of mind."

Rob is studying me. There's something uncomfortable about it.

He doesn't believe you.

"I'd like you to run an MRI," I say, too brusquely, and realize I'm fidgeting with my hands.

He doesn't comment. The more he observes me, the more anxious I'm getting. The doctor shines a penlight into my eyes and tells me to look off to one side. "Any other problems?"

"No."

He clicks off the light and steps back. "Did you suffer any loss of consciousness after the accident?"

"Very briefly."

"How briefly?"

"Seconds. No more than a minute."

That seems to give him visible concern. He runs a few tests to check my balance, coordination, and reflexes.

He's not going to green-light the MRI.

"Well, I don't see anything that might indicate neurological dama—"

"I'd still like to have the imaging test done."

"—However," he continues with a patient smile, "since you're still having symptoms, it's not a bad idea to go ahead and get the MRI done. I'll send the order to your insurance company for approv—"

"I'd like to have it today. I'll pay out-of-pocket."

"Okay, but—"

"I'd like to do it now, please."

Rob pauses, his expression wandering into doubtfulness.

"It's just that I have a lot going on at work in the next few days," I say, trying to appease him with a smile. "My wife is very worried about this, so the sooner, the better. It would really help me out."

Rob blinks a few times, nods, but doesn't speak.

He's going to report you.

He's going to tell them you're stark raving mad.

44

I lie flat on my back under the MRI's main coil, surrounded by a plastic tube, the molded ceiling just inches from my face. My head rests on something masquerading as a pillow, wafer-thin, the size, shape, and feel of a baking pan. Beneath me is a cold slab—the only thing separating me from it is a sliver of a sheet that makes my skin itch. In this confined space, with arms pinned so close to my sides, I couldn't scratch even if I wanted to. I hold in my hand a rubber ball. The technician told me to squeeze it if I feel frightened or need help, and that will signal her. Clamped to my head is a pair of headphones with music intended to make me relax.

It's not working.

I've never had an MRI. I didn't realize how unnerving the experience is. I don't like it here, want out, but this is very important. So I remain imprisoned within this plastic cave.

The violins swell through my headphones.

"Helloooo . . . ," I say to no one, hearing my voice fall flat.

"Yes? Is something wrong?" The technician's voice booms through my headphones.

I clear my throat. "Just checking to see if we're ready to get this started."

"A few more minutes," Speaker Voice grants with a mix of assurance and diplomatic irritation.

I keep waiting.

I've got no idea what Rob told them in order to get me in so quickly, but my sense is that he conveyed there was some sort of emergency because, while strapping me in, the tech kept assuring, "Don't worry. Everything is going to be okay."

I'm not so sure about that.

The machine lets out a series of resounding, mechanized clicks, rattling me from my thoughts.

Speaker Voice says, "We're ready to start now. Still doing all right in there?"

I don't recall ever stating that I was, but I tell her yes.

"Great. Don't worry. Everything is going to be okay."

I wish she'd stop saying that.

"Just remember, you have the rubber ball if you need anything."

"Fuck the rubber ball!"

It's that voice again, the one that won't leave my head and keeps wandering out through my mouth.

"Excuse me?" she says.

"I said, I've got the rubber ball."

"Okay." She sounds reluctant, doubtful. She pauses for a few murderous seconds. "We're going to start now. You'll hear a little noise and feel a few vibrations for this next part. I'll need you to keep still."

I'm strapped down like a captured beast. Jumping jacks are hardly an option.

As it turns out, "little" and "few" are drastic understatements. This spaceship is rocking like it's on a mission to Mars, banging, clacking, and rattling, the violin music rendered inaudible by the clamor. I grit my teeth, close my eyes, and try to endure.

Whoa. What the hell was that?

Did this thing just . . . ? No, it can't be. But I felt it, as if . . .

Holy shit!

This entire machine just skipped off the floor.

Oh my God.

Now it's not just skipping—it's tilting upward.

Oh no . . . oh no . . . OH NO!

My chest turns heavy and thick. Blood drains into my face, as the machine inclines sharply, feet rising, head dropping. My reflexes kick into action, and I feel my hand rapidly and repeatedly squeeze the rubber ball.

"Wrong ball," Donny Ray says through the headphones, in a mocking singsong tone.

I jerk at the sound of his voice. The machine continues to lift. Sweat rolls from chest to face to scalp, as gravity pulls it downward.

"SOMEBODY GET ME OUT OF HERE!" I say through a panicked scream. "SOMEBODY HELP ME!"

The MRI comes to a jarring stop, now pointing straight at the ceiling. The noise and vibrations cut out, and I'm immersed in stillness. My body is completely upside down. My pulse is hammering out of control.

"Christopher," a new voice says.

Wait, I know that voice. It sounds like—

I catch movement from above. With chin lowered to chest, I strain to see up through the end of the tube; then my heart erupts into a fast-footed beat, as black dots dance before my eyes.

"Dad?"

My father peers down at me.

"Dad, what are you . . . ? Where did . . . ?"

"You've been looking at things from the wrong side," he tells me through the headphones.

"I don't understand."

"You will, soon."

"Be careful on that road," Donny Ray chimes in. "It's a killer."

Then I hear laughter. It's my father. The horrifying laugh I remember so well. The sniggering and cackling one that always climbed into maniacal shrieking, echoing through the house late at night, twirling through my ears like jagged corkscrews.

I close my eyes and scream.

Through the headphones, I hear glass shatter. The white light explodes.

And then in a heartbeat, the MRI is back on the floor, and I'm outside the coil, looking up at . . .

"Jenna?" I say, clenching at the sheet. "What are you doing here?"

She answers with an expression devoid of emotion, or . . . No, that's not right. Something is there, something I think is . . .

"I have to go now," she says.

"Go where?"

"I can't stay here with you."

"Stay where? What do you mean?"

Jenna doesn't answer—and now she can't even look at me. She turns away. She walks. And as the distance between us widens, Devon materializes at her side, then hand in hand, they drift toward the exit doors and disappear.

"Devon! Jenna!" I shout, tears filling my eyes. "Wait! Don't go! *Please!* Don't leave me!"

And they are gone.

I hear glass shatter again. The white light explodes.

And then, in an astoundingly quick beat, I'm looking up at the tech.

"Are you okay?" Her expression is tempered with professional concern.

"I just saw—" My voice is thick, mind spinning out. I struggle for composure. "Yes. I'm okay. I just got a little panicked. Please . . . let's just get this over with."

But I know it will never be over. The terrifying confusion, the madness. Not now. Not ever.

This is just the start.

45

Everything around me is moving in wavy circles. A few moments later, my vision starts to settle, and I see I'm . . .

In the Loveland parking lot.

The last thing I remember is the MRI tech looking down on me. I check the dashboard clock.

That was nearly forty minutes ago.

More weirdness, more seeing and hearing things I shouldn't. More worry. Time keeps bending, my perceptions doing the same, and I'm no longer sure whether to trust either.

It's like a part of me is dying.

Or maybe I'm already dead.

I shouldn't be working in this condition. As my mind loses its contours, that only seems clearer. But I can't stop right now. Not when I'm on the verge of a breakthrough with Donny Ray. Equally pressing, I need to figure out what's happened to Nicholas and Stanley. I just have to hang on a little bit longer, wait for the test results, then once I know what's wrong, figure out some kind of strategy.

The MRI.

All at once I'm back there again, reliving the nightmare. My stomach hitches, my skin turns cold. My body is shaking.

The phone rings. I fumble to find it.

Jenna says, "I'm just checking in to see how things went."

"You're still here." My words fire out. "You didn't . . ." I stop myself, and for about five seconds, there is dead silence.

"Of course I'm here," she says through a laugh of reasonability. "Where would I go?"

"Nowhere. I just . . . I thought the call dropped."

"Oh . . . so how did the MRI go?"

"It was nerve-wracking," I say, trying to control the quake in my voice, fully aware the attempt is less than adequate. "Like being stuffed into a clothes dryer."

"Sounds not so fun."

"You have no idea." And really, she doesn't.

"Did they say when you'll hear back with the results?"

"Two days, hopefully."

"We'll just wait, then."

"Yeah . . . we'll wait."

"Chris."

"Huh."

"There's something else. Tell me."

"It's nothing."

"Sweetie, I know you better."

I don't say anything more. There's no use in trying.

"And I love you way too much to let you suffer in silence, so please, talk to me."

I've reached my tipping point. The ground beneath me is sinking. I'm drowning. I gasp for a mouthful of oxygen, struggle to find more, but it's like there's none left for me. Like the atmosphere is a thick, scalding soup, and the more I try, the more my throat closes up.

"Chris," I hear my wife very gently say.

"What?"

"Listen to me carefully." Her voice turns firm with just the right measure of tender guidance. "I want you to lean on me."

"I can't." My speech is slurred, and it sounds more like a cry for help.

"You can. Lean on me, baby. That's what we do—it's what we've always done."

"I don't know how to anymore."

"You do—you've just forgotten. I'll help. Can you remember what we used to do when things made us scared?"

And all at once, I do remember. The time in college when we got the news her father had died after a massive stroke. The temporary scare when doctors found a suspicious shadow on my liver. Those long nights we spent so vigilantly in the hospital at Devon's bedside after he contracted pneumonia, unsure whether he'd live to see the next day. Jenna would lay her head on my chest, listen to my breaths, and synch hers to mine. Together we would breathe, and together everything would feel better. All the fear, all the worries in our lives melting away, the two of us becoming one.

"Chris," she says, "go ahead. Do it right now. Breathe with me."

I try to draw air.

"That's it," she says, inhaling deeply with me, then letting it out. "You can do this."

My respirations are loud and frantic, hers soft and calm, but we are doing it. We are breathing together, and little by little, she is bringing me down.

"Keep going," Jenna says, inhaling deeper. "You're doing fine."

I feel my throat start to open up, the oxygen slowly finding its way back and replenishing my lungs. Soon, my rhythm finds hers and we dovetail together.

We are one.

In that exact moment, something within me breaks wide open, something more powerful than myself, and there is no longer fear, there is no longer doubt, there is only truth.

"I'm so scared," I say, voice fracturing.

"I know, sweetheart. I know . . ."

"It's the same thing. It's the same goddamned thing as my father."

"It is not," she says, her tone falling weaker as if hearing this is more than she can bear.

"It already is. I'm losing my son, and the worst part—the most agonizing—is that I know he'll never forgive me for this, that he'll end up hating me the same way . . ." I stop, not wanting to drive the knife in deeper.

"That isn't going to happen. It's just not."

"How can you possibly know?"

"Because," she says, "it's not Devon you need to ask for forgiveness."

"Who then?"

"It's yourself."

I don't answer—not because I don't have one but because I know she's just spoken the truth. Truth I've been trying to avoid for most of my life.

"Come home, Chris," my wife tells me. "Come back to your safe place."

46

The night was brutal.

I spent a good part of it staring at the ceiling, but all I could see was a life coming undone. A mind slipping away. A family falling apart.

While I'm grateful to Jenna for talking me off the ledge yesterday after my living nightmare inside the MRI tube, I also realize that even she can't erase the images and sounds that traveled through my crumbling mind. Something else I know: if those were more than products of a head injury, Jenna will be just as powerless as my mother and I were during my childhood.

I drive toward work with the fear that this new day may only throw more conflict my way.

When I arrive at Loveland, my concerns prove well founded: the parking lot is now less than two-thirds full. With the vacancies now so much more obvious, my thoughts skyrocket on the rewind.

Stanley and Nicholas.

The cafeteria.

This parking lot.

My suspicions were no overreaction, and with that comes a new reality, the size and scope of which are much bigger than I'd first wanted to realize.

Loveland Hospital is vanishing before my eyes.

I have to talk to someone.

Don't do it. Do NOT.

But something horrible is happening.

As horrible as your ass getting wiped out next?

Heat flushes my face.

Mind your own business. Keep your mouth shut.

My feet stumble over themselves. After finding my stride, I pick up the pace and rush toward the building.

Down the hall toward my office, worries trail me and refuse to let go. I need to see whether Melinda has e-mailed the information I'd requested, so I can get to the bottom of all these strange happenings. But halfway there, Jeremy materializes from a bathroom door. He takes one look at me, then strolls my way. I've got no time for him right now, but his demanding expression says I don't have much of a choice.

"Christopher," he says. "Something very strange is happening."

"I'm sorry?" I try to avoid choking on my words.

"I keep checking my e-mails for updates on your progress with Donny Ray's evaluation, but for some reason, I'm not finding them."

"Oh, yeah." I coerce a laugh. "That."

"Yeah, *that*. Any idea at all why *that* might be?"

"It's with good reason," I say. "I guess I've been a little involved and forgot. I'm actually making great progress with him."

"I don't need to remind you how important this case is, do I?"

"No, sir. You most certainly do not."

"And that tomorrow is our deadline."

"No need to remind me about that, either. I'll meet it."

"Excellent. So, keep me updated, all right?"

"Absolutely, and again, my apologies."

Jeremy smiles, but I can't find a shred of satisfaction in it. He walks away, and I rush into my office.

I know how he feels in one respect. Anxious for an e-mail from Melinda on her progress, I check my screen.

Nothing.

Now I'm downright irritated.

The instant I step onto Alpha Twelve, disorientation greets me. From one end to the next, patients enter and exit rooms. Others wander the hallways. Several more stand around and chat with one another.

What in God's name is happening here?

This floor maintains the highest level of protection Loveland can offer, and patients are never allowed outside their rooms unless accompanied by a staff member. This isn't just a concern—this is a safety hazard, a security breach gone haywire.

A clammy and firm hand cups my right elbow. I jerk around. Mere inches separate Gerald Markman and me.

"We are all sculptors and painters," he says wearing a ravenous, craving expression, "and our material is our own flesh and blood and bones."

He licks his lips. I pull my arm away and take off running toward the nurses' station, outrage, nausea, and utter fright sparking through me like loose live wires.

And there I run head-on into yet another peculiarity because the nurse on duty is someone I've never before seen: twentysomething, with pink cheeks and an eager expression.

"Can I help you?" she asks.

"Is Melinda around?"

Mystery Nurse tucks a thatch of hair behind one ear and tilts her head.

"Melinda Jeffries," I reiterate.

"I'm sorry, but I don't know who that is."

I look at her fixedly. "What do you mean, you *don't know*? She's the head nurse on this floor."

"They just moved me here," she says, as if this addresses my concerns. She throws in a shallow smile that seems vaguely apologetic.

"Did anyone explain why they *just moved* you here?"

"No. I'm sorry. They really didn't." Her smile dims. "Is there something else I can help you with?"

I motion around me. "You can tell me what's happening on this floor."

"I'm not sure what you mean."

"The patients. Why are they not secured inside their rooms? Why are they just wandering around?"

She looks confused. More than before.

"I can't believe this!" I fumble for my phone.

"I need an officer down to Alpha Twelve. *Immediately*," I tell security. "It's complete pandemonium here. All of the patients have broken out of their rooms!"

I consider the nurse, then look at the time display on my phone screen. I'm late for my session with Donny Ray.

"Did you even bother to let anyone know what's been going . . . Oh, never mind!" I snap at her. "*You'll* be hearing from your supervisor!"

She blinks and draws back from me.

47

I grab an extra moment outside the consulting room to decompress and remind myself that I'm in my professional element. That this is where I'm most comfortable. That I know how to do my job, and that the evaluation is due tomorrow.

I can do this.

I walk inside. Donny Ray is already sitting at the table. Once again, something about him has changed, but this time it's not just his physical appearance—it's subtler, a slight shift in demeanor, as though he's shed yet another layer of discomfort.

Wish I could feel the same way.

I have to keep my concerns about Alpha Twelve and the shrinking hospital population outside this door and tread very carefully. I've worked too damned hard to build trust, and fast as that trust can build, it can just as easily come tumbling down without warning or provocation. The plains of human suffering are slippery slopes. Every traveler is so frail and unsteady, vulnerable to even the slightest threat of doubt or uncertainty. The goal here is to change his emotional climate. To normalize the feelings he has about his past trauma so that he's able to talk about them.

I lean back in my chair a few inches, gather my wits, and offer Donny Ray a neutralizing smile. "I've been thinking about what you mentioned yesterday."

He shakes his head.

"About your mom. How you described her. It kind of reminded me of my own mother."

"In what way?"

"That thing she would tell you? About your town being small?" I look down and rub my forehead. "Something about how there's nothing to do every minute?"

"But every minute counts?"

"Yeah." I point to him and nod. "That's it."

"Did your mom say that, too?"

"No. I was thinking more about what you said after, how she chose to look at life."

"Yours did the same thing?"

"Man, did she ever. In fact, I used to make a joke about it—well, it was actually more like a complaint disguised as humor. How when bad things happened, she always pretended that they hadn't."

"So, what was the joke?"

"That I always imagined her entry into the world went something like this: the doctor gave her a slap on the ass, and instead of bursting into a scream, she turned her head away and let out a despondent sigh."

Donny Ray suppresses a chuckle, then looks bashfully at the floor.

"It's okay to laugh," I tell him, "it was meant to be funny. I mean, that's kind of how I survived all those miserable years."

"You had a rough childhood, too?" He seems surprised.

"*Rough* would be putting it mildly—in fact, if I didn't laugh, I would have cried all the time."

He watches me in deliberative silence. "That bad?"

I nod slowly. "Yeah . . . that bad."

He doesn't speak, but his expression relaxes. I allow the calm to linger. Not just because that's what a good psychologist does, but also because I actually need it. Because for a few seconds, some of my own pain managed to sweep to the surface.

When I look back at Donny Ray, he's scrutinizing me.

"Anyway," I tell him, "this really isn't about me. What I'm trying to say is that I wasn't aware we had that in common."

"What happened to you?" he abruptly says, as if the need to know has broken through his uneasiness and given him the confidence to ask.

"It's a long story, Donny Ray, and it's not why we're here."

"I know why we're here," he says, voice sturdy with resolve that surprises me. "What happened to you?"

I feel my expression go slack. I take in his attentive gaze, those eyes of steel that have become pools of empathic awareness. Like something is tugging at him to crawl through that narrow, confined space and reveal his own pain.

While it would be very unprofessional to tell Donny Ray about my tragic past, I can't deny there's a piece of me that would like to. A piece that knows his pain so intimately and might even help him find a way out of it. If I could, I'd tell him that I understand how, once inflicted, the pain caused by a parent never leaves. How it becomes the biggest part of you.

But I can't do that. I can't, because we're not here to talk about my problematic childhood. Still, for a moment I get lost in it all. The memories. The emotions . . .

When I refocus on Donny Ray, he's watching me with concern and slowly shaking his head, and I see sadness. I see understanding and sympathy. But most of all, I feel as though he knows what I've been thinking. He parts his lips slightly, like he wants to say something but can't.

I realize this session has slipped from my control. I've got to bring it back. But as I reach for my notebook, I find it's not there.

I look at my empty lap in bewilderment, and then turn my gaze around the room.

My notebook rests beside the computer about ten feet away.

I hear that strange noise again, then a shadow swoops down the wall and across my lap. I look toward the ceiling, and this time I catch a split-second glimpse of—

No way. It can't be.

"What's wrong, Christopher?"

I turn to Donny Ray.

What just happened?

48

"Christopher?" Donny Ray says again.

I fight like hell to navigate through my fog of confusion, to regain normality, even though I'm fully aware there's nothing about this situation that's anywhere close to being normal.

Don't you dare slide off the rails, I demand of myself. *Jeremy is waiting. The MRI results are waiting. Focus now. Go crazy later.*

Donny Ray is still staring at me.

"I was just . . ." I steady my voice and try to reestablish the flow we've lost, so I can move this session forward. ". . . I was just thinking about what we were discussing."

"About all your pain?"

"No." Flustered, I look at him. "About your mom. I'm wondering what it was that she pretended not to see."

Donny Ray's voice reveals nothing but anguish when he says, "Lots of things."

"Can you tell me about them?"

He focuses on the door, runs his hand along a spreading five o'clock shadow. "I'm not sure I want to."

"How about one of the things, then?"

"I . . . I'm . . . I don't think I . . ."

"It's okay. You don't have to right now," I say, thankful to at last find a toehold on lucidity. "I just want you to know that you can."

"It's just that . . . I'm so . . ."

"I know," I tell him. "I get it. I really do."

"He did things," Donny Ray says.

"Who did?"

"My father."

"What kinds of things?"

"To both of us. He did them to us both . . ."

"To you and your sister," I confirm.

Donny Ray twists his body away from me. Now he is literally fighting for each breath, back heaving, broad shoulders rising and falling. "It was just Miranda at first, but I didn't know. I . . . I didn't know that was what he was doing to her."

"When they left you alone."

A fast nod.

Again, I think about the ice cream cone, and my stomach turns queasy.

"Then, after she was gone . . . after that happened . . . I figured it out, because he started doing it to me. I became her replacement." Donny Ray turns back to me, tears welling, mouth trembling, and in a defeated whisper, says, "All that anger toward Miranda . . . I was so damned wrong, and it was too late to tell her."

"Where would this happen?"

"The shed. I remember the shed." He falters, then stops.

I hold to the silence. He's on the verge of opening the door to his childhood nightmare, and I don't want to shake him out of it.

"It was my safe place where I would go," he continues, "and it was a good place, but he turned it into a really bad one."

Gently now. "What did your father do to you inside that shed, Donny Ray?"

"There was this lightbulb . . . and it . . . it hung from the ceiling by a chain. And I'd concentrate on this dirty naked bulb, swaying back and forth while he did it to me. And I'd count . . . I'd count each swing until he was finished. One time I got up to two thousand and fifty-seven."

Nearly an hour and a half of sexual abuse, I calculate. An hour and a half of deep emotional and physical turmoil, inflicted on an innocent child. Turmoil that was likely repeated until that child's mind was broken. Destroyed. I swallow hard to fight back my nausea.

Donny Ray hunches over, face in hands, rocking his body to a slow and steady rhythm. Forward and back . . . forward and back. I know he's still in that horrible place, and I have to take him out of it.

Very softly I say, "Those feelings you had of being alone? They must have been so much worse, after."

His shoulder muscles pull taut—they are bulging with tension.

"And after losing your sister . . ."

"I loved my sister. I miss her so terribly."

Within this new context of Donny Ray's own sexual abuse, I again ponder the flat affect he uses while describing Miranda. It's not that unusual for victims to detach from emotions associated with the incident. Only after intensive therapeutic work are they able to rejoin with those feelings. What has me scratching my head is that Donny Ray displayed such powerful emotional response to his abuse, and yet while addressing Miranda, there seemed to be nothing. And now I go back even farther to my initial thoughts about a possible unconscious pathology and the trauma trigger. Is there something about Miranda that's far more painful than Donny Ray's abuse? Something he's not yet able to tell me? Maybe even something he can't recall?

I don't know . . . can't be sure.

Moving on in pursuit of that answer, I ask, "Where was your mother when all this was going on?"

"Hiding," he snaps, and the anger returns. "Hiding like she always did. Pretending that none of it was happening."

I try to separate my personal identification with him, because I understand it from a firsthand perspective, although in a completely different way. "And after you left the shed? What would he do?"

"After was worse."

"Worse, in what way?"

"I didn't get the ice cream cone."

"What did you get?"

"The punishment," he says, voice crackling with contempt. "He'd punish me for seducing him, call me a filthy, disgusting whore boy."

I close my eyes, open them. "I'm so sorry, Donny Ray. I can't begin to imagine—"

"No. You cannot imagine. Nobody could unless—" He grits his teeth, as if doing so might help keep the humiliation, the anger, contained. "But that wasn't the punishment."

"How did he punish you?"

"He'd drive me to the center of town, shove me out of the car, and leave me there."

"Making you feel more alone than you already were."

"It was the dress," he says, choking.

"The what?"

"He made me . . ." Donny Ray gnashes his teeth and lets out a barely audible moan. "My father made me walk through town to get home . . . wearing my dead sister's dress."

I draw what feels like my first taste of oxygen since he began telling his horrific story.

"I felt like a freak show. I was ashamed. I was angry. I was so . . ." A tiny yet excruciating whimper passes through his lips. "All I wanted to do was crawl into a hole and die."

"But you couldn't."

"There was no lightbulb to look at then," Donny Ray Smith tells me. "Just everyone staring. Laughing."

And in that instant, his eyes return to their previous state.

Blue fury. Cold as steel.

49

One of the first things I learned during my early clinical studies was that trauma is attracted to trauma. While my childhood experiences bear no resemblance to Donny Ray's, the family dynamic feels awfully familiar: a father who inflicts deep psychological pain on a child, and a mother who checks out, only to inflict yet another layer of damage.

It would be difficult for any psychologist to hear a story like Donny Ray's and not feel affected by it. We are, after all, human. We have emotional vulnerabilities just like everyone else, and while we've been trained to compartmentalize in order to help others, every so often a patient comes along who holds up the mirror to us. When that happens, it can be difficult to ignore what's looking us in the face.

Still, I refuse to believe that I'm losing objectivity with Donny Ray—I'm simply using my own human experiences as a tool to get information I need.

There's a difference.

It doesn't mean I can't separate my feelings. It just means I need to be mindful of my own past while assessing him.

And perhaps my instinct after our previous session was right. Maybe I can parlay our connection into finding the missing link: does Donny Ray remember murdering Jamey Winslow?

I begin sorting out my thoughts, hoping to integrate new knowledge with the old. I don't think there's any question that Donny Ray's father murdered Miranda. He had the means and the opportunity, and the files indicate the cops thought so, too. Was she intentionally waving good-bye to her brother that day for the last time? After seeing Donny Ray's detached reaction twice while he spoke of Miranda, I have to wonder whether he might have actually witnessed her murder. This could explain why he appeared so disconnected.

Which brings me back to Dr. Philips' notes. She entertained the possibility there was some kind of psychological disorder at play but never could pinpoint the pathology. Since the doctor made no mention of Donny Ray's sexual abuse—or the subsequent punishment his father inflicted—I have to assume she was unable to get him to open up about it. That might be the critical cornerstone she failed to uncover.

But what does this new information mean?

I allow my intuition to wander. Young incest victims don't just notice the inanimate during their abuse: the inanimate becomes their entire world. I revisit that eerie image of the lightbulb, how all this little boy could do was focus on it, obsessively counting the number of times it swung from a cord while his father violated him.

A violent and intolerable shiver rides through my entire body.

Logic tells me that from what Donny Ray described, during those moments, he could very well have entered into a dissociative state. But plenty of kids detach from reality during traumatic events, and it doesn't turn them into killers.

There has to be more.

What kind of incident might have pushed Donny Ray into such predatory killing behavior that he can't recall? The repetitive rounds of sexual abuse would certainly qualify. And being abandoned in public afterward, wearing his dead sister's dress, piled one trauma on top of the other, which would be more than enough to push him over the edge.

But how would the effects of that experience express themselves? Is becoming a serial killer a guaranteed outcome? I'm not sure yet, but my mind is trending toward the idea that the other victim in this—Donny Ray's sister—may be able to tell me.

I look to the Internet and search the news coverage of Miranda Smith's disappearance. The first thing that pops up is a school photo of her. I zoom in and see that, much like Donny Ray, she was positively striking in appearance. Same raven-colored hair, same well-defined features. But Miranda's eyes were mirror opposites of Donny Ray's: dark as night, yet in their own way, just as intense.

I begin reading an article and learn that she disappeared on her way to school one morning.

Wait a minute.

I flip back to the notes on Donny Ray's last victim, Jamey Winslow, who also went missing on her way to school. After pulling up the news story about her murder, I at first think it's the wrong link. Then my stomach seizes.

No way.

Jamey Winslow bore a remarkable resemblance to Miranda Smith.

I bring up more stories about Donny Ray's other victims, and one by one, with each photo, my mind whirls into a tailspin. Every one of them resembles Miranda Smith—some not as markedly but all with the same color hair and dark, intense eyes—each disappearing on her way to school.

Each wearing a blue dress.

How did I miss these connections while reading through the files? Then I remember . . . I'd planned to go back and look at the girls' photos but got sidetracked when Donny Ray's juvenile record was missing. Then his attorney was missing, and after that, so too was Dr. Ammon.

I never saw these images.

My thoughts fly into reverse and land on an earlier session with Donny Ray. How he seemed lost in thought, staring at that picture on the wall. A picture that happened to feature a little girl wearing a blue dress. He wasn't just lost in thought—he was lost inside his own mind.

A clear pattern: relentless and consistent layers of abuse, followed by behavior that mirrors it in a most striking and disturbing way.

A causal relationship.

Dr. Ammon discounted Donny Ray's inability to recall murdering Jamey Winslow because his head injury proved inconsequential. And while Dr. Philips was definitely on to something, any progress went flying out the window along with her credibility after the hospital sex scandal broke. But the bottom line is that Donny Ray Smith may be telling the truth about having no ability to recall killing Jamey.

Possible diagnosis: dissociative amnesia, brought on not by a head injury, but instead by acute and repetitive psychological trauma.

50

Don't tell Adam.

"What are you talking about? We're working this case together. Of course I'm going to tell him."

You cannot. He's part of the Big Plan, him and his bootlicking disciples—they're all working to destroy you.

"What?" I pull open the door.

"That's what I'd like to know," Adam says, frowning at me from his desk. "I just heard you called a security incident down on Alpha Twelve about an hour ago? For no apparent reason?"

"What do you mean, *no reason*? Of course there was a reason."

Motioning for me to close the door, he says, "We need to talk."

I grab a seat across from him. "When I got there, all the patients were wandering in and out of their rooms and through the hallways. Not one locked door, not a single security officer in sight. It was the most bizarre thing I've ever seen. So *of course* I called an incident."

Adam's eyes are hazy with doubt as they search mine.

"What is it?" I ask. "What's wrong?"

"Chris, the rooms in Alpha Twelve are never locked, unless a patient is under special order."

"What the hell are you talking about?" I laugh but there's no amusement in it. "Of course they are!"

He shakes his head. "That would be illegal."

"But it's a safety precaution. They're not supposed to . . . Wait. You think I just *made up* this policy?"

"I'm not saying that." But his expression states otherwise.

I stare at him for about five seconds. He stares back at me, and sticky tension stretches between us.

"Anyway, I'm sure security has the whole mess under control by now, so we're good there."

But judging by the crease in Adam's brow, my assurance offers little relief.

"I've got something much more important to tell you," I quickly move on, "something huge that could blow Donny Ray's case right out of the water. We just had a breakthrough. I've found the trauma trigger that Philips missed. Donny Ray has a pathological need to repeatedly murder his sister, then make her disappear. I strongly believe that's what caused his dissociative amnesia when Jamey went missing."

Adam's eyes flutter.

I start telling him the history of Donny Ray's abuse, along with an explanation about the picture on the wall of a girl wearing a blue dress. How every victim resembles Miranda. He shakes his head as I continue, but it's hard to tell whether he's following me.

"So here's how the events might have played out." I lean in toward him. "He sees a girl who looks like his sister, who also happens to be wearing a blue dress, probably the same color dress his father made him wear."

"You say *probably*."

"Well, we weren't at that level of detail in the interview. He was racked with deep emotional pain, and I wasn't able to ask him about it."

"Okay, go on . . . ," Adam says and starts twisting the ring on his finger.

"The blue dress strongly relates to his psychological trauma. He experiences the humiliation and shame all over again, and that activates the rage he's unable to express. And in that state, since he can't take out the rage on his father anymore, Donny Ray instead transfers it to Miranda, possibly because, through his subconscious and distorted reasoning, he blames her for leaving him alone to shoulder all the abuse."

"Possibly . . ."

"Well, yeah. I don't know that for sure yet. I'm just hypothesizing."

Adam concedes with a tentative nod.

"So anyway, he kills the girls instead. And here's something else. Donny Ray said his head injury happened after falling onto the family tractor's bucket loader, but he can't recall the exact date, only that it happened the summer his sister went missing. Tractors can be used to bury bodies, right? Maybe Donny Ray saw his sister being murdered. Maybe he was even forced to help dispose of Miranda and doesn't remember hitting his head after blocking it out. That would create three layers of trauma. And it could explain why he hides the girls' bodies."

Adam flinches, then blinks a few times. "Chris, I feel like you're overreaching into a lot of places with no firm foundation."

"What do you mean? Why?"

"First of all, the bucket loader thing. Don't you think the detectives considered that possibility?"

I tell him I already thought about that, how there's nothing in the report to indicate Texas cops followed up with the local hospital to get the exact date of Donny Ray's head injury, which means they probably missed the connection and never looked further.

"The detectives couldn't find enough evidence to charge the father," I explain. "So what if they were unable to complete the chain of events? I mean, the dad was clearly disturbed, and he could have been clever enough to cover his tracks."

"But you're still assuming a lot of things." Adam is smiling, but there's no twinkle in his eyes. He looks frustrated, also a little concerned. "And you're playing cop again."

"How am I *playing cop*?"

"Speculating that Donny Ray's head injury happened while he was helping his father bury the body? Other than a bucket loader, there's nothing to support the theory. You have to admit, that's a fantastical leap. It feels more like you're trying to help solve Miranda's murd—"

"*Fantastical?*"

"And you're using some picture on the wall as a springboard into dissociation, when you don't even know if Donny Ray's father made him wear a blue dress. Besides, I never saw anything in the police report indicating the other victims were wearing blue dresses when they disappeared. So how are you reaching that conclusion?"

"I missed it the first time myself, but go look again, and you'll see. The information's all there in the police report."

"Okay, but weren't you the one who reminded me we're not even supposed to factor in the other cases?"

"Adam"—I feel my throat tighten around his name—"they gave the information to us for background purposes. I'm just throwing around ideas. I'm brainstorming, thinking of possible scenarios. And you're completely missing the entire point. Philips couldn't get Donny Ray to open up about his abuse. That's what she was trying to do, and *that's* a really big deal, because it explains a lot of things."

"But what I'm trying to tell you is, without solid footing on that reasoning, you still can't prove whether his need to kill the girls is driven by disassociation or psychopathy, which brings us back to the original question of whether or not Donny Ray is malingering—and on that note, how can you be so sure he's even telling you the truth with this sexual abuse story? How do you know this isn't just an attempt to step up his game plan with you after things fell apart at Miller?"

He thinks you're unloading a pile of horseshit.

"Why do you keep throwing doubt at me? I'm a psychologist. I know what I'm doing."

"I'm not saying you don't." Adam stops, tries to speak, then starts again. "And I'm not throwing doubt at you."

"Then what *are* you doing? What exactly are you trying to tell me here?"

"That you're hopping all over the place with a theory that doesn't hold water. It's not like you, Chris. You're usually so—"

"That's not true! It all relates. It's all extremely relevant. I just need to figure out how."

"Okay . . . okay." Adam raises both hands, aims his palms at me. "Fine. But you still need to connect a lot of missing pieces, and your evaluation is due tomorrow."

"I'll find them," I sharply say, "*before* I jump to any rash decisions."

"Chris, stop that."

With arms locked tightly against my chest, I look away from him.

"Listen," he says, "I didn't mean to upset you. It's just that you came in here sounding so hellfire sure about all this, then after you explained it, the inconsistencies confused me. That's all. We're friends, remember? This is what we do for each other. We watch each other's backs."

I study Adam's face for a few beats to determine whether he means what he says.

He's patronizing you.

I don't like it.

He's judging you.

Things get very quiet. Then Adam asks, "So how did things go with Rob yesterday?"

"Wow, that came out of nowhere fast."

"Not really. You never called back to let me know how it went. I was just following up. I'm concerned."

But it feels like his concern is more about my mental and professional competence.

"He got me in for the MRI," I say.

"Hey, that's great. Did it go okay?"

"It's over with." I shrug. "That's the best thing I can say about it."

"Do you know when you'll have the results?"

"Tomorrow."

"Will you let me know as soon as he calls?"

I hesitate. Again, it's not what he's asking, more what seems to be trolling just beneath the surface. A little too much urgency. Like he's getting leery of me.

He knows you're losing it.

I try to relax my posture, but it seems as though Adam can tell the action is forced.

"Hey." He lets out a small laugh, obviously meant to disarm me. "Isn't it okay for your best friend to be worried after you've had a head injury?"

He's setting you up.

51

Driving home, those awkward moments with Adam wheel toward annoyance.

I fully realized my theory about Donny Ray wasn't concrete yet; there was no need to point it out. He said he was just trying to help but instead came across as extremely overcritical.

The simple fact is that while Donny Ray's previous psychologist had an inkling of what was going on, she obviously wasn't skilled enough to ask the right questions, therefore she never got the right answers. I have far more practical experience in the field of forensic psychology than she. I've been doing this for years and doing it well. Talking to Adam, you'd think I was some kind of rookie fresh out of school, seeing a zebra where there was only a horse. I'm greatly bothered that, instead of acknowledging my discovery, Adam demonstrated a lack of respect for my abilities. He doubted me.

That's because Adam despises you.

I can't help but question whether his doubt came from a bad place, if beneath his voice of concern was a whisper of professional competitiveness. He's already completed his assessment and concurred with Ammon that Donny Ray is malingering. If my theory is right—if Donny Ray dissociated during Jamey Winslow's murder, and his amnesia was caused not by the head injury but instead his previous psychological trauma—that would make both of their opinions irrelevant. Mine would prevail.

Adam has always felt threatened by you.

This is very disappointing.

I have every intention of closing the missing links he mentioned, and when I do, Adam will realize he was wrong. He'll feel embarrassed, and then I'll flaunt my success in his face. I'll be the one who gets to shame *him*. See how he likes it.

Don't forget when he asked about the MRI. It was a vicious move.

As if he thinks the accident has in some way compromised my professional judgment. That simply isn't true. The injury has compromised many things but not my ability to properly assess Donny Ray's case, and I resent the implication.

I just don't understand what's gone wrong inside Adam's head.

52

I walk into the house and find Jenna talking on the phone. She takes one look at me, and I can tell she senses the residual steam rolling off my back. I head for the refrigerator and try to play it down, but after looking inside, I can still feel the heat of her gaze on me.

"I'm not sure what to tell you," Jenna says, continuing her conversation. A minute or so later, she hangs up.

I look back at my wife, and now I see more than concern. She stares at the phone as if it might answer her confusion.

"It was Kayla," she says.

"Kayla?" I repeat and feel a stab of discomfort. She never calls here. We don't exactly have that kind of relationship with her, especially after my disturbing outburst at her home. "What did she want?"

"Something about a globe?"

Oh, shit. The globe.

I'd forgotten all about the damned thing. It's still upstairs in the closet, inside a pants pocket.

You need to lose that thing, buddy.

I'm not your buddy.

Jenna waits for my reaction.

"A globe...," I repeat, knowing my statement to be a weak avoidance effort. Then I shake my head because there's not really much more that I can say. Anything else could potentially cause a slipup.

"She noticed it went missing from her living room right after we left, then struggled for days over whether to mention it." Jenna wrinkles her nose. "The whole conversation felt really awkward."

"So she thinks we stole it?"

You did steal it.

"She didn't say that, but I can't see any other reason why she'd call to mention it."

"She's probably just still angry about the way I treated her. You know how Kayla loves her drama," I reply, giving pause to the thought of secretly returning something that, in retrospect, I haven't the slightest clue why I stole in the first place. Too risky, I decide. Its reappearance after another visit to the house would point the finger at me even more.

Jenna appears to be thinking about my comment, but I'm unable to determine whether she agrees with it.

"It'll turn up," I try again.

Her nod is speculative.

I shift my attention toward the floor, but there I only find more discomfort, because Jake's food is only half eaten. By the time I get home, his bowl is typically licked clean. But not tonight.

"Honey," I say, "have you noticed Jake acting different lately?"

"Different, like how?"

"He seems a little lethargic and withdrawn."

Jenna shakes her head and shrugs. "He seems fine to me."

"And there's still food in his bowl."

She looks down and examines the uneaten food.

"Strange," I say, "right?"

Jenna slowly raises her gaze to meet mine. She doesn't answer, but we've always been able to read each other, and the misgiving that streams across her face speaks volumes.

The bowl is empty.

53

"The dog knows."

I wake up with a start.

That voice again, but this time, I could swear it didn't come from inside my head. This time, it sounded as if someone were speaking from right beside me.

Beside me?

I survey my surroundings. I'm in the family room. I look at my watch. Dinner was close to an hour ago.

"Jake knows."

I nearly fall out of my chair because now the voice comes from a far end of the room. I spring to my feet and inspect every inch of that corner.

"Not there," the voice taunts as it zooms swiftly overhead and toward the other corner.

"Where the hell are you?" I pull furniture out of position, search under tables, and lift the rug, trying to find it. "Stop hiding!"

From the floorboards beneath my feet now: "I'm not hiding. You are."

I leap from my spot as if it's just caught fire. "Quit chasing me! Leave me alone, goddamnit!"

The voice laughs from the entryway.

I pivot in that direction. Jenna stands there, and from the distress washing across her face, I know she's been there long enough to watch me frantically race around the room, shouting at no one. Her mouth hangs slightly open. Her arms are glued to her sides.

As for me, my feet feel anchored to the floor like lead. I can't speak. I'm embarrassed and humiliated. I'm shaken, because in one fell swoop, all the comfort Jenna was able to restore after the MRI yesterday, all the hope she helped me rebuild, feels lost. Not just for me, but from what I'm seeing, for her as well.

"Mommy!" Devon calls out from his bedroom. "Where are all my baseball hats?"

"Probably wherever you left them, sweetheart," Jenna yells back, but her eyes never waver from me.

"They were all on my dresser," he says, "I just saw them there this morning!"

Jenna shifts her fretful attention to the staircase. "Ten baseball hats?"

"Yeah, and they're all gone!"

"I'll help you in a minute," she says, then turns back to me.

Reprieve over.

"I should be getting my results from the MRI tomorrow," I offer quickly and nervously. "We just have to ride this out a bit longer, and then we'll have answers."

Before Jenna can respond, movement over her shoulder distracts me. Jake crosses the entryway.

Carrying one of Devon's baseball hats in his mouth.

I look back at Jenna and see my fright reflected on her face. She doesn't understand what I'm thinking, but it doesn't matter—I know she feels it. My wife takes a step away from me, and I see a shadow drift along the planes of her face. Something that looks like uncertainty. Like doubtfulness. No, it's more than that. It's—

"Chris," she says, voice shaky and holding unsettled eyes on me. "I don't know what just happened, but it's making me very nervous."

She's not alone on that.

54

NOW YOU SEE IT, NOW YOU DON'T

My father began seeing and hearing things that weren't there—sometimes people, sometimes small animals, and sometimes beings that defied the laws of biological reason.

He also began screaming at them.

After that day in the car, I already knew the score, knew exactly where we were headed. To a place with no promise of a new day and no escape, just new ways to experience old and troubling emotions. A life of being tossed between extremes, none of them good.

My father was very sick, and that was a secret Mom could no longer hide from others, even as she continued the fight to hide it from herself. One day, Dad wandered out of the house in his pajamas and strolled to the next-door neighbor's. After welcoming himself inside, he plopped down on their sofa and launched into a loud and frightening diatribe about six-legged, subhuman creatures, cohabiting and reproducing inside sock drawers. Frightened and unnerved, they called my mother, who rushed over to explain that he'd become disoriented after getting a flu shot: they didn't buy it, and news of my father's lunacy quickly traveled through the neighborhood. Everyone watched us now with guarded suspicion.

We were all struggling against the same truth, each in our own way: my mother fighting mightily to ignore it, me feeling threatened by it, and my father hopelessly lost in it. The more difficult my dad became, the more my mom would bounce between two rocky states, either digging into her toolbox for another mental contrivance or isolating herself within the dark clouds of depression. When things became most intolerable, she would exercise the option of committing my father for "evaluation." Then off he'd go, shipped away for the county to deal with.

"They're going to make him better!" she insisted every time, her smile so tragic, tears so desperate. "You'll see. They'll fix him—they will—and then we can finally have him back!"

But it was like sticking a Band-Aid on a bullet wound. We always did get him back, but he was never anywhere near fixed, and in some ways the hospital visits only made him worse. He'd arrive home medicated, stupefied, and for a short time more manageable, but eventually his disturbing behavior would resurface and escalate further. Even while he was gone, I didn't find much relief, just a permeating sense of oncoming doom that germinated within me like a fast-growing seed. So many nights I cried myself to sleep, feeling lost in my helplessness. Lost on this mental merry-go-round with him, cycling through tragic hopelessness and going nowhere fast.

Our family threads were quickly unraveling, a river of denial swirling and pulling them looser as my father continued to come undone.

And in the process, he was taking us all down the same path.

55

As my car drifts toward work, restless worry hangs ahead of me like a bad vapor.

I told Jenna the MRI results would bring answers and give us hope, but if I'm going to be honest, my statement was more an act of desperation than assurance. An MRI can't detect schizophrenia, so I'm praying it will reveal a brain injury, because at least that might be treatable. Against schizophrenia, I don't stand a snowball's chance in hell.

It's sad—if not completely ironic—to hope that a damaged brain could save me from going crazy, but fighting for sanity feels a lot like struggling to maintain balance on the tip of a double-edged blade. Each day I slip a little closer to the end, trying to keep my mind from destroying my family before it destroys me. I don't know how much longer I can hold on. Judging from Jenna's reaction last night, it would seem she's beginning to wonder as well. I could almost see cracks spreading through the courage she's worked so hard to maintain.

My breaking mind is also breaking my wife.

I try to ignore the thought, but it won't let me. Then, as I pull into Loveland's entrance, ten feet of tarmac brings a distraction I didn't at all want.

My foot briefly slips off the brake pedal.

Oh, hell no.

Yesterday, the lot was two-thirds full, but today there are more empty spaces.

More trouble.

Keep your nose out of it.

"Get out of my damned head!" I shout, hands clapped over ears as I barrel through Loveland and toward the consulting room. "I have to tell someone!"

Tell no one. Too many people are working against you.

"Nonsense! If others are disappearing, everyone can't be in on it."

The ones who are disappearing don't know anything, and the rest are part of it.

"I'm going to Jeremy with this."

Jeremy's the last one you want to tell. What proof do you have? He'll know you're going crazy. He'll put you away.

Rounding a corner, I squeeze my eyes shut, grab hold of my hair. "But something has to be done!"

"About what?"

I look up. Evan McKinley stands outside the consulting room. He leans to one side, looks past my shoulder, then comes back to me.

"Nothing," I say, struggling to put a lid on the voice. "Just thinking out loud." I force a smile.

Evan forces one back.

He steps away from the door, and I work to tame my twitchy nerves into submission. I tell myself I've got to stay focused, that the evaluation is due in just a few hours. I've got to find out what color dress Donny Ray's father made him wear, then confirm that it's the trauma trigger for his disassociation. But upon entering the room, Donny Ray doesn't seem onboard with my plan.

Not even close.

He stares ahead, unfocused, his body completely still. I follow his gaze, and where it ends chills me. Again, he's honed in on the picture of that girl in the blue dress, and, just as before, seems transfixed by it. No reaction to my presence—in fact, no reaction to anything at all. I pad forward, keeping my attention on him, then take my seat. His eyes are glazed over, arms hanging loosely on both sides, fingers limp and spread apart.

"Donny Ray?" I say, trying to capture his attention.

Nothing.

I look at the picture, then back at him. He's in some faraway place, and wherever that is, I need to bring him out of it.

"Donny Ray," I say again, this time with volume and urgency.

And again, he shows no response.

I lean in closer so we're face-to-face, snap my fingers, speak louder. "Donny Ray. Can you hear me?"

He blinks a few times, looks startled, as if just now realizing that I'm here, or that he is, or . . .

I pull back a few inches and continue watching. His eyes seem a little clearer but still clouded over by confusion, so I give him a minute to acclimate before saying, "Donny Ray, do you know where you are right now?"

He circles his gaze through the room, then brings it back to me. He nods but still seems marginally unsure.

"Can you remember the last thing you saw before this?"

His face is a blank slate.

"I need you to stay with me here," I tell him. "Can you do that?"

Another nod, this one sluggish.

He's still noticeably detached from his surroundings, and I need to ground him. Searching around, I say, "Donny Ray, can you find three things in this room that are red?"

He searches, too, and as he tells me, I see his awareness sharpen.

Excitement ripples through me. Conviction. Donny Ray has just been in a state of disassociation, triggered by the blue dress in the picture—a confirmation that my theory is dead-on. With time at a premium, this evidence couldn't have come at a more perfect moment.

I grab a bottled water off the computer table and hand it to him. "I need to ask you about what just happened, and I need you to remain alert. Are you able to do that?"

He takes a greedy swig from the bottle, gasps for air, then gives me the okay to continue.

"What you mentioned when we first met, how you forget things. How they don't fit together. Is that what you're experiencing now?"

Donny Ray clears his throat and says, "Yeah . . . uh-huh."

He's lying. Don't believe him.

What? No. This is one of the missing pieces of evidence I've been looking for. I don't have time for you. Zip it, and let me do my job!

Going back to the question he was unable to answer earlier, I ask, "What's the last thing you remember before seeing me here?"

He looks at the door and scratches his head. "Evan sitting me down."

I point to the wall. "Do you remember seeing that picture at any point?"

He blearily narrows his vision on the girl in the blue dress, then nods.

"Was this before or after Evan sat you down?"

"After."

"Okay. Going back now, can you give me an idea when experiences like this started happening?"

"Young."

"*How* young?"

"I'm not sure."

"Any idea at all? Maybe an approximate age, even?"

He takes hold of his shirt with one hand, and, with the other, starts twisting it. Then he shakes his head.

"Was it before or after Miranda's disappearance?"

"After."

Close enough. The disassociation probably began around the same time as his abuse, but since he blocked a lot of that out, it wouldn't be unusual for him to be hazy about the circumstances that followed. I feel confident enough to move on.

But as I prepare, the noise I've heard before rattles above, much louder now. A thundering roll, followed by fast and frantic pounding that nearly knocks me from my seat. Next comes the shadow, so large that it nearly covers the entire room with darkness. I look up, and my body instantly pitches back, then jerks into paralysis.

The teenager in the red hoodie speed-crawls across the ceiling, chasing after his rubber ball.

I look back at Donny Ray. He watches me, brows crinkled, head crooked.

I cannot afford to let reality slip from my grasp or lose my patient's confidence. I've got to hold it together at least until I'm finished here.

I shove my thoughts through the flurry of confusion, find my way back to our conversation. "Do you have any recollection of losing time when Jamey Winslow was murdered?"

"Yes."

"What exactly do you remember?"

"Waking up in bed. With blood on my clothes."

"How do you know it was the same day?"

"Because I panicked and ended up being late to work, and I saw it on the news later."

"Okay." I push back my sleeves, lean in toward him. "I'm going to ask a lot of you today. We'll need to discuss your abuse again."

Donny Ray swallows hard. His Adam's apple rises, then falls.

"The dress your father made you wear. Was there more than one?"

He closes his eyes and slowly shakes his head.

"Can you describe it for me?"

When he opens his eyes, he's fighting back tears. His lips part, and I see the slightest quiver. "I . . . I don't want . . . I can't . . ."

"I have to know, Donny Ray."

He looks to one side and toward the ceiling, the lights above reflecting off tears that fill his lower lids. "It's too . . ."

"What? Tell me."

"It's so . . ." He stops again. "Humiliating!" he says through a strangled voice, still refusing to look at me.

"I know . . . I understand, but I wouldn't ask unless it mattered. I need this information for your evaluation. I need you to help me."

Donny Ray collapses forward, reaches around his legs, and pulls them tightly together. With cheek resting on knee, veins grossly protruding from his neck, he rocks his body. Like he's back there again, enduring his father's relentless cruelty. Like this is all too painful.

I fall back in my chair and wait, knowing how difficult this has to be for him. To suffer that kind of shame after such horrid abuse. To be hurled back into that dark place and describe such a lurid and repulsive detail.

Donny Ray tries to pull himself together—or I think that's what he's doing. His posture rises and stiffens, but he still can't look at me.

"Lace," he at last tells me through sputtering lips. "It was lace."

"I need to know what color it was."

"I . . . I don't . . . I can't."

"Please try. This is extremely important."

He leans forward again, rocks harder. The side of his face that I can see is stained by tears that fall quickly and seem endless.

"White."

The floor falls out beneath me. In a few heartbeats, my theory has caved in onto itself. Adam was right. I'm sunk.

My voice is unsteady when I ask, "Was . . . was the dress all white?"

Donny Ray finally looks at me. He pushes the bangs off his face, swipes away a tear. "No, the dress wasn't white."

I'm confused. I ask him to explain.

But he has trouble forming words, like they're lodged in his throat. He clamps his hands to each side of the chair. Muscles strain against skin. A bead of perspiration rolls down the front of his neck, then disappears beneath his shirt collar. Now he looks angry—no, it's more than that. I'm witnessing rage, a brand so raw and caustic that it almost feels like my own.

And in a fast second, Donny Ray's eyes open so wide that I can see the whites. His fiery blue irises rest at their center, aimed directly into mine, their heat so intense that I can barely stand to look at them.

A guttural sound rumbles from deep inside his throat, and Donny Ray growls, "You. Fucking. Monster!"

I try to remain calm—or at least look that way—because I know he's not just remembering what happened. He's at last experiencing the rage he was never allowed.

"What was white?" I ask, gentle but firm. "Tell me what was white."

Just as fast as it appeared, his fury morphs into a new emotion. His angry eyes go dull and unfocused beneath half-opened lids. His shoulders droop, posture crumbles.

Then, in the tiny voice of a child, weak, pleading, and barely audible, Donny Ray mutters, "The bow . . . The bow was white."

And there is nothing but aching silence in this room.

Donny Ray looks down. Tears fall into empty palms as he says, "A giant bow . . . the purest white. It was the only time I ever saw my father's hands clean. He'd stand over that bathroom sink—he'd stand there and scrub them—for twenty minutes before fixing the bow on the front of that dress, and . . . and I always knew what was coming next . . . then he'd spray it with starch, wouldn't even let me use the seat belt on our drive to town."

Donny Ray stares vacantly while the impact of his narrative lands. "Every day, I pray to God that hell never gives the man a second of peace. Not a goddamned second."

I can't argue with his sentiment. I inhale and exhale. My heart is breaking, but time is flying. I have to move this forward. The picture on the wall feels as though it's screaming at me. I lift my head to look at the girl in the blue dress and nearly choke on bile. The girl in the picture is no longer peaceful. Now a thin line of scarlet blood trickles down her leg, collecting into a growing pool by her feet.

Tick tock, tick tock.

Overwhelmed by a fusion of nausea and terror, I have no choice but to close my eyes and open them, hoping my insanity will hold off until I can get what I need from Donny Ray. Slowly, the blood near the girl's feet and on her leg evaporates. The picture is restored to order, and for the moment at least, I am able to tackle reality.

So now I must ask. "The dress, Donny Ray. What color was the dress?"

"My favorite color. He did it on purpose."

"Donny Ray, what *color* was the dress?"

He spits out the word as if it tastes rotten.

"Blue."

56

I sit in my office and stare at the computer screen.

Evaluation complete. Diagnosis: dissociative amnesia, brought on by acute and repetitive psychological trauma.

Though I know every missing girl is connected to Donny Ray's horrors of the past, as instructed, I've kept them out of this, only focusing on Jamey Winslow. The rest I've moved into a separate file, should I require it at a later time.

The only thing left to do now is hit the "Send" button.

After all the years I've been doing this, after the multitude of evaluations I've completed, I always have the same reaction right at this moment. I second-guess myself. I waver. Never once, not even for a moment, have I taken the weight of my responsibility lightly, and this is no exception.

I know I'm right—that's not the problem—still, I fully recognize the impact of this one action. Donny Ray will go back to court, and even though his fate will be left for judge and jury to decide, my diagnosis will significantly impact that process.

I look up at the clock. Deadline fast approaching. Time almost up.

I think about Adam's doubt, but with the blue dress connection now complete, so too is the link to Donny Ray's pathology. Adam was right in one respect. I don't have to play cop. Whether Donny Ray was forced to cover up his sister's murder is in fact irrelevant where my diagnosis is concerned.

And with that comes another confirmation. Adam shouldn't have doubted my professional judgment, should have known me well enough to trust my abilities. He insulted me, and I feel confident now that his motivation was indeed fueled by professional jealousy.

Adam wants you to fail.

He threw a thin shroud of concern over his question about my MRI results, but the shadow it cast on our entire friendship has left that connection severed.

A swell of anger and sadness surges through me, then with more force than necessary, I punch the "Send" button.

57

Evaluation sent. Job done.

On the way to Alpha Twelve, I have time to process what pressure and a looming deadline wouldn't allow before now.

Adam didn't believe me, but I believe Donny Ray.

As a professional, I got what I needed, but as a human, I can't help but feel as though in the process, I only inflicted more pain on a wound that never healed. I took something from Donny Ray Smith. Another piece of his already-fractured psyche.

I want to give it back.

Or at least try. I'm fully aware that telling him my decision won't cure his ache—that kind never really heals—but maybe, even in some small way, my news will help.

Hold on. What the . . . ?

I peer down the hallway of Alpha Twelve. Except for the rooms that Nicholas and Stanley once occupied, every door is closed and secured. What in God's name was Adam talking about when he told me patients are never confined to their rooms? Come to think of it, weren't all the doors locked tight when I came down to the consultation room earlier?

Adam is jacking with your head.

I march forward with an angry huff, intent on giving Donny Ray the good news.

You're not supposed to share that information with patients.

"You think I don't know that? It won't hurt anything."

I reach Donny Ray's room. Evan stands outside with an expression I can't quite gauge.

"Still thinking out loud, Doctor?" he asks.

A glance over my shoulder tells me that, while I wasn't within his line of sight, my voice probably carried farther than I would have liked.

"I'm just under a lot of stress right now, Evan," I mutter, then motion for him to unlock the door.

He does, and I distractedly march past him.

Inside, Donny Ray sits up in bed and stares out the window, hands woven tightly in his lap, one thumb moving back and forth over the other as if soothing an old and persistent injury.

I step forward. He turns his head toward me and tries to smile, but the corners of his mouth betray him, pulling it downward. I grab the chair in front of his desk and spin it in his direction, then take a seat. Donny Ray waits for me to speak.

"I want you to know that I fully realize how much it took to tell me what you did, and I appreciate your efforts, and . . ." I stop myself, because this all sounds so obvious and in the scheme of things, so meaningless. "I'll just get right to the point. I've completed your evaluation, and it's with the court now."

Donny Ray nods, tension and uncertainty rapidly amassing into worry.

"It's my opinion that you suffered from dissociative amnesia after Jamey Winslow went missing."

His mouth drops wider as comprehension gathers. "I didn't think you would . . . I never thought anyone would . . ."

"Believe you?"

He closes his eyes and nods.

"It'll still be up to the courts to decide if you're not guilty by reason of insanity."

"But it's not about that. It was never about that."

I look at him curiously.

"It's about the truth. It's about knowing that somewhere in your mind the truth is hiding out, and you can't find it, because there are all these reflections, and they're blinding you. We helped each other find the truth."

Maybe we can both find it.

Donny Ray's statement on the day we met—one that no longer causes confusion.

The door opens. Evan pokes his head inside and says, "Dentist's appointment in ten minutes. I'll be back to get you in five."

Donny Ray acknowledges Evan, then gets out of bed and walks behind the wall that separates his living area and washroom. Seconds later, I hear the sink running and check my watch: it's getting late. Now that the anxiety from this evaluation is out of the way, I'm hoping my mind will stop slipping so quickly. I scoot the chair back into place, shove closed a bottom drawer, then move toward the door.

But a few steps out, I stop to look back over my shoulder, then return to the drawer and pull it open. I reach for the book tucked off to one side and feel it tremble in my hands as I read the title.

Shakespeare's *Hamlet.*

I swallow hard, open it to the bookmark, and four words scream back at me. Four very ominous and telling words.

That sleep of death.

The room curls in around me and my vision gets murky and my chest pulls so tight that I can barely draw air. I spin around to find Donny Ray standing there. In one swift move, I drop the book out of view.

"Christopher, what's wrong?" His posture stoops and he angles his head.

I try to keep my hand from shaking, my mind from screaming, and every muscle in my body from jumping. "You just startled me, is all. I didn't hear you coming."

Donny Ray's dimples fill with light as a smile starts to build. "Good Lord. I was really worried, because for a fraction of a second, I thought maybe it was about that book you've got lodged into the back of your rib cage."

I freeze.

He says nothing more. He doesn't have to, because from those eyes comes an intense blaze of fiery evil, the magnitude of which sends every inch of my skin crawling with heat. I lower the book to one side, back away from him, and he flashes the smile of a killer.

"It was you. All along it's been you. *You* fed them that sentence."

"I've really got a bunch of wacky-assed, fucked-up neighbors around here," Donny Ray says through a bouncy laugh that makes my toes curl. "And how about those crazy doors on Alpha Twelve? The way your mind keeps locking and unlocking them?"

I have to get away from this monster, as fast and far as humanly possible.

Halfway to the door, I hear, "Christopher?"

I'm unable to stop myself from turning back.

He holds up my cell phone with one hand. "You've lost something. Again."

I look down and pat my shirt. The phone isn't in my pocket. How did it get into his hands?

"Who's this?" Donny Ray asks, studying the image on my home screen with interest I don't at all like.

I say nothing.

"Your son, right? He's a very beautiful boy," the child killer tells me. "That dark hair, those deep, brown eyes . . ."

But it doesn't feel like a compliment.

"You must love him more than anything."

It feels like a threat.

"Do not cross that line with me, Donny Ray," I growl. "Don't do it."

"When the situation warrants, Christopher."

"The *situation* is moot. Fortified walls and the army of security personnel inside this hospital say your threat is useless."

"Twenty-three twenty Hillsborough Lane," he says with a smirk rotten as spoiled vinegar. "Green house, white shutters."

His description leaves me short-winded. "How do you know that?"

At the door, Evan fidgets with his keys in the lock. I glare at Donny Ray. "You'll never get out of here. Never."

"Gerald might disagree."

"What's he got to do with this?"

"If I can get to them, I can get to you."

Evan enters, but the silence that covers this room like a wet stinking blanket stops him. He looks at me, looks at the patient, and seems even more confused.

Just as Donny Ray passes by, he winks at me, then reveals that boyish grin, now cloaked in a thousand shades of darkness.

58

A wicked chill bumps up my spine as I watch Donny Ray leave his room under Evan's guard.

"Evan," I call impulsively, and he walks back my way. Donny Ray waits patiently in the hall, leering at me.

I motion Evan in close. "Keep a good watch on him today."

Evan says, "I can assign a rotation to him."

"No, do it yourself." He looks surprised. I make my voice confidential. "I trust you, Evan, and this patient is very dangerous right now. He needs close watching."

"All right, Doctor," he says and walks back to where Donny Ray stands. I watch them disappear.

I'm alone.

Now I can let myself tremble.

My initial suspicions were right. Donny Ray engineered all the odd happenings in Alpha Twelve that day.

Donny Ray is a psychopath.

He was trying to throw me off-balance. But why? Why did he force confusion on me, when I was the one person who could help his case?

Because he doesn't need your help.

"What the hell are you talking about? Of course he does."

Throwing you off your game is the only way to make you see the truth.

"What truth?"

The voice doesn't answer, but Donny Ray's comment from just moments ago gives me an uncomfortable nudge.

It's not about that. It was never about that. It's about the truth.

The only truth I know right now is that Donny Ray Smith stinks of danger. Not only is he a psychopath—he's an extremely clever one. After Philips got into trouble at the Miller Institute, I became his next sitting duck, and he's been playing me like a god-damned fiddle ever since.

The picture on the wall. The girl in a blue dress. His moments of detachment. That tragic story of abuse. All were building blocks for his carefully orchestrated plan. And he was nearly successful, until he slipped by leaving his drawer open.

Or did he?

I'm quickly learning that Donny Ray Smith doesn't make mistakes. Which leads me to the question of whether he wanted me to see that book. Was it just another installment in his plan to drive me over the edge?

I reevaluate everything that occurred during our sessions. The story about his mother, which echoed my own. I now see how he used it to manipulate, to garner sympathy, so I'd fall onboard with him even faster.

But how did he know so much about me?

I reconstruct my memory of our meetings. The missing pen. My out-of-whack actions and movements. The breaks in our conversations.

The lost time.

I was too blinded by my confusion in the beginning to see it, then later by my empathy, but with both now gone, everything is falling into place. I understand how Donny Ray got so much information about me. It's because I've been unknowingly spoon-feeding it to him. He's been using my memory lapses to extract the information. But with that realization comes another one far more disturbing.

My address.

Oh, God. How could I have allowed this to happen? In those conversations I don't remember, what else did I unknowingly tell the monster with a hunger that can make ten kids disappear? What did I hand over that could allow him to put my own son's life in danger?

You must love him more than anything.

The way he looked at Devon's picture.

He's a very beautiful boy.

The moment my phone got into his hands, Donny Ray knew he was holding a psychopath's pot of gold: information he could use. A perfect tool to intimidate and keep his secret safe.

His secret.

I've just greased the wheels on a psychopath's insanity plea. If the jury believes Donny Ray disassociated while killing Jamey Winslow, he'll go to another psychiatric facility, far less secure than a prison. I can't even bank on the other cases to put him away because there may never be enough evidence to charge him.

I have to do something. I've got to make sure this dangerous felon is sent off to prison for the rest of his life—or better yet, is executed—and never has a chance to come anywhere close to my son.

But how?

I'll let Jeremy know, then the court. That's it. I'll tell them I've got new evidence that changes my decision.

And what evidence would that be?

I rake a hand through my hair, feel the sweat pooling on my forehead and scalp. "I don't know!"

You've got nothing. Donny Ray's been leading you around by the nose. Face it. You've been hoodwinked.

"There has to be something. I'll find it!"

Too late. Done deal. The deadline has passed. Retract your report and everyone will know you got blindsided by a psychopath.

"But I've got to stop him!"

How? By letting the court send him to work over another psychologist? You were his test monkey. He'll have an even easier time convincing someone else.

"Holy . . . You're right. I'm stuck. I've got no time to find more evidence, and without any, I'll look like an even bigger idiot in trying to explain what happened."

You've got a much more pressing issue to deal with.

"What's that?"

Keeping him inside Loveland.

"He was bluffing. He can't get out of here."

I bet Gerald would disagree.

I take off running toward Gerald's room.

And there I stand before yet another wide-open door; beyond it, a room stripped of Gerald—The Husker who degloves people—and all his belongings. With utter astonishment I look toward the counter where Mystery Nurse sits. Asking her what happened to the patient feels useless at this point. Her mind seems about as lost as he is now.

I swing back to Gerald's door, and it's like staring at a horrifying question mark.

If I can get to them, I can get to you, Christopher.

I think about Stanley and Nicholas and second-guess myself. Both spoke that *sleep of death* phrase to me, then both vanished. If Donny Ray was responsible, can he do the same thing for himself?

I shut myself inside my office and hunt for answers.

I begin with the first disappearing act: Nicholas' mysterious transfer to some obscure hospital I've never heard of in Billings, Montana. After looking up Smithwell Institute's number, I dial it and tell the receptionist what I need. She hands the call over to a nursing administrator named Trina Mullen.

"What's the patient's name again?" Mullen asks, computer keys clacking in the background.

I repeat it.

The clacking stops. "That's what I thought. Nope, not showing a patient here by that name at all."

"We sent him four days ago. He would have reached you by now."

"If he were coming this way, we'd have documentation, and I'm not showing a thing."

"But *our* documentation shows otherwise."

"Maybe there's a mistake."

"Somebody's made one, but it's not us!" I slam the phone down, nerves raging beneath my skin like red-hot needles.

Nothing works here! This place is broken!

I'm starting to wonder if Stanley was right.

I move on to his disappearance and dial St. Mary's, but after speaking to the nursing supervisor, all I get is a repeat performance. She's got no idea what I'm talking about, no record of Stanley ever being brought there.

I hang up, stare into thin air, and wonder what the hell is going on. One record mishap, I could possibly understand, but two in a row? For two patients who subsequently dropped out of sight from the same floor and just a day apart? That's no coincidence—that's highly suspect.

My fingers break into a frenzied spider dance across the keyboard as I search for Nicholas' hospital records, hoping perhaps there might be some kernel of information I can pull from them.

They're not here. Gone.

And when I look for Stanley's and Gerald's, it's the same damned thing.

Someone deleted their files.

There's no way Donny Ray could have done that.

Unless someone on the inside is helping him.

I think about Melinda. She's likely become one of the casualties as well, so I check the employee roster, and there I find solid confirmation: her information is also gone. Even the work schedules, both past and present, show no sign of the woman ever putting in time here.

She's been erased.

Was her disappearance a strategic one? While searching for the information I'd requested, could she have stumbled across something that put her own life in grave danger? I have no proof, but there's one thing I can absolutely be certain of: it's not just the people who are being erased from Loveland—it's also every trace of evidence to prove they existed at all.

Perspiration gathers at my neckline. I don't yet know who's pulling the strings around here, but something very nefarious is happening inside Loveland, far worse than even I'd imagined.

You've got to do something.

I've got to do something.

You've got to take matters into your own hands.

59

Do NOT tell Adam.

"Look, I get that he was an ass for doubting my professional integrity, but there's nobody else around here I can trust."

You cannot trust him.

"I have to talk to someone about this! I have to stop what's happening here!"

Adam is standing at his bookcase when I come storming in. He startles and spins around. Several books fly off the shelf and tumble to the floor.

"What the hell?" He motions toward the pile of books. "Ever heard of knocking before entering?"

"There's no time for that," I say and make a beeline for the chair. "We've got trouble. Big trouble."

Adam's vision never leaves me as he walks to his desk, and even after taking his seat, he's the image of watchfulness knuckled by doubt.

I rub a sweaty palm against my pant leg, then scoot the chair a little closer toward his desk. "First of all, you need to know that I played things down at the outset, because I didn't want it to seem like

I was overreacting, but since then, I've come across new information that's far more definitive." I recheck the door behind him, then lower my voice. "Adam, something very strange is going on around here, something bad, and I just don't know who else to tell, and I'm really worried, and something has to be done before it gets—"

Adam stops me with a raised hand, and I see consternation play across his face when he says, "Chris . . . what's happening to you?"

"I'm trying to explain that!"

"No, I mean, I've never seen you like this."

"Like what?"

"Look at yourself. Your shirt is soaked in sweat, you're all wild-eyed and running at ninety miles an hour. You're a mess. Can you at least slow it down?"

"Adam, there's no time to slow it down! More people are disappearing!"

He angles his head away from me.

I tell him that, in addition to Nicholas and Stanley, Melinda and Gerald have also gone missing, how all their records have disappeared. How Smithwell and St. Mary's have never heard of our patients. Then I detail my observations of the parking lot and cafeteria, visible indications that the hospital population is substantially thinning.

Adam doesn't respond. His eyes dart back and forth between mine.

"You don't believe me."

"I'm not saying that."

"But you look like it, Adam. You really do."

"It's just . . . all I'm saying is, let's bring this down a few pegs, okay? There's got to be a logical explanation."

"That's what I've been looking for! It's not there! *That's* the problem!"

"First of all, I'm still not clear who these missing people are that you're talking about."

"They're the ones from Alpha Twelve! I've already told you about them!"

Circumspection reels across Adam's face as he swings the computer monitor toward him. He starts typing.

I wait and watch.

Seconds later he looks up, and at last I'm relieved to find he's just as surprised.

"See, Adam? See what I mean?"

"Actually, I don't."

"Wait . . . *what*?"

Slowly, he swivels the monitor around, aims it toward me.

I look.

"Chris," he says, "the people you're talking about don't exist. There's nothing here to indicate they ever did."

"That's what I've been trying to tell you! Their records have been deleted! Just like *they* were! Somebody at Loveland is trying to erase them. They're being transported to some—I don't know— some secret location, or maybe it's even worse than that, but you saw those people, Adam. You saw them just like I did."

He nervously tugs at one sleeve.

"Oh, come on, man. You did. You saw those people. You were right there with me. Gerald? The scary dude who skins people?"

His eyes narrow.

"And Nicholas? The guy who was playing with himself in his room?"

His eyes go broad.

"This is—" I shoot straight up in my chair and it flips over onto the floor. Adam slides his away from me. "—This is crazy! I can't believe you're even telling me this!"

"Chris," he says. "You're freaking me out. Please sit. And calm down."

I reach to right the chair. I sit. "And you were right about Donny Ray Smith. He is malingering. He's a psychopath. He was working me the whole time. I messed up by sending in my evaluation. I said he disassociated during Jamey's murder, but I was wrong."

"You did *what*?" Adam's jaw drops.

"But I think he might know where the missing people are going, and I'm trying to figure out how. The point is, he's dangerous to everyone. But we're not going to let him hurt us."

I expect satisfaction and approval, but Adam's next reaction startles me. It's more than hesitation, more than doubt. Pitiful sadness spiked with deep mistrust, palpable and unnerving, like overhearing a trusted friend speak badly about you behind your back.

I tried to warn you . . . He's part of it.

"Chris," he says, "I'm very concerned about you. Has Rob called back with the results from your MRI yet?"

"Really, Adam? *Really?* You're actually going to use that against me now?"

"I'm not using anything against you. I'm just trying to say—"

"What, Adam? What is it? That you think I'm losing my mind?" *You are losing your mind.*

I slam my hand down on the desk, startling him. "You're supposed to be my friend! You're supposed to support me!"

Adam doesn't say anything—he's stunned into silence.

My cell phone rings.

"I have to take this," I say, disgust in my voice that doesn't come close to scratching the surface of what I'm feeling right now.

Adam watches me coldly as I leave.

60

My cell rings again.

I look at the screen and my shoulders pull tight, then adrenaline kicklines through my body. So much happening right now. So much flying at me with merciless speed. I swallow hard against my angst and try to prepare for what I know is coming.

"Christopher, it's Rob. I just got the radiologist's report from your MRI."

"Hey," I say, unsteadiness rocking through my voice.

"Good news. No damage showing at all."

My heart sinks. "That's really great, Rob. Thanks so much again for expediting things. I appreciate it."

"Not a problem at all. Happy to deliver good news. A lot of times, well . . . you know."

"I do," I say and abruptly hang up on him.

He's Adam's friend. You can't trust him. He's lying.

"No . . . I'm afraid he's not."

If only Rob knew that good MRI results mean my diagnosis is so much worse. That my ultimate fear is coming true, screaming at me.

That I've been turning into my father all along.

I've been praying that a brain injury would at least afford me a chance to mend my damaged mind. But there is no injury. There is just the excruciating truth. Now there can be no more hiding, no pretending. The voice in my head, the hallucinations, are symptoms of schizophrenia.

I slog down the hallway, for no other reason than to try and clear my head. Most of my life, I've told myself that if I could just make it past thirty, I'd have beaten the schizophrenia odds. Onset becomes increasingly unlikely after that age. Each birthday felt like a bigger celebration, but only after reaching thirty-five did I finally manage to find a measure of relief.

I should have been safe—I should have made it.

It's the tree's fault.

I stop walking. I clench my jaw and slam my fist against the wall.

"The tree!" I shout to nobody. "The goddamned tree!"

One turn of fate. That's all it took to reverse the tide, to push me into these relentless waters. One moment to destroy my life.

So, what now?

"I need confirmation and a diagnosis. That's what. I need a treatment plan. Maybe it's not as severe as—"

Are you crazy?

"Well, yeah, obviously."

You keep trying to help them destroy you. Tell a doctor now, and you'll get slapped with a one-way ticket to Loonyville.

I start walking again, now at a fast clip. Getting an official diagnosis would be the worst thing I could do. The consequences would be immediate and disastrous. I'd lose my license. I'd lose my work. And I'd lose any chance of figuring out what's happening in Alpha Twelve or if Donny Ray actually poses a threat to Devon. No, I can't seek diagnosis or treatment now, not until I devise a plan.

What's the plan, then?

I could get my hands on some Clorazil and self-medicate in the meantime. It's one of the most effective drugs available right now. But how? I'm not an MD, can't prescribe meds, and I can't exactly ask one of the doctors at Loveland to do it. Besides being unethical, it will only draw attention to my problem. And with all drugs being so closely monitored at this hospital, sneaking them would be next to impossible. Every capsule and tablet within our walls is accounted for, every single one scanned after leaving the Omnicell dispenser. Even when staff members drop a pill and have to replace it, they're required to provide a written explanation.

So I'm screwed. I have to go on without medication or support. And now there's yet another problem I can add to my list, this one far more urgent.

Time.

"Chris, wait!" I hear Adam say from behind me. "We're not done talking!"

I don't turn to look back at him. I walk faster.

"Chris, please!"

Don't do it. He's recording you. He's trying to steal information from your mind. He needs to get lost. Tell him that.

"Get lost!" I yell and keep my attention aimed forward, then break into a panicky dash.

"Chris! Don't do this!"

DO NOT answer. Lose him!

I take an abrupt turn down the next hallway, but Adam keeps after me.

"Let's talk this out!" he shouts from several feet back.

You don't need to hear it.

"I don't need to hear it!" I yell.

"Chris! We've been friends for too long. I'm just worried about you. You're completely misunderstanding things."

It was no misunderstanding.

"It was no misunderstanding!"

"Chris, please. Look at me!"

You don't have time for him.

"I don't have time for you!"

My parting comment as I burst through the exit doors.

I make fast tracks out of the parking lot, but hitting the road is like making a mental U-turn that only drives me deeper into worry.

I lost it with Adam.

I didn't mean to. I just got angry, and though I felt justified in it, couldn't control myself. But he saw those people who are now missing.

Or did he?

I don't know anymore. About anything.

Now I have to go home and tell Jenna. I have to deliver the news that will break my family. With that thought and so many others, I keep driving, vision set ahead, mind heavy with so much grief.

61

I walk through the door and into what was once my settled little world, fully aware that I'm about to throw it further out of kilter. Jenna takes one look at the tears I'm fighting back, and I can tell she already knows.

Her smile is so full of love . . . and so sad.

"Daddy! Daddy!" Devon speeds into the room, his face lit up with an abundance of exuberance at the sight of me.

And I can't take this—not any of it—because standing before me are the two people I've built my life around. Two people whose own lives, whether I like it or not, I'm about to destroy.

I kneel down, and my son throws his arms over my shoulders. I press his tiny body against mine, take in his little-boy smell—a combination of bubblegum, the outside soil, and a myriad of other things that come his way as he tackles each new day—and never before have those things meant so much, because I know these are the things that will very soon slip away from me.

As he slips away from me.

Jenna has been watching us, and I can tell she's feeling everything that I am.

For Devon's sake, I do my best not to show the penetrating ache that cuts through me. There are limits to how much pain can be hidden, and I'm pretty sure I've reached my threshold. All at once, tears I can no longer hold back fill my eyes. I pull him closer, but it doesn't seem close enough. It never will be.

We never will be.

I cling to him, to these feelings, knowing they will soon be few and numbered. After a few seconds, my little boy pulls back and looks at me with so much sadness.

"What's wrong, Daddy?" he asks.

"Nothing is wrong," I tell him. "Everything is just right."

And that's the problem, because I know that soon, everything won't be.

Jenna walks toward us. Keeping a protective watch on me, she says to Devon, "Sweetheart, why don't you go clean up for dinner? Then bring down that lovely drawing you did at school today for Daddy to see."

Devon takes off toward the staircase. After watching him disappear from sight, I turn toward Jenna. She places a firm hand on my shoulder and keeps it there.

"The MRI is clean," I say and feel her hand tighten. "It's happening. It's my dad all over again. It has to be schizophrenia."

Jenna falls into a silence that speaks what she cannot say. She knows where we're headed, to the one place both of us hoped we never would have to go. I'm unsure what to say. I feel so lost in my helplessness.

She guides me to the couch. We sit.

"Chris, we will be okay," she says. "We can handle this."

Her assurance breaks my heart. It kills me because as strong as I know my wife is, as hard as she tries to be that way for my sake, I can't bear putting her through this agony. Facts don't lie. History doesn't lie. Even though Jenna has heard all the horrific stories about my childhood, she didn't live through them, can't possibly imagine the kind of emotional torment that's about to come barreling down on us. It's something I can't begin to describe, with so many deep and complex layers that unless you've been trapped between them yourself, they're incomprehensible.

I bury my face in her shoulder.

"We'll get through this, baby. I promise we will," she tells me, "and I'll be right by your side when you go back to see Rob. He'll refer us to someone who can help you."

Rob.

I haven't thought about him since our call. If I'm diagnosed, I can kiss my job good-bye. I need to make arrangements before that happens. I have to figure out who's pulling bodies out of Loveland, but even more critical, I must ensure that Donny Ray can't follow through on his threat against Devon.

Jenna pulls from our embrace and offers a smile of warmth and encouragement, which sends me closer to the edge.

So I do what I did with Rob, with Adam, with myself for most of my life—the thing I swore I'd never do to my wife.

"I just can't do this right now . . . ," I say through my cracked voice and even more broken thoughts. "I'm sorry."

I hide from the truth by avoiding it, and with stunning precision, become both my father and mother rolled into one.

62

THE RIPTIDE OF TWO CRIPPLED MINDS

Having a parent die suddenly is a pain sharp and swift. Watching him submit to a slow death is even more excruciating. But when the mind goes before the body, it's like attending a funeral every day.

Sometimes I wished my father would just die and get it over with.

At the same time, a war raged within me between anger and guilt. I'd been cheated out of what should have been a continued and loving relationship with my father, and during the moments I found strength to be truthful with myself, I hated him for it. But that only made me feel worse, because I knew he hadn't asked for this, and that his situation was far more tragic than my own.

That I had become the victim of a victim.

The father I loved so much was becoming the complete antithesis of everything I most admired, but it wasn't just my dad who was falling apart. I could see my mother doing the same, unplugging from the world, drifting off into some distant place. Her everything-is-fine identity was evaporating like some thin, resinous smoke, and what lingered in its wake was the grimmest of pictures: a woman broken open by tragedy, only to find out there was nothing inside, that there never had been. Now, I was caught in the riptide of two crippled minds.

My mother could hide a pink elephant behind a thumbtack, but the saddest irony of all was that my father would be the one to finally end her magical thinking. For so many years, he'd allowed her the reality of her dreams—now he was tearing down that reality. My mother could no longer dismantle the truth because the truth was dismantling her.

I began catching glimpses of who she really was. Not the passionless woman I'd always thought her to be, but instead, and much like me, nothing more than a frightened child. And like a child, instead of facing the truth, Mom simply took the path of least resistance.

With each passing day, she fell deeper into paralyzing depression. The Southern Beauty I'd always known was fading away, her face weathered by grief and rapidly advancing far beyond its years. On most days, she sat at the kitchen table, staring sightlessly out the window and chain-smoking cigarettes. It was on those days that I felt the most pity for her, because I honestly believed she loved my dad to whatever degree she was capable. My father was her everything, her only source of strength, and without him, she became nothing. She began pulling further away, avoiding Dad whenever possible, and offering little of herself to him.

One day, I came home from school and found he'd been sequestered in the guest room.

"It's better for him this way," she said, as if he were a puppy quarantined for pissing on the rug.

But he wasn't a puppy, and it wasn't better for him—it was better for her.

Late one evening, I walked by his new living quarters and saw him mumbling incessantly to himself. My mother breezed past me carrying a laundry basket filled with clothes. She went inside, tossed some unfolded pajamas into my father's lap, then, just as quickly, she was gone.

Dad held the pajamas up and stared at them, confused, as though having no concept of their purpose.

My heart sank.

I walked inside, reached for the pajamas, and helped my dad get ready for bed. After I finished, he looked up at me, a lone tear falling down his cheek.

"Th . . . th-th-th-th . . . thank . . . ," my father said in a stuttering whisper. "Thank . . . you."

I placed a gentle hand on his shoulder, and through my utter anguish, I nodded and smiled.

Walking out into the hallway, I heard an odd noise and followed it to my mother's bedroom. The door was wide open, the light still on, so I moved closer.

She sat at the edge of her bed, holding my dad's shirt against her face, letting it grow damp in her hands.

Breathing in his scent.

Quiet sobs escaping from her lips.

63

After dinner, I retreat into the family room and stare at the television, but all I can see is disaster playing out before me, the walls closing in as my sanity fades away.

I see my father.

But from a completely new perspective. The heartbreak he must have felt. The pain that was impossible to comprehend through my young eyes. Now, in the cruelest of ways, fate is at last letting me empathize.

Jenna's approaching footsteps pull me from the thought. She takes a seat beside me but keeps her gaze forward, as if searching for the right thing to say. I hold silent as well, maybe because I can't find words myself, maybe because I know that none exist.

She places a hand on my leg, leaves it there, and we sit, neither of us speaking.

"I know you're worried about Devon," she says a minute or so later, obviously still processing her thoughts among our windstorm of chaos.

I want to tell her about Donny Ray's threat against Devon, about the disappearing people of Loveland, but I'm afraid it will come out all wrong and frighten her. I can't afford to burden her load. She hasn't even had time yet to absorb the news of my schizophrenia.

So I keep that part to myself.

"I can't lose my son," I say, simplifying matters that are far more complicated than she can possibly realize.

"You will not."

I try to reply, but the words get tangled in my throat.

"You won't lose Devon, because you love him so fiercely. You love him in ways your father never could."

"But that won't save him from schizophrenia. Nothing will."

"It can."

"How?"

"Because," she says, fighting to smile, "your past is exactly what *will* save him. Chris, you knew this could happen, and you've worked hard to build a strong foundation for Devon in the event that it did. The intensity of your love for him comes from that fear. Because of it, you've strived to enjoy every moment with him and to make sure he did the same. No matter what happens, those memories will never go away—they will always be. They're unshakable, and they will keep him safe. That's so much more powerful than anything your father was able to do, because he never saw his schizophrenia coming. He never had all the time that you've had to prepare for this."

I hadn't thought of it that way.

Jenna moves her hand into mine, its soft warmth something I very much crave during this moment, something I very much need.

"Go see Devon," she says. "Go see him right now. Don't be afraid. Don't deny him or yourself the one thing you know will see you both through this. And keep doing it, Chris. Keep doing the only thing you can right now. Keep loving him."

I look into her eyes and find in their certainty the truth I'm always searching for.

Truth that saves me each time.

64

Standing in Devon's doorway, I find him getting ready for bed. He pulls the PJ top over his head, then glances down and lets out a helpless sigh: it's inside out and facing backwards. I smile through my sadness because the look on his face is so precious.

"Daddy," he says, "I did it wrong."

"It's okay, kiddo. It happens."

"Can you help me?"

"Of course." I move toward him. He raises his arms, and I pull off the top.

"Ready?"

"Ready," he replies, arms still held high, and together we fix the PJ crisis.

Devon thanks me with a big hug, but after pulling back, he reads my expression, and his own starts to drop.

"What, Daddy?"

I shake my head, but I'm fighting back tears.

He gives me an inquisitive look, then scurries into bed. Jake is nowhere to be found, but by now I'm used to his need to appear nearly invisible. I sit beside my son, trying to gather my nervousness and thoughts.

"Daddy, what's wrong?" he tries again.

I look down at the blanket, run my hand over it. "There's something I need to talk to you about."

"Did I do a bad thing?"

"No, it's nothing like that at all. It's just . . ." I sidle a bit closer to him. "It's just that sometimes there are things I need to tell you."

"What kinds of things?"

"Well, for one, how much I love you."

"I already know that," he says, as if I should, too. "You tell me all the time."

"Because I want you to understand that my love will always be here for you."

My offer of assurance feels so heavy coming out. An echo from so long ago, the same thing my own father would tell me, only this time with a much more tragic spin. "Even . . . even if someday I'm not able to tell you that myself."

"You mean like if we're not together anymore?"

"Yeah, like that or . . . or there could be times when it may seem like I don't love you."

"It will never seem that way, Daddy," he says.

"But it could."

"How?"

"Like if I accidentally hurt your feelings without realizing it. I'd want you to know that it's not your fault. It will never be your fault."

"But why would you do that?"

I reach for a blanket corner, roll it between my fingers, and try to figure out how I can explain this complexity to a six-year-old boy. "I haven't been feeling so well lately and because of that, I've done some of those things already."

"Like at dinner that one time?"

"Yeah, like that. Did it frighten you?"

He shrugs. "A little, but not anymore."

My smile is sad. "I'm so sorry I made you feel that way, buddy."

"It's okay, Daddy. It was just an accident."

"It was. But I don't want you to ever be afraid to talk about it when something like that happens, so if it does again, will you do me a favor?"

He nods.

"I'd like for you to tell me, and if you feel funny doing that, be sure to tell Mommy instead, so you don't have to—" I stop, because my chest feels heavy just thinking about what his bleak future will hold. A future no child should ever have to endure.

Devon chews his bottom lip, a reflection of worry that makes this conversation so much harder.

"Anyway . . . the thing is, I've been trying to get better, but I may not be able to, kiddo. I may not win this one . . ." My voice weakens, and tears fill my eyes, because I know what I'm actually doing is telling my six-year-old son good-bye. That he will soon lose his father.

"Are you going to leave me, Daddy?" Devon asks, his tiny voice so soft that I can barely hear it.

And that's all it takes to finally rip me apart. To break me. Because telling him this is excruciating enough, but hearing him understand it is infinitely worse. I can't look at my son. If I do, I'll never get through this. I turn away and the tears start.

I feel Devon's soft little hand slide into my palm, his tiny fingers between mine. I hear his weak and troubled breaths.

"Daddy, I love you," he says very quietly.

I find the courage to look back at him, his pink cheeks dampened by tears.

For a long time, neither of us speaks, and I know that this moment, painful as it is, will be one of the few that are left, that it's so very precious.

Then, as if reading those very thoughts, he says, "We'll stay like this forever, Daddy, okay? Just like this."

What he said at the lake on that beautiful day, now with deeper and more tragic significance.

Devon throws his arms around my shoulders and hangs on tight like he never wants to let go, and I hold my son against me just as hard.

Several minutes later, after we pull apart, he says, "Is it okay if we don't do liftoff tonight?"

"Are you sure?

"I'm sure."

"How come?"

"Because I don't want to save the world, Daddy. I just want to save you."

65

To deceive is like striking a match. It can be dangerous and destructive, deadly even, and the people closest to you are most at risk. The flame burns slowly at first, and then before you know it, erupts into a ferocious explosion, consuming everything that matters. In the aftermath, you're standing in a cloud of smoke, staring at the charred and smoldering ruins of what once was.

On this morning, I sit at the kitchen table and stare out the window, but I don't see much, other than a world losing hold. A world rapidly shrinking and falling apart.

I think about Devon and what this illness will do to him, what it did to me as a boy. And about Jenna. How every step of the way, she's been here for me, offered her support, and above all, her unfailing love.

How I've betrayed her trust.

Instead of keeping my family from falling apart, I've only accelerated the process. Not on purpose. Not by any stretch of the imagination with intent to cause harm, but just the opposite. Still, none of this negates that instead of being truthful with Jenna last night, I kept her in the dark. Now the guilt rests squarely on my shoulders, and that one act is snowballing. I'll have to keep lying in order to delay getting diagnosed, to buy more time so I can save Devon from Donny Ray.

My gaze shifts blindly across the yard as I try to work through the clutter of racking emotions. If I could reverse time and take it back, I would, but life only moves in one direction, and what lies over your shoulder cannot be fixed. Straight ahead of me now is a trap: anything I do to try and repair this situation will only drive me deeper into trouble.

So I just keep staring out the window.

Sudden movement brings my vision into focus, and I barely glimpse Jake as he emerges from a clump of bushes and exits the yard. I narrow my view, notice the pile of dirt he just left, then something else catches my interest, green, and barely visible beneath the loose and disturbed soil. Keeping my eyes fixed there, I slowly rise from the chair, then move toward the door.

Outside, I edge closer toward the green object, each step like crossing unsettled ground.

I reach the spot and realize I'm staring down at a swath of cloth buried in dirt. I drop to my knees, start digging, hesitantly at first, but with each handful of earth I draw, my speed gradually and steadily increases. I uncover the green thing, yank it out, and hold it up.

A pair of Devon's shorts.

I claw frantically at the soil, dirt and mud flying all around me, fingers turning bruised and raw from the stony granules digging beneath my nails.

I pluck out one of Devon's T-shirts. His shoe. A baseball cap.

I keep digging.

When it's all done, I stand upright, body stiff from soreness and uncertainty; clothes, hands, and face coated in grime. I stare at the ground covered with the items, all of them belonging to Devon.

At least fifteen pairs of socks. His ten missing baseball hats. Five pairs of shorts. Six T-shirts. Two pairs of sneakers. It just goes on and on. All my son's clothing that started to go missing the night I collided with that tree. Clothing that Jake has been diligently and meticulously stealing away, transporting to this special place.

Burying them like valued treasures.

Mystery finally solved.

Because I at last know why Jake has been speaking to me mind-to-mind, what he's been trying to tell me all along—something that's now coming to fruition.

My son is in danger.

The dog knows.

"But *how* did he know?"

I look over my shoulder and find Jake sitting by the corner of the house and watching me.

"You don't have to worry anymore, boy," I tell him. "I hear you now. He'll be safe. I'll make sure of that, if it's the last thing I ever do."

"Chris?"

Jenna's voice throws me into a jolt. I turn and find her watching me, expression one of profound disquiet. Her attention wanders between the piles of dirt, my son's belongings scattered between them.

"What are you doing?" she asks. "What is all this?"

"Devon's stuff that's been going missing." I nod at the items. "I found them. It's been Jake all along. He's been burying them out here."

Jenna looks back at me, eyes broadened by worry. I don't want to scare her, but she already looks deeply troubled, and Jake has just raised the stakes. I can no longer keep my lies going. It's time to at last come clean, correct my mistake, and let her know that our son is in danger.

"There's something I have to tell you, honey. I know why Jake's been burying Devon's—"

"Chris," she interrupts, and it's not just worry I see now. It's . . . "What's wrong?"

She steps closer toward the piles, looks them over, then turns back to me.

"Baby . . . ," she says, shaking her head, eyes filling with tears, "there's nothing here."

66

On my way to work, I'm nervous and tense. No, I'm more than that—I'm rattled to my core. I know what I saw, but Jenna's reaction tells me I didn't.

She was lying

"You shut up about my wife! She'd never do that!"

I don't know what to think, can't trust what I see anymore, but I trust Jenna, so she has to be right.

And speaking of trust, as Loveland draws closer, I find my thoughts returning to Adam—or rather, to my extreme anger toward him. No matter what's happened, I've always been there for him. When he and his first wife were going through the divorce—even though I knew he'd created most of their problems—I stood by his side. I was there for him. When he told me in the strictest of confidence that he'd made a bad call with a patient that could have cost him his job, I kept that quiet, consoling him, saying it could have happened to any of us. Now I've uncovered a major conspiracy at Loveland, a plot that could ultimately put us and everyone else's lives in jeopardy, and what does he do? He hesitates. He dismisses me. He doesn't even listen.

That's because he's in on it.

And after I've worked so hard to uncover this clandestine, underground operation, instead of trusting me, instead of supporting and praising me for it, Adam further tries to discredit me by pulling out the crazy card.

I'm incensed with Adam. I'm insulted. I'm deeply injured.

Before I can let those feelings simmer, my worries abruptly shift when I again approach the most execrable entity I've ever laid eyes on.

The Evil Tree.

The Evil Tree that has turned my life upside down. Ever since I nearly hit the beast, it's been trying to draw me back to finish the job. And in this moment, I decide that I'll no longer give it the pleasure or benefit of my attention. I can't avoid passing it on my drive to and from work, but I can attenuate its powerfully magnetic draw by depriving it of my energy.

At fifteen feet away, I accelerate, keeping my sight focused on a spot far ahead of me.

At ten feet, I'm tempted to take just a quick peek but tell myself that's all part of its power, that giving in will only cause me more grief.

Five feet, and my forehead sweats. My hands are shaking.

Just as our planes intersect, as if through a volition all its own, my head turns toward the tree, and my eyes lock onto it.

And I know—without any doubt—that the thing owns me now. It has finally won this battle.

I shouldn't have looked.

67

The parking lot at Loveland is half empty.

Things are moving quickly, my insanity racing up the backside. I have no idea what the disappearances mean yet, but I'm going to figure it out today.

When I get to my office, another surprise awaits me, no less disagreeable. Adam sits behind my desk wearing a mournful look that I can only interpret as a sign of approaching trouble.

"What are *you* doing here?" I ask, outrage and disgust tainting my words.

He rests his hands on my desk, leans slightly forward, and says, "You refused to hear me out yesterday. Now I'm going to *make* you listen."

"It's not like you've given me much of a choice."

"Chris, knock it off. You're the closest friend I've ever had. I care about you. I'm on your side. And I don't like what happened between us."

"I wasn't exactly loving it myself."

"It's just . . . I'm worried about you, man." He lingers on me for a moment. "Is there something happening I should know about?"

He already knows what's happening. He's part of it.

"You already know what's happening. You just chose not to support me."

"That isn't true. You completely misread what I—"

"Misread what?" I step toward him, feel my vocal chords flex with anger, my tenor pulling tighter. "Misread when you treated me like I was crazy?"

You are *crazy.*

"Or maybe it was the part where you disregarded that I was clearly upset. Or how about when, instead of listening and being a friend, you jumped to the conclusion that this knock to my head has jarred my common sense loose? Which *misread* are you refer- ring to here, Adam? I'm confused. Help me out."

Falling silent, holding his unreadable eyes on me, he reaches for the computer screen on my desk. Turns it toward me.

"We're not doing this again, Adam. We are not. I know what the records say, and I've already explained why."

"Just read it, okay?"

I look at the screen and see an e-mail from our personnel director. I read it.

Dr. Wiley,

Per your request for information re: Melinda Jeffries. Our records indicate nobody by that name has ever been employed by Loveland Hospital or any of its affiliates.

Regarding Nicholas Hartley, Stanley Winters, and Gerald Markman, none has, at any time, been registered as patients here.

My chest constricts. My stomach tugs into a knot. I look up from the screen and realize Adam's been watching me the whole time. He reaches under his desk and pulls out the red folder I saw him slam shut several days ago.

I lurch back at the sight of it and feel my temples flare with heat.

He slaps the folder onto the desk and opens it. Inside is a series of photographs. Adam spreads them out on the desktop, then looks at me.

I study the photos of young girls I've never before seen. I look up at Adam and say, "Who are they?"

Very softly. "Chris, they're the missing girls. The ones Donny Ray is suspected of killing."

"That can't be. You have the wrong pictures."

Adam doesn't respond. He just looks sadly troubled.

"But . . . but none of them look like Miranda Smith."

"None of them ever did. And I checked the police reports. Not a single one wore a blue dress on the day she went missing."

"NO!" I slowly back away from him, fists pulling tight, nails digging holes into my palms, "I saw those faces, Adam. They looked just like her."

"Chris, something is happening to you. Maybe it's because of the accident or . . . or maybe it's worse than that. I don't know, because you've stopped telling me things, but I'm really worried. You're getting paranoid, and we've got to find you some help."

Get away from him!

I bolt for the door.

"Chris, wait!"

"No! Someone, or *something*, is taking over this hospital. Everything I've told you is true." I jab my finger sharply at him. "You're trying to keep me from getting to the bottom of it! You're trying to sabotage my efforts! But it won't work, Adam. I won't let you!"

"That's not true. I'm not doing anything of the sort!"

"And *I'm* not paranoid!"

Before he can say another word, I'm gone.

68

SOMEONE IS OUT TO GET ME

Paranoia became a prominent feature of my father's schizophrenia.

It began with fits of rage and persecutory declarations, which erupted into stomping, screaming tirades that put the fear of God in me. Things would break and shatter, Dad would wail louder, and I'd run to my room for cover. With the door locked, I'd bury my head beneath a pillow, tears sopping the sheet, panic and terror writhing through every part of me. I thought things couldn't get any worse, but that was just another of my flawed survival tactics.

One day, as I watched TV in the family room, the screeching and wailing started, more ferocious than ever. While my father's violent complaints were difficult to interpret, his sentiment was not. It was wrathful and convulsive, frenzied and maniacal.

Instinctual fear drove me upstairs for safety, and he was quickly on my trail. I lurched into the bedroom, but before I could slam the door, he crashed through with an expression that I could only interpret as crazy-eyed and murderous intent. I was trapped. My only way out of that room was the second-story window with a merciless drop onto our concrete driveway.

He let out a bloodcurdling scream and charged at me, shouting, "STAY AWAAAAY. STAY AWAAAAY!"

I dropped to the floor, curled into a ball, and prayed for salvation. I felt his body launch itself over mine. I heard the window shatter. I heard a sickening howl that barely sounded human.

When I lifted my head, he was covered in blood and rolling around in broken shards of glass, moaning like some tortured animal. Just moments before, I'd been terrified of the man. Now my heart ached for him in ways I never knew it could.

A neighbor called for an ambulance, and they rushed him to the hospital. He spent several days recovering from his injuries. After that, it was back to the psych ward, then he came home again, medicated, temporarily stabilized, and ready to bring more disorder and heartbreak into our world.

My mother wasn't home during this latest fiasco, so in her mind it never happened. Not once during his hospital stays did she visit him or even pick up the phone to check on his status.

When he returned home, face and body covered in stitches, she refused to look at him.

69

Everyone is against you.

"Nothing works around here!" I shout, storming through the hallways. "This place is broken!"

Stanley was right.

I dash into the bathroom, lock myself in a stall. Face buried in my hands, I cry.

I don't like being inside Loveland anymore. It keeps changing, keeps slipping away from me. I'm no longer safe here, and the more reality disappears, the fewer places I have left to hide from myself.

Do not trust anyone here.

"We've got to get out of here!" I yell and hear the echo of my voice bounce off walls, so loud that it surprises even me.

Ever since the accident, insanity has been haunting me. This voice has been haunting me. Donny Ray has been haunting me. But most of all, time has been haunting me.

"It's ticking under my skin!"

More echoes. More anger. More utter helplessness.

"Pull it together, Chris!"

"But I don't know how!"

Without thought, I push open the stall door, and, before I know it, I'm running back toward my office.

I dash inside, slam the door shut, then lean against it. I try to grab hold of myself and the starburst of thoughts firing through my fractured mind.

I stumble toward my desk, collapse into the chair. I get up, pace back and forth, and run a hand through my sweat-soaked hair.

I scream at nobody.

"I HAVE TO CALM DOWN! I HAVE TO CALM DOWN! BUT HOW?"

I go back to pacing and try to figure out how to figure this out. I have to figure this out. I have to hold on to my sanity.

I know my schizophrenia is inevitable, but I can't let it drive me into complete madness, not until I make sure Donny Ray no longer poses a threat to my son.

I've got several things to do. I can't change my diagnosis with the court, but I can make sure the psychopathic demon never sets foot in public. That means figuring out whether he's actually responsible for the disappearances at Loveland and whether he can get out as well.

My options are limited to one. I need to confront Donny Ray, determine whether he's walking the walk or just talking the talk.

I scramble toward the door, but a shifting beam of sunlight off to my side stops me. I look toward the window, and the air catches in my throat. Outside, a tiny blue dress flitters in the wind.

Blue lace. Big white bow.

One word scrawled across the chest.

MUD.

Written in mud.

70

MUD.

The same word, written the same way I imagined I saw it on Devon's covers that night.

How Donny Ray knows about that would be an easy guess. I probably told him during one of our sessions while he was taking over my mind. His message served two purposes. To mock my stupidity, rub it in my face, while at the same time, to accelerate my mental deterioration. By hanging that dress outside my window, Donny Ray raised the stakes on his threat against Devon. He wants me to know that nothing can keep him inside Loveland.

Not that his guerilla tactic is going to work. He could have accomplished this latest feat in any number of ways. The most obvious, bribing another patient with better roaming privileges into doing the dirty work while I stepped away from my office for a few minutes. Regardless of how he executed this latest ploy, Donny Ray has indeed raised the stakes. He's thrown me his challenge, and I'm accepting it.

Game on, asshole.

But the stakes ratchet up another notch when I walk onto Alpha Twelve and see six open doors. More empty rooms, fewer patients. Loveland Hospital is quickly deconstructing, which tells me time is gaining on my heels. But not for long, not if I have anything to say about it. I'm going to put a stop to this chaos, right after I put a stop to Donny Ray.

"Keep your eyes on me the entire time I'm inside this room," I tell Evan before entering. "Do not leave your post for a second. If you see anything that looks even a little off, get in here, immediately."

"Yes, sir." He checks his weapon, then reaches for the key to allow me access.

I enter, and the door closes behind me. I look back at Evan. He steps a few inches away from the window, gives me a solemn nod.

Donny Ray sits at his desk, but he's not facing it. The chair is spun around and aimed out, so his body is situated the same way mine was the last time. This doesn't look like a coincidence. This looks like he's been waiting for me and is ready to play. I raise him one and take his prior spot on the bed.

I won't mention the dress—there's no point to it. Showing my annoyance would only strengthen his advantage. We both know the score, and Donny Ray has made it perfectly clear he'll use anything—even my son—to make sure I keep my mouth shut about his sociopathic manipulation. Now this game of fox and goose has begun.

But it seems Donny Ray's plan is much the same as mine. He's looking into my eyes, and I'm looking into his, both of us watching, waiting each other out. That's fine. He may have a sharp and cunning mind, but I've got the upper hand when it comes to knowing how those operate. All I can do now is observe his every action, every statement, and hope to get an inkling of what his next move will be.

Donny Ray eases his chair backward and forward so it emits a series of slow, high-pitched creaks. Then he abruptly stops.

"Is something the matter?" he asks, making the first move.

"Maybe I should ask you that question."

"Maybe I should ask you that question," he repeats.

"You know damned well I didn't come here to talk about me."

Still holding those stony eyes on me, he goes through three additional rounds of chair squeaking, slower now, the sound appreciably louder and more drawn-out. I feel my lips twitch. It's grating on my nerves.

Don't mess with this guy.

Shut up. I know what I'm doing.

You've walked into dangerous territory. You still don't know who he really is.

My calf muscles jerk and pull tight.

He resumes with his rocking for a few more seconds, then stops again. "You seem unsteady, Christopher."

"Let's keep this professional from now on, okay? It's Dr. Kellan."

He nods toward my feet.

I glance down and see my pen lying on the floor. I look up at Donny Ray.

With a playful grin, he raises his hands in surrender. "Wasn't me this time."

I reach for the pen, put it back in my pocket.

"Those things are trouble for you," he says.

Watching me, Donny Ray calmly places a hand on each side of the chair and pulls his body upward, cut muscles flexing beneath a thin, black T-shirt. With a look that could pass as pure innocence, he pushes the bangs away from his face and tops the performance off with a schoolboyish grin. But I know these are the false flags of a psychopath, mirroring societal norms rather than actually having them.

A chameleon.

A child killer, and, on some level, I can't help but feel his actions are intended to flaunt that contradiction at me.

It's making my blood boil.

He resumes the movements, still studying me, rocking faster now. Back and forth . . . back and forth. The chair is chirping at me, and the sound is getting deeper under my skin. I try to maintain my composure but he's chipping away at it. I can't take this any longer.

"Knock it off!" I shout.

He grins again, but this time there's nothing innocent about it. The mask is off. I'm at last seeing the real Donny Ray Smith—the demon—but only because he's chosen to let me, and only because he knows this is the exact moment it will levy the greatest damage. As I've learned, every word he speaks, every facial expression, is a carefully calculated move designed to control and deceive. To do harm.

Donny Ray walks to the door. Peering through the window at Evan, he says, "We have to get out of here."

My pulse erratically changes because he's just said the same thing Stanley did before his disappearance.

I labor to hold my voice steady. "Donny Ray, what are you talking about?"

"You know." Keeping his back to me, he bobs his head up and down.

"I really don't."

"Nicholas and Stanley are already gone. Melinda and Gerald, also."

"Yes, that's more than obvious. And your point?"

"You let them go. We should go, too."

"I didn't let anyone go, and it was never my goal to get you out of here. I was here to help find the truth. Remember that? The truth? That thing you seemed so passionate about?"

"Yes, I know it well." He shifts his weight from one foot to the other. "But I don't think the truth is what you want."

"I have no idea what you mean."

He leans in closer toward the window then waves to Evan, and I let out a small laugh, marveling at the arrogance that allows him the luxury of taunting a uniformed police officer.

Donny Ray finally turns around and gives me his attention. "You know exactly what I mean." He cocks a brow. "The *truth* has been right in front of you all this time. You're avoiding it."

"Stop talking nonsense and get to the point."

"Stop talking nonsense and get to the point."

All this time, he's been carefully handpicking which of my statements to parrot back as a method to throw me further off-balance, but I'm not playing along anymore.

"And quit mimicking me," I say, at last drawing the line. "It's disruptive."

"I'm just trying to help you."

"Let's make one thing perfectly clear, Donny Ray. I'm the doctor, and you're the patient. The only help you can offer is to dispense with the mind games."

"I'm the doctor and you're the patient. The only help you can offer is to dispense with the mind games," he answers back. "Speaking of the truth, have you figured out yet what's happened to all the people around here?"

I supply no answer. He wouldn't have asked if he really wanted to know. Direct isn't exactly his style.

"Who do you think is making them all disappear?"

The look on his face and tone of voice are ambiguous enough to indicate he's posing an innocent question, but I can read the subtext. Donny Ray wants me to think he's making the people of Loveland vanish.

I can't wait him out any longer. Things are moving too quickly all around me, the body count dropping, my mind crumbling. It's time to force the issue.

"You can also dispense with all the mundane weaving and skirting," I tell him. "I'm not at all impressed, and it only makes you appear more tragic and sad."

"You're looking into a mirror, Christopher," he says and takes a firm step toward me, expression suddenly stern. Dangerous.

"You smack of impotence and desperation, Donny Ray—actually you stink of it. So here's an idea. Instead of putting all your weaknesses on parade, how about if we just cut bait and get to the point. You can start by telling me why you came into my life."

He moves closer toward me. His smile is tight and angry. "I came into your life to tear it down, and I'm not going to stop until I break it. That sweet, *beautiful* little boy of yours is the last thing holding it up. But not for long."

I stand straight up, every part of my being wanting to reach for his neck and rip out his windpipe. Rancor like I've never before known collects in my throat, and from it comes a low gnarling sound I barely recognize as my own.

"I will take you out, first."

"That's just not going to happen," he snarls back.

"You're full of it, Donny Ray. You've got no power inside this institution."

"I have all the power."

"Yeah? Prove it."

His biting expression melds into a knowing smirk. "Your proof is waiting just outside the door."

The window is empty. I rush forward, then stare at the vacant spot where Evan once stood. I glance up and down the hallway, and it feels like a brick has just dropped into the pit of my stomach because there's no sign of him anywhere.

Evan has become one of the missings.

"Christopher?"

I reel around.

"You never asked what I did with the bodies," Donny Ray Smith tells me.

He's not talking about the missing girls.

71

Donny Ray has been emptying out Loveland.

But how?

You already know.

"Know what?"

I told you. It's an inside job. He's got an underground army at Loveland. They've been helping him yank all those people out, and they're going to keep helping him. You have to do something, fast.

I have to do something fast, have to figure out a plan. I've got to stop him.

I begin weighing options. My first priority is to keep Devon safe. I can do that, so long as I keep Donny Ray locked inside these walls.

Wrong.

"What?"

You can't keep him inside Loveland. You never could.

"Why not?"

Because you built these walls in your mind. He can penetrate them whenever he wants. Do you honestly believe he can't walk right out of here himself?

"That's nonsense. He would have already left."

He hasn't left because he doesn't want to, yet.

"Why not?"

I've already told you that, too, and he just confirmed it. Donny Ray didn't come here for the evaluation—he came here to destroy you. The Big Plan. Now that the job's almost done, he can split whenever he wants.

"Oh, God. You're right."

Donny Ray has the power to leave *now* and go after Devon. I have to regroup, figure out a strategy to stop him. I sprint down the hallway, fear and urgency chasing after me like a pack of wild dogs with the taste of fresh blood.

Better run faster.

"SHUT UP! JUST SHHHH . . . SHHHH." I try to complete my sentence, but it's fighting me. A sound I've never before heard bursts from my lips—a high-pitched, pulsating squeal, followed by a deep, throaty laugh that barely sounds human.

"WHAT'S HAPPENING TO ME?"

I know what's happening—my mind is breaking, that's what. I'm losing it. I'm one step from the edge, but I've got to stop Donny Ray first.

You can't stop him.

"I have to!"

But you can do something else.

I punch the gas pedal. My tires squeal with fury as my car peels out of the parking lot. Donny Ray and his underground army may have their Big Plan in place, but I'm about to sling my own scheme right back at them.

I'm drastically outnumbered, ridiculously handicapped, but there can be no underestimating the fierce determination of a father set on keeping his son out of harm's way. I may not be able to stop Donny Ray from leaving Loveland, but I can make damned sure he never gets anywhere near Devon. I know my work is cut out for me, that my plan will require monumental skill, rigorous planning, and extensive calculation. It may take most of the evening to get this job done, maybe all night, but sleep deprivation offers no challenge. I'm driven by fear and doggedness, my determination not only fierce but unbreakable.

So, we have our plan. How are we going to work this?

"First, I have to secure our home, then make sure that Devon is watched around the clock. I'll need to gather plenty of information in advance so I can predict Donny Ray's movements before he makes them."

"You mean like this one?"

My lungs go airless. My world tilts sideways, everything in it swimming rapidly around me. I look into the rearview mirror, and Donny Ray sneers at me from the backseat. I split my nervous attention between him and the road, gradually easing onto the brakes.

"It's okay," he says, motioning forward with a hand. "No need to stop now. I'll talk. You listen."

Oh, God. He's with me.

"I've always been with you, Christopher. You just couldn't see it. But I'm glad. You needed to take me out of Loveland."

You have to take me out of here!

The exact demand he made the day we met, now with horrifying significance, because I've just done the one thing I was trying to prevent. I've indeed taken Donny Ray out of Loveland. I've aided in his escape.

But is this real?

"Reality can be a strange thing," he says, "you know? Daddy taught me that. He used to say it's not about what you see, but what you choose not to. Of course, that didn't work out so well for Miranda. Never could stand the little whore, so I chose not to see her, and *poof*! She was gone!"

No, I refuse to believe this is real. He's not here. Now I'm having paranoid delusions that Donny Ray is following me. He's finally infiltrated my mind.

"The reflections in your mind have been blinding you, Christopher. They've been pushing you closer to the edge." He looks out at the road ahead and nods as if agreeing with his own thought. "But that's the plan. We're moving in the right direction now. We're getting close."

Bit by bit, Donny Ray has been dismantling Loveland. Now he's moved into my mind, so he can tear that down as well.

"I'm tearing down the walls, Christopher. I'm rocking your world." His grin is glib; so, too, is the small laugh he exhales. "And my work is nearly complete."

"I won't let you have my son!" I shout. "You're not taking Devon away from me!"

"Really? Because it looks like you're driving me right to him."

I slam on the brakes, veer off the road, then pull to a screeching stop along the shoulder. "Why? Why are you causing me all this agony?"

"Your agony started a long time ago." Donny Ray's expression shifts into what looks like pity, or compassion, or whatever warped and phony mask his mind is wearing at the moment. "That's why you called me here, to rid you of it."

"I don't want your help! Get out of my car . . . or my head . . . or—"

"And now that you've let me in, I'll never leave you."

"You're evil!"

"I am truth."

"You're a lie!"

"That's how I am—The Truth. Once I'm exposed, you can never bury me." He nods toward the road ahead.

I aim my vision through the windshield, but before it can find focus, the glass shatters, and the white light explodes.

72

I jerk my head up and gasp.

What in God's—?

I'm still in my car. I check the clock and realize that time has again escaped me, to the tune of about . . .

An hour?

More minutes stealing away when every second is golden.

My mind untangles, vision settles, and up ahead, I see . . .

Oh, hell no.

I'm parked directly in front of the Evil Tree, its gnarled branches woven together and looming overhead like a giant black web, trapping me.

A strong wind blows, and as if awakened from restless sleep, the Evil Tree comes to life. Leaves hiss venomously. Swaying branches throw shadows across my car like toxic vapors. And from the most cellular level of my being comes the purest of truths. That I've unwittingly landed at the hub where every evil in this world intersects.

I've got to get out of here.

I crank the ignition key, but abrupt and rapid movement outside the windshield distracts me. I turn my head just in time to see an object catch light, then disappear into darkness—darkness that still holds my attention as I question whether what I just saw was more than a reflection on the glass.

Another movement, this time to the right. I swing in that direction and find my answer waiting there.

Holy—

At about ten feet, the rubber ball wobbles to a stop, then a brilliant streak of crimson blazes into view.

No freakin' way.

Standing before my car, bathed in the glow of headlights, is the teenager in the red hoodie.

Staring at me, stricken with abject fear.

At just a few feet away, I can see his face clearly. I'm positive that up until the accident, I'd never seen this kid before in my life.

"Who are you?" I shout at him.

He snatches up the ball and takes off running. Just as quickly, I sling my door open and clamber from the car.

"Not a chance!" I yell and chase after him. "You started this! You're not getting away from me this time!"

Still clutching the ball, he beats a path toward the lake as if his life depends on it. I follow on his heels, but the kid's a speed demon, covering ground at a rate that makes it difficult to keep up.

Several feet ahead, he dashes into a cluster of scrub oak, but I stay on him through the tangle of jagged twigs that poke and scratch and snap into my face. I claw my way out, but all I find past the clearing is more mystery. There's no sign of the boy, not even the sound of his footfalls. I look to my left, then to my right. On each side, tall and sturdy boulders surround me, far too steep and slick for him to climb. Clamping a hand to each side of my head, I look out at the lake and observe the undisturbed water, smooth as glass.

Gone. Again.

"WHAT THE HELL ARE YOU TRYING TO TELL ME?" I shout out to the boy. But the only answer I get is my same question, reverberating back as a whispery echo.

A thunderous crash goes off, and my stomach sucks up into my throat, because I recognize the sound of metal crushing on impact.

"Oh God, my car!"

Then the glass shatters, and then the blinding light explodes.

73

It takes less than two blinks to realize that I'm flying up the road.

The road? What in God's name is going on?

It's not only the minutes taking leaps—so, too, are circumstances and events, quickly eddying into the path of utter disorder and confusion. With my mind decomposing so rapidly, any effort to keep track of reality is a job unto itself. I have to get this plan into place before my world collapses.

I jam a foot onto the gas pedal and feel my body jerk back as the car shoots forward, reeling me at unforgiving speed toward home.

I drive recklessly up my street, careen into the garage, then pull to a screeching halt. Jenna's car isn't here. She's probably picking up Devon from school, which will work in my favor. I've got no time to talk right now, no time to explain, just plenty of work to do.

I burst through the door and into the house. I rush up the staircase and toward my office. Inside, I get busy logging on to my work account to extract the information I'll need.

An hour later, I have at my ready—scattered about the floor and pinned to the walls—a full-blown paper arsenal of facts, figures, statistical data, and maps, detailing Loveland's infrastructure, along with anything else I could gather to track Donny Ray's daily patterns. I've also gathered the blueprints for this house and marked all points of vulnerability in red. In effect, I've got a war room equipped with information I'll use to keep Devon safe.

I move to the window and part the curtains to see if the security patrol has arrived. Not yet, but I expect them shortly. From the office closet shelf, I pull down a metal lockbox. After opening it, I reach for my gun and slide out the magazine. If Donny Ray does manage to make it to this house, that bastard won't live past our driveway.

Things are going smoother than expected. I'm pleased. All that's left to do now is study up on the information I've gathered, make certain it's ironclad.

A car pulls into the driveway. I spring from my chair, then relief gives me a dose of calm when I hear Jenna's and Devon's voices coming from the kitchen. I can't talk to them right now, can't afford any interruptions. With so much work to get done before morning, the clock is banging double time inside my head. I scramble to the door, turn the lock inside the knob, then get back to work.

About ten minutes later, I hear the pitter-patter of Devon's feet on the staircase, accompanied by Jenna's steps, firmer and more anchored. My son scurries off to his room, and shortly after, two raps hit my door.

"Chris?" my wife says. "You in there?"

"Hi, honey." I shuffle some papers, more for effect than actual purpose, then the doorknob jiggles.

"What are you doing in there, and why's the door locked?"

"Oh, that." I force a laugh and hope it sounds casual enough. "I've got a big project starting up tomorrow. At work. It's extremely important. I have a lot of research to get done this evening. I didn't want Devon busting in and disturbing me."

"But what about dinner?"

"Too busy. Can't come down right now." To evoke further credibility, I hit the print button, and the machine rattles off pages. I slam a desk drawer. "Just go ahead without me, and I'll grab something later."

"I can bring you up a plate."

"No, that won't be necessary. I'm fine for now, really."

Finally, some peace, and I'm relieved, but then Jenna knocks once more.

"Honey, please!" I yell at the door. "What is it? I'm trying to work in here!"

"Sorry to bother you again, but I forgot to tell you something earlier," Donny Ray says. "You're wasting time with all that bullshit. Loveland is history. The war's right here."

Wood cracks and the walls around me boom into a powerful quake as Donny Ray violently and repeatedly slams his body against the door.

74

I snatch up the gun from my desk, then charge forward, shouting, "GET OUT OF MY MIND! I'LL KILL YOU, GODDAMN IT! YOU HEAR ME?"

With gun aimed high and ready to fire, I yank open the door, but when I see what's on the other side, my stomach clenches.

Jenna stands in the hallway, face blanched by shock, staring at the gun in my hand. She doesn't speak, but her quivering lips tell me all I need to know.

I lower the gun to my side and say, "I'm sorry . . . I thought—"

She looks past me and into the room, and her expression cascades into wide-eyed fright. She drops a hand to her side, and the globe that I stole from Adam's house falls, shattering into pieces on the floor.

"Honey, I can explain that. It's not what you—"

Jenna shoves past me, then takes unsteady steps toward the center of the room. She scans the walls, papered with a plethora of charts, of graphs, of floor diagrams, a peppering of pushpins holding them all up. Red-scribbled markings everywhere. Arrows and special symbols, discernible only to me. Directives scrawled like graffiti: POTENTIAL ESCAPE ROUTE! PRIMARY STAGING AREA! STOP DONNY RAY!

"This probably looks a little strange to you," I say, taking long strides toward her, "but it isn't what you—"

Jenna stops me in my tracks, because riding through her eyes, on her face—everywhere—I see things I've never before witnessed. I see naked fear. I see heartbreak.

I see my wife looking at someone she doesn't know.

"Please just listen to me!" I say with hands raised in the air, swallowing hard against my distress and agitation.

Jenna studies the walls again, then turns back to me. With tears welling, she says, "Chris, we need to get you help right away."

I stare at her for a few seconds, then start pacing the floor, vision fixed there as I talk. "No. You have to hear me out. I'm very sorry if all this looks frightening, but you'll understand much better once I explain." My body involuntarily and abruptly jerks. "Now, please listen very carefully when I tell you this. A flagrant evil has descended over Loveland. People—scores of them—are vanishing. The employees, the patients, *everyone*. They're being transported to some secret place. I don't know where yet, but I do know who's behind it all. Donny Ray is doing it. He's moving them out."

I stop pacing to look at Jenna, and now she appears more frightened. I can't blame her, and I hate being the one to bring this frightening news, so I come back, reach for her hand, and get full confirmation of that fear. With her arm so stiff and unyielding, I'm now fully aware how unsettled all this is making her.

"Sweetheart," I say, trying to temper my voice, looking at her with compassion, "our son is in grave danger, but please don't be scared right now, okay? You just have to trust me. I've been giving this a lot of thought. I have a plan. I'm going to save him from—"

"Chris," she says and starts backing away from me. "Please. Stop."

"Stop what?"

"Stop doing all this."

"I don't understand. I'm trying to tell you right now what's been—"

"I know what's been going on."

"Wait . . . What? You already know? About Donny Ray? And about Devon?"

"Adam told me everything."

"Damn it!" I shout and look away with an angry smile. "I should have known he'd get to you first!" I turn quickly back to her. "But don't believe him. Don't believe anything he says. He's lying to you. Adam is in on it!"

"Adam is trying to help you!" she says, tears rolling down her face. "Chris, I'm frightened of you. *We're* frightened of you."

"You're—of *me*?" A loud and frenetic laugh escapes through my lips. "How could . . . I don't understand this at all. I'm trying to protect you!"

"Please, you have to put a stop to all this, to what you're doing to yourself . . ." She takes in a shaky breath. ". . . To everyone."

I launch forward, then spin back toward her. "But it's not what you think. I'm doing it all for a very good reason. I have to save Devon, because—"

"Chris!" she yells. "Listen to me! Devon is not the one who needs saving. He's never been the one!"

"Yes he does!" I grab hold of my hair, shake my head vigorously, then through clenched teeth, "He needs it! He needs it very badly! I have to protect him!"

"No, baby . . . ," she says, voice cracking. "The problem isn't happening at Loveland. It never was. All this time, it's been happening in your mind. You're trapped inside it, and now everything is falling apart. *You're* falling apart."

"That's not true! It's just not! You have to believe me! Devon will die if I don't do something! Look, I know"—my body jerks again but harder this time—"I know I've been having some problems lately, but this part is actually real."

"None of this is real," she says, sadness so plain. Sadness I can't at all comprehend.

"You . . . You don't believe me?"

"Not because I don't want to. Because I can't."

"Please . . . *Please!* Don't do this to me, not now. Don't abandon me. You're the only one left who can help me. I need you!"

The sound of tiny footsteps interrupts us. Jenna gives the open doorway a wary glance, then rushes toward the wall and starts pulling down my papers.

"Wait!" I shout at her. "Don't touch those! I've been working all afternoon! It's extremely important!"

I leap toward my wife. She startles and lets out a shriek so appalling that it knocks me off-balance. I stumble forward, try to regain footing, and grab hold of Jenna's arm, but she shoves me away. Her breath is heaving. Her cheeks are soaked with tears.

Devon screams.

I turn around and the blood drains from my face.

My son stands in the doorway frozen by terror, sobbing to the point of hyperventilation.

Directly behind him, I see Donny Ray Smith, a smarmy smirk spreading across his face.

"Nothing in this world can hold me, Christopher," he says. "Nothing at all."

"I'LL FUCKING KILL YOU!" I shout and vault toward them.

Donny Ray lowers his hands, but before he can touch my son's shoulder, I crash into him. We fly backward onto the floor. I land on top of him, and we wrestle for control, but the man is so much stronger. In one powerful move, he flips me over and slams my back against the floor.

Jenna screams.

"Give up the boy!" Donny Ray says, legs straddling me. "I'm taking him!"

I can't see anything, can't even feel my own body. I only feel rage—rage so powerful that it explodes within me like a thousand bottle rockets. In a flash, I spring upward. Donny Ray flies into reverse and smashes into the wall, but before he can regroup, I'm on him again, hands gripped tightly around his neck.

"Daddy, stop! I can't breathe!"

The sound of Devon's voice startles me. I see my hands clutched around his neck. I see him choking for air.

I see his shock and horror staring me in the face.

"Oh no . . . *God* . . . OH, NO!" I shout, instantly releasing my hold on him, unable to fathom what I've just done, or for that matter, how. But I don't get a chance to figure it out, because something heavy and hard hurtles into the back of my neck. The room swarms into a spin all around me, and my vision blurs as I drop to the floor.

I lift my head in time to catch Jenna racing through the doorway with Devon draped over her shoulder. My son's frantic, sobbing screams echo down the hall—soon after that, I hear the sound of tires as they burn rubber on the driveway, and the walls of my once-unyielding world, cracking, crumbling, and falling all around me.

75

THIS IS HOW IT ENDS

I was more and more on alert after my father came home from the hospital looking like Frankenstein. The message on my radar was clear: Danger. Madman going madder.

One night a series of violent slams rattled my door in its frame. Walls shook. The hardwood quaked. Things flew off shelves and crashed onto the floor.

Then, this.

"I'LL KILL YOU, GODDAMN IT! YOU HEAR ME? I'LL FUCKING KILL YOU!"

I crawled under the bed and held my face to the floor, the only thing beneath me, a puddle of tears.

This is it. We're here. This is how it ends.

The door crashed open and with surprising force, slammed into the wall—but that paled in comparison to the view of my father's feet, furiously stomping toward me. There was nothing to do except wait for what was coming next. I knew it would only be a matter of seconds before he killed me.

Instead, his angry howls descended into dull and helpless

whimpers. Then he spoke again, but this time his tone was weak and pleading.

"Please . . . Please . . ."

I swallowed air, turned my head toward him, and tried to listen.

"Please . . . don't . . . ," he murmured through tortured sobs. "Please don't take him from me. Don't take my boy."

I peered out and saw my father sitting on the floor. Body hunched over, arms wrapped around knees, face pressed against them. Moaning and weeping.

And in an instant, it all made sense. The towel crammed down the drain. The nightmarish receiving tower constructed of knives. The charts, the diagrams. The stern warning he'd given through the window glass.

The man in the drain.

Through all his madness, there was only one desire left in his shattered mind, one determined need. To keep from losing me.

Even after I'm gone, my love will still be with you. You'll always feel it deep inside your heart.

I crawled out from under the bed and scrambled to him.

He looked at me, and beneath his tearful eyes, I saw it—I saw love—pure and whole and real.

My father and I embraced, holding tight to each other before this moment could slip away from us, as we both knew it would.

With his face pressed against mine, our tears and sobs mingling, he whispered into my ear.

"Christopher . . . you are my everything."

76

I come to with my face flat against the floor, and it takes a few seconds to ground myself in the moment. Then my bruised neck delivers a harsh reminder. I lift my head and look at the papers still covering the walls and scattered throughout the room.

One thing I can feel grateful for is that this time I know it was simply a matter of passing out from injury and exhaustion, rather than losing minutes that become more precious all the time.

I heave my body off the floor, and memories of what happened here rise to the surface, nearly bowling me back over.

I tried to kill my son last night.

It wasn't intentional, just a product of misunderstanding. I was only trying to protect Devon, but through my mind's jumbled jigsaw of skewed perceptions, I did just the opposite.

I became my father.

No, I was worse than him, and as that reality settles, a boundless and exponential ache swells within me. It doesn't matter what I tried to do—it matters what I did. Fear is indelible, it's irreversible, and once inflicted, you can never take it back. That kind of damage, I know so intimately, because more times than I could count I was victim to it. Damage that is now intricately woven into my wiring. Damage I've now handed on to my son. Jenna said I worked long and hard to prepare Devon for the possibility of losing my mind, but in a matter of minutes, I managed to reverse that process.

I'll never get over this one. Never.

Donny Ray.

I saw him. He seemed so real. But seeing Devon materialize beneath me—my hands clenched tightly around his tiny neck as he choked for air—says otherwise.

Then comes the ultimate and most brutal shot of reality. My wife and son are gone. They have left me, and now I am truly and unequivocally alone. Just my unraveling mind and me as we continue to helplessly whirl through this terribly broken world, struggling to draw a flimsy line between reality and fiction.

I look out through the window at my world of pain, everything so monochromatic, so desolate, mere shadows of what I once loved, all of it stripped away.

How do you walk on faith when there is none left?

I try to put one foot in front of the other, but as I move through the house, with each step, nothing but emptiness greets me, both from throughout and within.

Bridge burned.

But maybe not, because there's one thing that I know for sure. Donny Ray Smith still poses a true and present threat. He wasn't in this house, but he's still out there, and he's still after my son. If I can save Devon, perhaps I can save this family from ruins, and then maybe, just maybe, I'll be remembered not for my rapid descent into insanity but for the powerful love that drove me to such extremes. Then they'll know that, all along, my intentions were pure and good.

I'd really like for that to happen.

Not that I'll ever get to see it. By then, I'll probably be locked up inside some institution, warehoused away like the spent human cargo I've fought most of my life to rescue.

There will be no time left for that, either.

Another item for my growing list of failures, but I'll happily give that one up. I'll give up everything as a price for saving my son.

This is all his fault. Donny Ray did this to you.

"No . . . I did this to me."

That's what he wants you to believe. It's not just your world Donny Ray wants to tear down.

"Huh?"

Think about it. In the car, right here in this house, Donny Ray is drilling deeper into your mind. Soon, he'll have complete control.

And in a flash, it all makes sense. "That bastard . . . he tried to make me do his dirty work. The one thing I've been attempting to prevent. He tried to make me kill my son."

The one thing he knew would finally push you over the edge.

"And it almost worked."

And he's going to keep infiltrating your psyche until every thought belongs to him.

Panic sizzles through me, with seething outrage fast on its trail. "I have to stop him."

Donny Ray lied to you last night. The battle hasn't moved here—it's still alive and thriving at Loveland. You have to change up your strategy, think fast and act even faster.

"But how?"

You know what you have to do.

77

WHEN EVERYTHING ISN'T ENOUGH

My father told me that I was his everything, but the statement would have more impact than even I could have known.

It was his good-bye.

I found him the next morning in his basement shop, hanging from the rafters.

The coroner said he'd been dead for hours. More than likely, he'd hanged himself just after our tearful embrace. A final attempt to keep me safe. Not from the man in the drain, but this time, from his dangerous mind.

My father's most drastic—most heartbreaking—move of all.

About six months later, at the age of seventeen, I became an orphan when my mother also passed away. The doctors told me she'd suffered a massive heart attack, but I'll always believe they got that wrong.

She suffered a massive heartbreak.

Now I understand the agony they both must have felt.

78

Sorrow bursts into rage.

It's raw, hard-driving, and knows exactly where to land. Seeing my son's pain and knowing I caused it—that was the last straw. I'm declaring war on Donny Ray Smith with every intention of becoming the victor.

I eject the magazine from my gun, fill it with rounds.

"This one's got your name on it, motherfucker," I say, snapping in the last bullet. "The others are for anyone else who tries to stand in my way."

I slam the magazine back in, grab the waistband holder, insert the gun into it.

Within a matter of seconds, I'm peeling out of my driveway. As I wheel down the road, my mind snaps into a state of hyperfocused awareness, thoughts more lucid than they've ever been, but it's not just that. Every sense has taken a definitive and determined shift, far above any state of normal human capacity. My vision is razor-sharp, and even though the car windows are closed, I hear sounds that I normally shouldn't.

A conversation between two people as they walk along the sidewalk.

A leaf, rustling across the grass and carried off by the wind.

I don't know from where this gift of penetrating, extrasensory perception derives, but I'm grateful for its help.

Faster. You don't have much time. You have to take out Donny Ray before he takes over your mind.

My foot strikes the gas pedal. My car throttles forward at breakneck speed.

The parking lot is less than a quarter full when I arrive at Loveland, the remaining cars scattered about like Matchbox toys.

Donny Ray is snatching up bodies even faster now. You know who he's going after next.

"Not a chance."

You've got very little time to turn this around.

I reach down to make sure the gun is snug to my waist, then pull my blazer down over it. Moving toward the building, my pace is accelerated, my thoughts are urgent. Rage is mounting.

Closer to the entrance, I spot workers wheeling equipment onto a truck. With premonitory heed, I stride toward them and see the trailer is packed to the edge with machinery, file boxes, and scores of computers.

They're absconding with the evidence.

A drop of sweat rolls down the center of my back. Nerves rattle like pennies in an old, rusty tin can.

"This is not good," I say, watching one of our security guards pass by. He shoots me an ugly gawp.

Don't look at him. He's one of them.

I study the guard with suspicion, then turn and walk away. "Things are getting more complicated than I'd expected. I need help, some kind of backup."

There is nobody.

Another truck pulls up behind the last. More workers get out and roll dollies toward the building.

You have to hurry. The entire operation's gearing into full swing. Donny Ray's army is about to move in and clear everyone out of Loveland, then he goes next.

I break into a run toward the hospital entrance.

Inside, only a handful of people occupy the main floor. I move past the employee lounge and take a peek—nobody there. I run by the administrative offices and find only two people working. I walk toward my office, and just one person passes me along the way. Awareness steps up: bumping into the wrong person could stop me from getting to Donny Ray, and even more, place Devon directly in the path of danger.

But I don't know how to act. I'm carrying a loaded weapon.

Play it very cool.

Adam and Jeremy step out of Adam's office. Even from this distance I know they're not engaged in casual conversation—both wear expressions serious enough to raise my concerns.

They're talking about you.

I take tentative steps forward and observe both men as they continue their discussion. I can't help but notice the tension. I'm unsure what's causing it, but I do sense it's not between them.

At about ten feet away, I go for cover behind a stack of boxes and keep watching. Adam tosses a glance at my office door and says something. Jeremy looks too, then responds with a frown and shakes his head.

You've got some serious trouble brewing there.

Two doctors walk up behind me. They're speaking too loudly and make eavesdropping impossible. I pretend to inspect some boxes, then once they pass, return my attention to Adam and Jeremy.

Adam just gave Jeremy the red folder.

Fury rips through me. That folder again.

It's filled with the information Adam's been gathering on you. He also handed over the tapes.

"What tapes?"

Of all your conversations with him.

I lower my gaze to Jeremy's hands—one holds the red folder, the other a brown paper bag with his name on it. I should have known. Jeremy's in on this, too. Now I've got the top dog working against me as well. The two men nod to each other, then Jeremy walks away.

Adam just ratted you out. Now Jeremy knows your mind is slipping. He's going to put you on psych leave.

"That bastard . . . ," I mumble, vitriol burning in my throat as Adam heads in the other direction. I reach for my gun, aim it at his skull, then cock the trigger.

Don't waste your bullets. Donny Ray is your target—anything else will only keep you from getting to him.

I lower the gun.

More obstacles. In addition to time ticking away, now I'm a marked man. I bound toward my office, dash inside, then lock the door behind me.

I'm safe.

But not for long.

79

Things have become significantly more complicated than I'd expected. I had no idea they'd be tightening the screws all around. Getting to Donny Ray will be much harder with Adam, Jeremy, and God-only-knows-who-else watching over me.

Every camera in this hospital is monitoring you.

I have to offset this new wrinkle, move about silently to avoid detection.

A fast-moving target is the hardest to hit. Get out of this office.

I feel for the gun at my waist, straighten out my blazer.

I'm ready to roll.

I head for Ground Zero.

On my way to Alpha Twelve, I approach Security Checkpoint One.

Stay calm. Act normal.

The hospital's been too cheap to invest in metal detectors, and the guard doesn't know I'm packing heat. Besides, Adam told

Jeremy about me just moments ago, so I doubt the news has trickled down to security yet.

At the gate, I pull out my card, swipe it through the slot, then after passing through without incident, quietly exhale my relief.

But after opening the door to Alpha Twelve, my jaw plunges. This place is in the process of being cleared out. Workers cart furniture from rooms. A maintenance guy stands at one of the circuit breaker boxes, flipping switches and looking down the hallway as lights flash on and off. Two patients wander slow and aimless amid the confusion, vision set ahead, faces nearly expressionless. Mystery Nurse sits at the station mindlessly typing away. As usual she's oblivious to what's going on all around her.

A loud *thwack* off to my side startles me. I jump back and see workers tossing debris into a construction bin, but beyond that, something far worse regenerates my worries.

Oh, no.

Jeremy stands about fifteen feet away, head bobbing in every direction, eyes wandering the floor, and when he's not doing that, he's busy talking to staff members.

He's looking for you.

Slowly, I back myself around the corner.

And he just came from Donny Ray's room.

"What was he doing there?" I whisper.

They're getting ready to take Donny Ray out of Loveland.

"And handing that crazed lunatic a license to kill again."

I set my sight on Donny Ray's room. The door is wide open, light shifting across the floor, with unfamiliar voices wafting out. Butterflies batter inside my stomach. Nerves climb the ladder to jittery.

They're strategizing on how to stop you.

I look both ways, wait for the path to clear, then zoom across the hallway and into a vacant patient room across from Donny Ray's. I peer out from behind the door. I keep watching.

Several minutes later, a shadow drifts up the hallway, then a guy wearing an orderly's uniform materializes. I'm pretty sure I've never seen him here before, but there's no question he's got *dirty* written all over him. He walks into Donny Ray's room, and about three minutes later, a second unknown man enters, also wearing the uniform.

Outside reinforcements.

I swallow hard, then people start filing out of Donny Ray's room at an urgent pace.

Hurry! They're on the move!

Just as I storm the hallway, Donny Ray himself comes walking out of his room. He wears freshly pressed jeans and a pinpoint oxford, his hair neatly styled, his shoes brand new. Two very large and disagreeable looking thugs in plainclothes flank each side of him as all three head straight toward the exit.

MOVE! Jeremy gave him his walking papers—they're back-dooring him out of here.

Adrenaline pumps through my veins like dirty motor oil as I rush toward them. I won't allow Donny Ray to leave this building alive. I cannot. My son's life depends on it. I've got to keep him safe.

They continue walking him forward. I pull out my gun and spring toward them, heart jackhammering against my rib cage as the distance between us narrows.

At about eight feet away, I raise my weapon, but one of the thugs locks onto me.

"He's got a gun!" the man cries out and points.

From behind me, I hear a stampede of feet beating a path my way. I aim my gun at Donny Ray, spit my words out like poison. "YOU'RE NOT LEAVING HERE! I'LL KILL YOU FIRST! DO YOU HEAR ME? I'LL FUCKING KILL YOU!"

Just as Donny Ray and his clan duck for cover through the doorway, I get a clear line of sight to him. I firm my hold on the trigger, but before I can pull it, an overpowering weight against my back hurtles me forward. My gun accidentally goes off, then I rapidly and repeatedly keep squeezing out more rounds.

A volley of gunfire flies across the room, ricocheting off the floors, the walls, everywhere. Plaster and tile crack and explode all around me. As I crash facedown, the gun flies from my hand and slides across the floor. Not a second later, I feel more crushing weight barrel down on me, so heavy it knocks the wind from my lungs. My forehead and cheeks are throbbing and numb, my nose and mouth oozing with blood. I hear frantic commotion, footsteps and voices all around me. A few heartbeats later, someone roughly yanks my arms back, slaps cuffs on my wrists, then pulls me sharply into standing position. Two men grab hold of each arm and fling me forward, and I stumble along with them.

"Sure!" I shout at the men. "Let a child killer walk the streets, and take *me* away! That makes a hell of a lot of sense! You people are depraved! You're a disgrace!"

The men answer with a backbreaking jerk as they fling my body forward.

Then, with a face full of blood and chuffing for air, I at last get a glimpse of Donny Ray Smith.

Lying motionless on the floor.

Face to tile.

A puddle of blood rapidly spreading around his body.

Dead as dead can be.

80

Wake up, Christopher. Can you wake up?

I have to wake up. Someone is telling me I have to wake up.

I blink a few times, then look down at myself. Lying in bed, I examine the Posey Net that covers my entire body. Arms, neck, and legs pulled through the openings. Ankles and wrists secured with loop straps. I'm sweating, trembling with fear.

Footsteps move toward me, and I lurch back against the bed, hands clenching the guardrails, biceps flexing, breaths speeding. My restraints clatter; perspiration slides from sodden bangs down the bridge of my nose.

I raise my head, and the first thing I see are those evil eyes coming at me.

What the . . . Didn't I just . . . ?

My vision wanders.

His room. What the hell am I doing in his room?

Donny Ray now stands a few feet away.

"Why am I being restrained?" I shout at him.

"You've been deemed a danger to yourself and others," he explains.

I release an angry howl and violently try to jerk myself free; the bed rattles, squeaks, and shimmies. Recognizing my efforts as futile, I let out a tiny, helpless moan.

"It's okay," he tells me, keeping his body still and voice level. "Nobody's here to cause you any harm."

A low and inarticulate sound escapes through my chattering teeth.

He waits in silence and watches me. A few moments later, my breaths slow and my jaw relaxes, but I turn away to refuse him eye contact. Hearing him move closer, I react instantly, shooting my terrified gaze directly at him, but now Donny Ray is the one who seems startled, staring into my eyes with what can only be recognition mixed with curious confusion. He examines my other features.

I keep hopscotching through time, don't understand how I landed here, but one thing is absolutely certain. The man who's been turning my world into an empty shell has now drawn me to the heart of the whirlpool, the epicenter of evil. The man who keeps broadening his web and pulling me deeper into it. I have no idea what he's doing, but there's not a doubt in my mind that Donny Ray has taken over complete control of this hospital. That there is only one way out of Loveland, and he's holding the key.

"You have to take me out of here!" I blurt, voice fraught with desperation, eyes begging.

"I need you to try and calm down," he says. "Do you think you can do that for me?"

A slow nod. A vulnerable expression.

A phone rings from somewhere off to the side. I jerk back. He raises a hand of assurance.

I settle.

Still mindful of my overall appearance, Donny Ray says, "I need to ask you a few questions."

I'm fearful but compliant.

"Do you know where we are?"

"We're at Loveland."

"Do you understand why we're here?"

"Please!" I shout. "Help me!"

"We're going to find the truth. Whether that helps you or not remains to be seen. Are you able to tell me your name?"

"But you already know all this! What does it have to do with—"

"I need your name," he says, this time as a firm mandate.

"Yeah . . ." I surrender. "Okay. It's Christopher Kellan."

"What's your date of birth?"

"June twenty-ninth, nineteen seventy-six."

"Can you tell me where you were born?"

"Johnson City! Why are you doing this to me?"

Donny Ray circles back to the original question I failed to answer. "Do you understand why we're here?"

I look down at my bound hands, look up at him and feel my expression change—something like nervous confusion diluted by distress. "I think . . . I mean . . . I just don't know anymore! As many times as I've turned things around in my head, I can't make sense of them. And then I keep forgetting things, and everything around me doesn't fit, and that just makes it worse . . ."

"*Forgetting things,*" Donny Ray repeats.

I close my eyes for a moment, then open them. "Like I don't know where I've been for a while."

He leans in closer.

Tears start as I shake my head. "I'm not afraid of you . . . I'm not . . . ," I tell him, but it feels more like an attempt to convince myself.

"You have nothing *but* fear, Christopher. Fear has taken you over, and because you keep hiding from it, you keep losing things, and you're going to continue losing them."

"What in God's name are you telling me?"

"What in God's name are you hiding from?"

"I'm not hiding!"

"Fear is the most powerful emotion we can feel, right?"

I don't answer.

"It's wired into us. It's primitive. It's instinctual." He rubs his wrist. "Do you have fear, Christopher?"

"Why does any of this—?"

"DO YOU HAVE FEAR, CHRISTOPHER!" His voice is sharp, no longer posing a question.

"We all do."

"No." Donny Ray sweeps a finger across his wrist, faster now. "I'm not talking about everyday fear. I'm talking about the primal kind. The kind of fear that scrapes at your bones. The kind that sends your mind screaming. Your fear is what brought us together. You know that."

The hairs on my arms start to rise. I'm quaking.

"And your heart will break, Christopher." His eyes are a blaze of blue boreal fury. His voice climbs in pitch, the tone getting smoother, the speech pattern transmuting into one I recognize.

"Who . . . Who the hell are you?"

"You'll have to accept that loss," he says in the voice of my son.

I examine his eyes, his face, still no more certain now about their familiarity than I was from day one.

"*Who are you?*" I ask again, barely able to get past the quiver in my throat.

"You know who I am," Donny Ray says, returning to his normal voice.

"Why? Why are you taking my son away from me?"

"To break your walls."

"I . . . I don't understand . . ."

"It's my job, Christopher. It's what I do, and it's what you need. This is how it's done."

"How what's done?"

"How you make someone see what they refuse to. You take away the things they love most. You make it all disappear. That's how we find the truth."

"By stripping away everything in this world that matters to me?"

"By stripping away everything in this world that you believe in. Now we can start rebuilding. Just you and me, partner, brick by brick."

"Get me out of here! Let me go!"

"Are you finally ready to make that choice?"

"What choice?" I say, but it comes out more as a plea.

"If I take you out of Loveland, are you ready to face what's on the other side of these walls?"

"Yes," I say without hesitation. "Please! Take me out of here!"

81

I see feet moving, but in my disconnected fog it takes a few seconds to realize they're my own.

Where am I?

It's like I'm walking through a void. Everything around me is oppressively still and silent. Even the air has an unfamiliar, motionless quality.

Is this real?

As my vision clears, ahead of me I see the Loveland parking lot. The only car left is mine, a little boat floating on a sea of blacktop. I turn toward the building, and more sedentary absence looks back at me. Nobody in the surrounding area, nobody coming in or out through the main entrance. I raise my vision toward the upper floors and find more vacuity: every curtain pulled open, every window like a black hole punched into rust-stained concrete.

Not a human anywhere. Everyone . . . gone.

Disappeared.

"Now it's just you and me."

I look to my right. Donny Ray is beside me, and I realize we've just walked out of Loveland together. He keeps his gaze aimed ahead. Like he's leading me someplace.

But where?

"Now we can get to work," he says with a single, affirming nod. "It's time, Christopher."

"You're not taking Devon from me!"

"It has to happen," he says gently, reassuringly. "You know it does."

"Why are you destroying my life?"

"I'm helping you *see* your life. The destruction you feel is a result, not a cause."

"I won't let you wreck my world!"

He stops walking. "Christopher, wake up. Can you wake up? The world as you once knew it has slipped away and lost its shape. But this is actually progress. It won't be long now."

"Long for what?"

"Your truth is waiting."

The glass shatters.

The white light goes off.

82

I'm parked under the Evil Tree.

This goddamned tree, this bastard that keeps pulling me back. I look up at the hideous beast, hovering so tall and proud, so arrogant, shielding what little light there is, casting me deeper into darkness.

A strong wind picks up, and the Evil Tree vigorously rattles its branches, shaking pollen over me like black rain.

Anger boils. Hatred reaches fever pitch. Outrage turns viral. I squeeze the wheel, chew my bottom lip, and hear a snarl deep inside my chest.

"YOU'RE THE REASON FOR ALL THIS! YOU'VE RUINED MY LIFE! YOU HEAR ME? YOU'VE MOTHERFUCKING RUINED IT!"

Tears stream down my face, and I erupt into hysterical laughter, so instantaneous that it startles me; then just as unexpectedly, that laughter turns into heaving sobs. Several seconds later a new emotion emerges, so powerful that it sends my body into a racking tremor.

Unadulterated fear.

You've got to get out of here.

"I've got to get out of here."

Go! Go!

I start the engine, hit the gas pedal, and my car flies into reverse, but the exact moment my tires hit pavement is the exact moment a raging storm swoops down, unleashing a wrath like I've never before seen. Wrath that, with each passing second, gathers furious intensity.

An angry clap of thunder explodes that could shatter bone. On its heels, a volcanic flash of lightning fractures the sky and sets it afire. Night turns to day, and ahead in the distance, my enemy again reveals itself. The tree speaks directly to me as if all along it's been waiting for this precise moment to deliver the message, one that couldn't be clearer.

This is where it all started, and this is where it all will end.

More wind, more rain, more thunder, then another pop of lightning falls over the tree, and I catch something at the base of its trunk, but through the shielding rain, can't tell what it is. I fling open the car door, leap out, and take off running, eyes focused on the one spot, wind belligerently shoving me forward.

And then I see him, and then my heart breaks into a thousand pieces. A sob escapes my lips, but a sharp gasp sucks it back in. "NO! NO, NO, NO . . . NOOOOOO!"

I fight my way through a thick wall of rain, feet stumbling into an unsteady zigzag.

I reach my son, my Devon, muddy and rain-soaked, lying across the trunk's base like a tossed-aside rag doll. I collapse beside him, reach around his cold and lifeless body. As I lift him up, he arches away from me, head falling back, arms hanging loosely at his sides.

"NO, BABY, PLEASE!" I press his face against mine and rock him. "PLEASE! NO!"

But I know that there is nothing left of my son. That my world has collapsed around me, and that the only thing that held it together is now gone.

I lower him to the ground. I study his sweet, wonderful face.

"My baby boy . . . ," I say, body shaking with the kind of grief that, before now, I never knew was humanly possible. I lean down, press my lips against his cold forehead, and a feeble whimper escapes me.

It's that sleep of death, Christopher.

At last, the meaning is revealed, because I know that this world is worth nothing without my son in it.

I don't belong here anymore.

I aim my gaze skyward. Rain mercilessly falls over me, battering my face and beating away the tears, but it's nothing compared to the immeasurable torture my mind is only beginning to comprehend.

"I'm going with you," I say through a defeated whisper.

I gather Devon up in my arms and carry him to the car.

With tenderness and care, I lay his body across the seat, then take one last look at my broken and beautiful son.

Tonight, I just want to save you.

But I couldn't save him.

It was just an accident, Daddy.

This one won't be.

I get behind the wheel, gun the engine, slam the car into reverse.

At fifty feet back, anger replaces pain, disgust overpowers regret, because I know that standing before me is the reason why my life has been so irreparably destroyed. My foot lands on the gas pedal. I hit the gearshift, hit the accelerator, and the car responds instantly, firing me forward at vicious momentum.

"C'MON, YOU BASTARD!" I shout with tears streaming down my face. "BRING IT ON! GIVE ME EVERYTHING YOU'VE GOT!"

Just as we're about to collide, a flash of light goes off between us.

And the last thing I hear is shattering glass.

83

The light fades, and I realize I'm . . .

What?

I'm back on the road again, driving the same path as before, rain pounding my windshield, wind sweeping up. I turn my head to the right and see that Devon is . . .

Alive?

Jake barks.

What's happening?

Jake barks again, this time with more insistence. I look over my shoulder at him.

Devon yells, "Daddy! Watch out!"

Plonk.

Something hits the windshield. I whip around and catch the rubber ball on a trajectory toward the road. But before it has a chance to meet ground, the boy in the red hoodie appears from out of nowhere and goes chasing after it.

The ball bounces on the asphalt, bounces again, then lands and begins to roll. The boy dashes after it, putting himself directly into my path.

I slam on the brakes. The car swerves. Devon cries out. Jake yelps. We miss the boy.

But the car wheels into a monstrous spin, then careens off the road. A muddy skid propels us even faster, and now we're headed straight for the Evil Tree.

Headlight beams mix with rain and obscure my vision. We are about to hit the tree when an explosion of white light blinds me.

I wake up seconds later, rub my eyes.

Wait. Seconds? Or is it weeks? Months?

I don't know. I don't know . . . Oh, God, I don't know.

Everything is tilted.

I look out my side window, see the tree a few feet away, and realize we narrowly escaped the collision by landing in a ditch.

My son lets out a whispery moan.

"Devon!"

His eyes are half open, his shirt quickly darkening with blood that runs from the gash across his neck. So much blood.

Jake lets out a frightened howl from the backseat.

I reach for an old T-shirt, a roll of tape from the glove compartment. I wrap both around Devon's neck, hoping to stem the flow of blood.

But it's too much blood, coming out way too fast. I scramble for my cell, try dialing out, but the signal keeps dropping. I crank down the window, extend my phone outside. The effort proves useless.

"Daddy, I'm scared," Devon says, voice so frail that I can barely hear it.

I crank the ignition key, slam the gearshift, punch the pedal. My car thrusts forward and the tires whine as we move out of the ditch and back toward the road.

But halfway up, it becomes clear we won't make it. There's not enough traction in the mud. And there is still no cell signal.

The wind howls, the rain picks up, and I'm so scared of losing my son.

"Daddy . . . please . . . help me . . . " His eyes are almost half closed, body swaying weakly, swaying sickly, the blood now pooling in his lap.

I slide the car to a stop, then turn the steering wheel hard, jamming the tires sideways into the turf in an effort to anchor us. Then I sling the door open and race for the road. Jake gives a sharp bark and jumps out of the door behind me, then trots in my path as I run.

Four agonizing breaths later, bars appear on my phone. I dial.

"911. What is your emergency?"

"My son—" I can barely get my sentence out, the most important I've ever had to speak.

I hear a strident groan coming from behind me, then the crackling of dirt as tires grind against asphalt. I reel around.

The car is sliding downhill.

And through the windshield I glimpse Devon, head dropped back, body joggling loosely to every crack and bump in the road.

"No! NOOOO!"

I chase after the car, feet pounding pavement, but I'm no match for the gravity that pulls my son downhill. Still, I keep running as the car picks up speed. Tiny stones pop beneath the tires like spiteful messengers of tragedy. Jake lets out a mournful moan. I can't hear Devon, but through the glass I see his mouth saying, *Daddy.* And though I keep running as fast as I can, I'm too slow to reach the car before it slams sideways into the tree.

"*DEVON! NOOOOO!*" I crumple to the pavement. My body collapses onto itself.

The white light goes off, this time as if exploding through my veins.

In a flash, I'm standing motionless and numb, mind dazed, as medics pry open the car door. They pull my son's body out and lay him across the base of the tree.

Again, the light explodes.

Jenna and I are rigid with misery in a hospital hallway, speaking to a doctor. His mouth is moving, but the message comes out so slow, so thick and muddled, that I can't understand it.

Until I do.

I let out an agonizing wail. Jenna collapses into tears.

And as I watch this event play out, the sudden yet inexplicable realization that I've experienced my son's death twice—first at Donny Ray's hands, and then at my own—destroys me.

Trying to offer comfort, the doctor reaches for my shoulder. I grab the pen from his lab coat pocket, then jab it into my wrist. And I keep jabbing. A river of red pours out of me and crawls along the floor. A river of pain, of regret . . . of loss.

And I feel my heart slow, my whole existence fragment. There is no sound, there is no light. There is unequivocally . . .

Nothing.

Nothingness that tumbles into an abyss, a deep, black, penetrating hole, as everything around me disintegrates into complete, encompassing darkness.

I disappear.

I am gone.

84

I'm back on the road, but now it looks different. On this road, the sun is shining, the air is clear, and I can see ahead for miles and miles. Tall meadows with grass the color of finely polished emeralds sway effortlessly to the decree of a gentle breeze. Distant mountains stand tall and proud, cloudless skies just above their peaks. I'm not sure where this road leads, but that hardly seems to matter, because I know it moves in the right direction.

"It's pretty, Daddy," Devon says.

I smile at him. "It really is."

"And perfect."

"Absolutely perfect."

"Daddy?"

"Yeah, kiddo?"

"Let's stay like this forever, okay? Just like this."

A statement strikingly familiar, and yet I'm not sure why, as if it comes from some other place. Some other time.

"Sure," I say. "We'll stay this way."

"Promise me, Daddy."

"Promise." I glance at him and the wisdom of youth shines back on me. I see purity, unblemished truth. And some part of me—one I can't even quantify—understands that there is indeed so much beauty in truth, so much relief.

We continue on our journey, no further conversation, nothing but joyful silence holding us together. My son and I, joined by something that feels like happiness, like freedom.

A tree comes into view ahead, its peach-colored blossoms sprouting like wings from branches that reach toward the heavens as if in welcome. We move past the tree, and I steal one last glance at it through the rearview mirror, watching it fade into the distance.

"Daddy, look," Devon says.

He's pointing through the windshield, toward the sky, eyes wide with wonder. I follow his gaze and see that two birds have joined us on our journey. Winging side by side in perfect unison, their paired movement seems effortless and yet so magnificent.

So meant to be.

We watch together. A few moments later, the two birds lift up through the air. One curves gracefully to the right; the other continues onward.

"There we go, Daddy," Devon says. "There we go . . ."

I smile.

But when I turn my head, I find an empty seat beside me. Now I, too, am traveling alone, and I know that my son really is . . .

Gone.

The flash of light goes off, but this time it fades to the rhythm of a gentle, beating heart.

85

"Christopher, wake up. Can you wake up?"

I have to wake up . . . Someone's telling me I have to wake up. My eyes flick open.

I wake up, or I come to life, or . . . I do something. I'm not actually sure. I'm not even sure where I've been. My mind seems so vacant, my body so . . .

I run my hands up and down beneath me.

Sheets. I'm in a bed.

My vision clears, and I see eyes. I study the face, a man's, but I don't recognize him. I lick my parched and cracked lips, try to swallow, but my tongue gets stuck to the back of my throat. It's like I've been asleep for years, like I—

"Christopher," the man says. He steps back to observe me, and I study his face more closely.

A decent man with kind eyes.

"Welcome back," this man says with his gentle smile.

I've been somewhere, probably for quite some time, but I don't—

"How long have I . . . ?" My question comes out weak and crackly, but before the man can answer, I fall away into darkness. I disappear.

I'm gone.

Again.

I blink a few times.

My body and mind feel . . .

Better? Just a little stronger, maybe?

The man is no longer here, and I wonder if he ever existed because nothing around me seems real—nothing is tangible.

I look to the doorway, light spilling through it, but my eyes can't adjust. I can't tell what's on the other side.

The other side.

A dark object moves through the light.

"Took a little breather there, did you?" the object says, and I recognize the man's voice, see his fuzzy outline, but before I can get a better fix on him, darkness snatches the opportunity away, falling over me, and again, my world disappears.

Again, I am gone.

I'm not sure what day it is. I'm unclear how long it's been since I first woke up, and I certainly don't know the length of time I was lying here before that.

I don't even know where *here* is.

Well, I know it's a hospital, and the man with kind eyes is a doctor of some sort. Someone might have explained more, but if they did, it eludes me. Time and memory are flexible in my grasp.

The next minutes, or hours, or days, continue this way. Periods of light—or life—followed by periods of darkness. During the times I am present, the man reappears. This man tells me things, and while I have a hard time retaining most of them, there is one that sticks with me.

You've come a long way, Christopher.

But on this morning, or this afternoon, or—I can't really tell the time of day—I feel significantly better. My mind is less cloudy, sight clearer, limbs a little sturdier. And I see . . .

Sunlight?

My vision wanders through the clearing haze and finds a window. I blink and squint as my eyes adjust to harsh rays bending through the pane. There are blue skies, and as I drop my gaze toward the ground, shiny reflections of light dance and bound back at me.

Cars. I'm looking at cars, lots of them lined up in neat little rows.

A parking lot.

I'm about to look back into the room, when something on the windowsill captures my attention. A book of some kind—no, it's actually a notebook, and now my curiosity widens, because I wonder what's on its pages. Curiosity that brings my legs to the floor and feet moving toward the window in slow, unsteady steps.

I reach for the notebook, open it.

And there I find sequences of numbers and letters running down the paper in orderly columns. I flip through the rest, and page after page, line after line, it's all the same—a seemingly endless array of alphanumeric codes in handwriting that looks familiar.

My handwriting.

I have no memory of jotting down this information, but there isn't much I can recall these days. I stare out my window at the parking lot, wondering what this all means, then do a double take at one of the cars. I look in the notebook, then at the car, then back inside the notebook. The vehicle's license plate tag matches one of the entries on this page.

I study the rows of numbers, stare out at the parking lot with its rows and rows of cars, and a vague wave of familiarity rolls through me.

I return to bed, and an overwhelming yet inexplicable sense of heartbreak fades into darkness.

86

"How are you doing there?"

The man is back. I am back.

"What . . . where have I—?" It's easier to speak now.

"Everything is okay," he says. "All of this is normal."

I'm not sure what normal is, because my world feels so indescribably abnormal.

"Tell me what's happened," I say. "Tell me how I got here."

"You've come a long way, Christopher."

"But where have I been?"

"That story," he says, "is even longer."

After pulling a chair close to my bed, he sits, and for the first time I notice the badge clipped to his shirt.

Dr. Donald Raymond.

Also for the first time, I realize how pale his blue eyes are.

"Donald Raymond," I say. "Donny—" My body stiffens.

"It's okay." He places a hand on my arm to offer comfort. "You don't have to be afraid anymore."

And something in his voice tells me I don't.

"It was . . ."

"Go on," he encourages, watching me with care.

"Like looking in a mirror . . . you were my . . . everything was . . ."

"Reversed," he says with a nod of gentle acknowledgment.

Doctor Raymond clasps his hands together and peers out through the window across my room. I can tell he's thinking that where we're going won't be easy.

"What is it?" I ask.

"Christopher, do you understand where you are right now?"

"A hospital."

He nods. "Do you know which?"

I shake my head.

"This is Loveland Psychiatric Hospital."

The name jogs my memory as images lift through the entrenched layers of my mind. "I . . . I think I remember being here."

"I expected you might. The thing is, those memories are going to be flawed."

"Flawed?"

"Mired by distortions—most of them, anyway. Now that you've come out of your previous state, we can straighten those out."

"Out of what state?"

"The one you went into a year ago."

"Wait . . . A year? I've been here for a year?"

"Your body was. As for your mind . . . that's a different story."

A vision streaks through my memory. I can't identify it. Something dark and swift, much like a bounding shadow. "It's like my brain keeps turning the memories on and off, and they happen so fast, I have trouble grabbing hold of—"

No sooner does the last word leave my mouth than it happens again. Another phantom memory slips through my consciousness, and a floodgate breaks open, images and sounds firing through it.

I see Loveland's dark walls swelling, pulsating, and closing in all around me. I see the shadowy hallways of Alpha Twelve, every door swung open, eerie white light spilling out through them. I hear screams, mad cries, and . . .

This place is broken!

I try to chase it all away, but sitting directly across from me now is a psychopath named Donny Ray Smith, drilling me with those eyes. He rises from the chair and reaches toward me. I lurch back, but before he gets close enough, like falling and glittery dust, Donny Ray dissipates.

Dr. Raymond returns.

"Christopher?"

I land headlong back into the moment and shudder, trying to get a grasp on my mercurial mind.

"It's okay," he assures me. "You don't have to be frightened anymore. Those memories aren't real. They were all products of delusional thought, caused by your illness."

"But what illness?"

"The one that made your mind shut down."

"What are you telling me? That I suffered from some kind of psychotic episode?"

He smiles gently. "For now, let's not talk doctor to doctor. You're used to being the one doing the diagnosis, but that will only confuse matters and make you more anxious."

I look into his blue eyes, and a line of logic begins to sharpen. I connect with the exact feeling I had after first realizing that Donny Ray wanted to take Devon away. But as that sensation grabs hold, with it comes so much fear.

"You . . . you killed my . . . ," I say, still attempting to narrow the gap between reality and make-believe.

He shakes his head. "You only thought so."

Confusion sends my vision circling the room, and I notice a painting that hangs on the wall. As I stare at the image of a young girl wearing a blue dress, another surge of memory strikes through me, then a hazy recollection drifts to the surface.

"You and I . . . we've been talking all this time . . ."

"We have, but your brain couldn't interpret our therapy properly. Your perceptions became mottled. It was in fact like looking into a mirror, but that mirror was cracked. Your mind was throwing distortions back at you."

The reflections in your mind have been blinding you, Christopher.

"I . . . I don't understand. Everything happened. I remember it all so clearly."

"I know it very much looked and felt like reality, and in your state, it became nearly impossible for you to tell the difference. I've been trying to help you find your way back. It's why you were brought here."

Your fear is what brought us together. You know that.

"But something's missing. What caused me to break from reality in the first place?"

Dr. Raymond frowns. He leans forward, carefully choosing his words. "Christopher, do you remember the car accident?"

"Which one?"

"I'm sorry?"

"Which accident? There were several."

"No." He shakes his head. "There was only one."

I look away, try to process his comment, but when I come back to him, I'm just more confused.

Dr. Raymond settles back in his chair. He pauses and thinks before speaking. "You were driving with Devon. You tried to avoid hitting another child and ran off the road. Can you recall any of—"

It was just an accident, Daddy.

My eyes widen as two wires touch and spark. Awareness explodes, and a threshold collapses. Memories give rise as if waiting all this time to break free, to hit air, to meet the outside world. Memories I now realize have been with me all along, yet I simply couldn't find my way to them.

I jerk forward and cover my face, but there is no hiding from this. There is only another awareness, a deep psychic pain as the tiny pixels come together, forming a picture of tragedy, the worst kind.

And your heart will break, Christopher.

My body rocks, shoulders curled over chest, hands grabbing for fistfuls of hair. "Make him stop, goddamnit!" I scream out. "Make him go away!"

"Let it happen, Christopher," Dr. Raymond says in a voice of measured and professional concern. "Let it all come out."

"I can't!"

"You can. These memories are going to seem fresh and new, but they're not. You're just facing them for the first time. You're integrating them. It's painful, but this is a very big step, Christopher, and it needs to happen."

It has to happen. You know it does.

"It hurts!" I say through agonizing screams. "It goddamn hurts!"

"I know . . . but this is where we start."

So we can begin rebuilding. Just you and me, partner, brick by brick.

But it doesn't feel like a start at all. This pain just keeps coming, consuming and endless. I'm drowning in the scattered and splintered pieces that clutter my mind, trying to make sense of what I know to be so utterly senseless.

Finally, I am able to speak again. "He's gone." My voice is thick and husky, throat tender and stinging. Then very weakly I say, "My son is gone."

"Yes," Dr. Raymond says with compassion I can both hear and feel. "He is gone. It's true."

We're going to find the truth.

"But why . . . How did all this . . ."

"You created a whole new world," Doctor Raymond tells me, "a sort of rubber one. In it, you could bend reality any way you wished. You could reverse time, bring Devon back, and in the process make your family whole once again."

"But I turned you into the enemy."

"Because I was trying to pull you out of that world—and in that world, you thought I wanted to take Devon away, when really, I was telling you that he already had been."

"How did I come out of it?"

"I began pushing you very hard, Christopher. One by one, I took your illusions away, until there was nothing left to see but the painful truth."

By stripping away everything in this world that you believe in.

"After that, your two worlds finally collided and merged. You found a window of insight and crawled through it."

Daddy, there we go . . .

Devon's declaration sweeps through me like a soothing and far-away echo. I see his beautiful smile, so vivid and powerful and tangible. But this time, it's no illusion.

This time, at last, I see truth.

The real one.

87

But there is still one truth I haven't yet found.

I've lost a year. I abandoned my successful practice as a psychologist. I abandoned my wife. I've lost Devon. But what makes his death even more unbearable is that I carry the responsibility for it. My guilt is insurmountable, and I know it will follow me for the rest of my life. I can never forgive myself, and I don't know if Jenna can either. How could she?

Insanity offered a temporary reprieve from the truth. But disappearing into my imaginary world meant leaving her in the real one to struggle alone through her grief. I didn't leave her intentionally, but that doesn't diminish the fact that my illness only added pain on top of more pain, making it all that more difficult for her. A broken mind did in fact shield me from having to mourn my son's death, but the escape was only temporary. That heartache is still here waiting for me, and now I wonder whether I'll have to deal with the loss of a wife as well.

The door to my room opens. Jenna stands behind it, still as beautiful as the first day I laid eyes on her. My breath whooshes out, and worry washes through me because, in her expression, I'm unsure whether it's joy or regret I see.

Whether she has come to say hello or good-bye.

Jenna steps toward me, and the closer she gets, the more I know she's speaking to me—not with words but through our unspoken language: *I love you. I've missed you so much.*

She hasn't given up on me.

Standing face-to-face, we're both frozen by the foreignness of this moment. The only indication of Jenna's feelings are tears that well in her eyes. Tears of joy, of happiness, or fear, or . . . I'm not sure what.

Neither of us speaks.

"Well," she finally says, showing me that adorable smile, "we always knew you were complicated."

I throw my arms around her. I indulge in this moment. I relish in it. The feel of my wife against me, the smell of her, the near-silent sob that shakes her body under my hold.

Jenna presses her cheek against mine. Skin to skin, as our warm tears mingle, her love holds me up, and at no other time have I needed it more. Because in this true world, I'm again with the one person who will allow me to go on, who is giving me my first taste of healing. We stay close in each other's arms for a long time, but as much as I need this, I know that Jenna does, too.

When she at last pulls back, I look into her eyes. My wife is indeed still as beautiful as ever, but I can tell that the past year has left its mark on her. I see sadness, so much pain and grief. A woman who first lost a son, and then, for a time, her husband. A woman who's been just as alone in her world as I was in mine, and in some ways, maybe even more. I want so badly to carve away that pain. But at a time like this, assurance seems impossible to find. I'm not even sure if any exists.

Still, I try.

"I'm so . . ." My voice fails me, and I make another attempt. "Sorry will never be enough. I don't know how to—"

"No, baby, don't," Jenna says with that gentle firmness I remember well. She pulls back so our eyes meet and wipes a tear from my face. "There is nothing to be sorry about. You hear me? Nothing."

A faint nod is all I can manage. Maybe because I don't believe her. Maybe because I can't. I look up, and in her tender compassion, find a glimmer of hope.

"Chris," she says, "all you ever did from the second Devon entered this world was love him. He left it knowing that."

"I abandoned him. I became my father."

"Sweetheart, you've got that one wrong."

"How?"

"You're not your father," Jenna says, "because you came back to me."

And with her absolution, I am both heartbroken and grounded. Her words open the floodgates to a swell of emotions, so powerful, so deep, so seemingly infinite. I am overwhelmed by her forgiveness, but that only makes me ache more for Devon.

I surrender to those feelings. I allow them, because I know the time is right, that in the safety of Jenna's arms is the best place to do it. I bury my head in her shoulder. And together at last, we suffer the loss of our son. And at last, I allow myself to fall apart.

Just as I reach the point where it feels like this pain will never end, Jenna moves her hand over my back and pulls me solidly against her.

"Chris," she whispers.

But I don't answer. I'm gasping for air.

"Chris," she says again.

I swallow hard.

"Breathe with me," she says.

I lift my head far enough to look into my wife's eyes, her tearful smile telling me everything I need to know.

And together we breathe.

We are one.

ACKNOWLEDGMENTS

This novel became a turning point in my career.

For years, I dreamed of writing the story; however, each time I stared at that blank page, apprehension always stood in my way. The reasons were many, but it was the extreme complexity of taking on a rubber world that frightened me most. Having two stories run side by side—one of which has to remain completely invisible—is a monumental task. This kind of high concept has been attempted both in movies and novels, but it seems as if just a few have managed to pull it off effectively. Naturally, this made me think, "Am I out of my freaking mind? If they couldn't do it, what the *hell* makes me think I can?"

But life has a way of shoving us outside our comfort zones and directly toward the things we most fear. Before I knew it, there I was, standing in the eye of the storm, at last committing those first words to the screen, shaky fingers and all.

That journey, however, would be paved with heartbreaking challenges. There were health issues and two badly severed fingers (don't ask—it's complicated). There were also numerous wrong turns, unexpected bumps, and so many tossed chapters that I lost count of them. There was screaming, fist pounding, tears, and for the first time in my career, countless nights I went to bed doubting my ability as a writer. But with those experiences came great lessons, the most important of which is that without fear, success is unattainable. That the hardest fought battles are indeed the most worthy.

Besides my stubborn unwillingness to accept defeat, what kept me fighting was the consistent and generous support given by those who surround me. From the ones who shared their knowledge, to the ones who seemed to know I could do this (even though

I didn't), each played an integral role in helping me bring you this story. To those people, I offer my most heartfelt gratitude.

Special thanks to the folks at Thomas & Mercer, specifically Kjersti Egerdahl, and especially Alan Turkus, who waited (and waited) with great patience and anticipation while I obsessively hammered away at this novel. The deadlines kept passing, and he kept extending them. Still, all the while, his excitement and enthusiasm over this story never wavered.

I'm grateful to have Scott Miller at Trident Media Group as my agent. Through every concern, he was not only receptive but also expeditious in taking care of business.

My developmental editor, Caitlin Alexander, was meticulous and thorough in her assessment of this book, weeding out the illogical, inconsistent, and nonsensical. Her insight was invaluable in helping to create added depth and believability to my story.

To say this book was a technical challenge would be a radical understatement. I walked into it knowing very little about forensic psychology but walked out with what I hope was the knowledge and credibility to make this story fly. For that, I owe my greatest thanks and complete admiration to neuropsychologist Cynthia Boyd, who talked me through the many complexities of psychopathology, disassociation, childhood sexual trauma, brain injuries, and a host of other topics far too numerous to list here. With my every phone call (also far too numerous), she responded with genuine enthusiasm and a most determined desire to be as helpful as possible. I can say without a second's hesitation that this book would not have been the same without her help, and I feel so very fortunate to know her.

Special thanks to clinical psychologist Franz Kubak at Oregon State Hospital, who helped me fill in the gaps so that I could portray Christopher's working environment and circumstances accurately and better understand the treatment of patients.

On that note, I've been trying for years to sneak into a psychiatric hospital, but unfortunately, it appears the only way they'll allow me entrance is as a patient. While this book drove me dangerously close to having that wish fulfilled, it wasn't close enough. I instead had to rely on the eyes and ears of the wonderful people who have dedicated their lives to helping the mentally ill.

Lori Wilson, also at Oregon State Hospital, has been my go-to gal since *The Lion, the Lamb, the Hunted*, and she is truly a gem. I pester her rather frequently with tedious questions, and amazingly, she never seems to tire of me. My only hope is that she can some-day help fulfill my research dream, if only for the sole purpose of getting me off her back.

To lighten Lori's load, I now have a new victim, Kathleen Lee, at Arkansas State Hospital. She, too, was so very helpful in answering my every question, further illustrating the remarkable kindness, dedication, and patience these fine professionals exhibit every day in their work

I have new understanding and compassion, not only for those who suffer from schizophrenia but also for their family members. I'm grateful to Terri Strong for being kind and generous in sharing her personal experiences with me so that I could portray Christopher's emotional struggles both as the child of a schizophrenic parent, and then as a victim himself. It is my hope that we can someday fully understand this horrible illness and find new ways to relieve the agony.

Attorney Richard Gates was kind enough to offer his expertise and knowledge about the insanity defense. He's an extremely busy man who, in spite of that, gave his time, further proving there are generous people everywhere.

To my beta readers, I offer enormous appreciation for helping me make this book the best that it could be.

And to my regular readers: you are the reason I write. Not a day goes by when I lose sight of that, and each day my respect and admiration for you only deepens. Thank you for giving me the opportunity to tell my stories. Thank you for your unfailing support and encouragement. It truly means the world to me.

And lastly, but by no means leastly (I know . . . not a word. I often make them up), to the people I affectionately refer to as my tribe. The ones who, without fail, hold me up, dust me off, and give me the strength to go on when life gets wobbly.

Kelley Eskridge (whom I promoted to tribal chief after she expertly talked me off the ledge several months back): You are my friend, my personal editor, and one of the smartest people I've ever known, and I am so damned thankful to have met you. I could go on and on, but please know how truly awesome I think you are.

Barbara Richards and I met eons ago during my first television gig at the CBS station in San Diego. She's still there and thriving—I'm long gone. Enough said. Some things are just meant to be. And while our professional paths took different directions, our friendship has only grown stronger through the years, partly because she's one of the funniest people I've ever met, and partly because she's one of the most honest and sincere.

Linda Boulanger and I texted back and forth for years before ever speaking a word to each other—and while my fingers often became numb and stiff (because, well, I'm a chatty one), I know her to be one of the kindest, most generous, and authentic people I've ever met. We did finally meet in real life last May at the OWFI conference, and she was every bit the awesome person I knew she would be.

The Rickrodes—Paul, Kay, and Deanna—you are my second family in every sense, and I am the son/brother you never asked for. I'm not really sure who inserted whom in whose life, but there you have it: we're stuck with each other, and I couldn't be more thankful.

To my dad: I love you and am so grateful for our closeness and mutual respect, which only gets stronger with each passing day.

To my mom: I miss you terribly but find strength in knowing you're still with me in spirit and that your love will always endure.

To Jessica Park, my best friend, my clarity, my kindred spirit. I love you in ways that no words could ever come close to describing. The day you walked into my life was the exact day I found new ways to experience so many joys that I never knew existed. You are truly a most precious gift.

ABOUT THE AUTHOR

Andrew E. Kaufman lives in Southern California with his two Labrador retrievers and a very bossy Jack Russell terrier who thinks she owns the place. An Emmy-nominated broadcast journalist, he eventually realized that writing about reality wasn't nearly as fun as making it up, and so began his career as a #1 international bestselling author of psychological thrillers.

Andrew became one of the highest-grossing independent authors in the country with combined sales reaching into the six-figure mark. *The Lion, the Lamb, the Hunted* was on Amazon's Top 100 bestsellers list for more than one hundred days, where it became the seventh bestselling title out of more than one million e-books available nationwide and number one in its genre.

He is also a contributor to *Chicken Soup for the Soul*, where he has chronicled his battle against cancer and the subsequent struggle to redefine his life, at last pursuing his dream of becoming an author.

For more information about Andrew's books, please visit www.andrewekaufman.com or follow him on Facebook: https://www.facebook.com/profile.php?id=100001249143819.